THE NIGHT SHADOW RIDER AND THE DYING LIGHT

THE EPIC HISTORICAL-FICTION SUPERNATURAL ADVENTURE CONTINUES

Book 3 of The New Seed Series

CHARLES ANTHONY SOLORIO

Note from the Author

Words are important. That is probably obvious coming from a writer! But words are *very* important. There are times when a writer struggles with making a difficult choice between using words that could needlessly offend versus using words that could needlessly draw the reader out from experiencing the writer's story.

I am personally invested in using the right words, as it is highly likely that I have indigenous blood running through me. In this story before you, I struggled with using the words "Indian," "American Indian," "Native American," or "indigenous person." There are legitimate issues, according to Native Americans I respect. I have chosen to use the word "Indian" in the following story in an attempt to not draw the reader out of the story with a word or term that was not used in the historical time period of the book.

I look forward to the day when we fully realize we are truly brothers and sisters.

PROLOGUE

Greetings to my brothers and sisters in hiding,

Can the remnant of the dying light break through the shadow swallowing our land?

I lift my eyes up from my chains. Where does my help come from? My help comes from You. I try to believe that You will return once again to our hard and thorn-stricken heartland and that You will use imperfect humans to bring forth Your perfect plan.

O God, why do our captors and murderers still live? Your answer of "grace" can be my greatest frustration. Your answer of "grace" is my greatest hope.

My fellow brothers and sisters in the last church hiding, I pray you are still alive out there to carry out the plan. I want to encourage you, though I die a daily death in this twenty-first-century concentration camp.

Months ago I lived on the other side of these walls, believing I was free. My family and culture raised me to swallow hidden beliefs permeating all institutions. Without a second thought I allowed those beliefs to spread into my chest and my head like an expanding darkness across a land under the shadow of the moon blocking the sun. I inhaled those beliefs into my lungs, and my heart beat for another. The shadow consumed me and persuaded me to move my hands and feet in unity with the march of the collective.

With their education, I earned new, impressive letters for my titles as an esteemed professor, to then raise up others in the ways of the state. As an elite professor at university, I towered above my students seated before their master teacher. I attacked those who believed in a rival God with their banned book. Even before it was illegal, I already knew the Bible was a book of treason against all kings who raised me.

Decades ago I knew who the Christians were before it became illegal to be a Christian. With the shadow moving over academia, a different light in their eyes penetrated and burned through me. I wanted that dying light to feed my ravenous lions. I challenged their faith. I saw them melt with my questioning, and I found my purpose in life. Their faith lay torn apart on a university auditorium floor, no longer possessing a pulse. My student crowds roared, and they went in for the kill. The Christians were defenseless as I held their academic futures in my hand. My well-trained students carried out my attacks, and it was as if I stood holding each naked victim's remaining torn clothing.

But then he came.

That student entered into my class, and I could not kill his faith. My disciples could not break him.

He spoke words I could never forget. I snarled, as his academic future in my cold fist meant nothing to him. I could not shake him. He did not tremble. I saw no fear in this one. The One within him emanated a love for me as I verbally assaulted him. I encountered a love for me that I could not break.

That love I had never experienced before dissipated part of the shadow in me. In my classroom I was the only one aware of a bright light that flashed and stole my vision. The crowd around me went silent.

While I was blinded, visions of the slaughtering of Christians buckled my knees onto the hard floor of my Colosseum. The ravenous crowd of students I raised up could not speak. My jaw seemed to unhinge, and a gasping sound escaped me as I then hissed and slithered, attempting to capture my next breath. There was sliding and dragging of feet as each student walked out of the room over the next few minutes.

He placed his hand on my head, and sobbing became my breathing and power as revelation entered into me.

My eyes that were blinded outward then turned inward. My inward-looking eyes opened, and what I had hidden came into view. How could a loving God allow me to live with what I tried to hide from Him?

My eyes fixated on how God loves us and how Satan hates the human race. For decades as a student and then as a professor, I'd raged against my country's history of colonization, slavery, and racism. I sobbed and shook my head. I had unwittingly colonized new heartlands for the original racist slave master, Satan, after he had colonized mine.

I cried out to God, "What have I done?"

My new inward eyes then simultaneously moved outward, and I, the professor, followed that student. I quit trying to teach my disciples and became a disciple of that student's God. I helped many of you reading this letter become offspring of God's underground church. That student taught us to blossom and grow under the protection of the Son while the oppressive and murderous shadow passes over us today.

I then spoke against the tyranny I used to be a part of. They canceled me from my job and prevented me from all social media access in the name of silencing "disinformation" and "hate," though I was educating all people of truthful information with a sincere love for all! The state I'd fought for in the name of tolerance and freedom from hate, turned to convenient intolerance against us and attempted to silence my love and His love for them.

Who are we anymore?

Are we descendants of the Mayflower, seeking life submitted under God away from the tyrant who desires to rule over us? Or are we descendants of the San Juan Bautista, slaves taken away to live under the authority and tyrannical rule of man?

You rightly ask, How did we get to this dark chapter in our Story? How did we end up with the leaders in our own country, and in every country, imprisoning Jews, Christians, and other dissenters into homeland prisons and concentration camps? How did we not see that some of our leaders intentionally overburdened our financial system to collapse it and, in the ensuing rubble, then made it into their own image? How did we not see that our country's security was compromised with our leaders personally profiting from working for other countries bent on destroying our country?

And I am the one imprisoned for committing treason?

Please pray for me, as today I am struggling with anger against our God as the memories and sights of our nation's leaders and captors hunting my family, capturing us, and torturing us attempts to rule over me this day. We are the last of God's remnant. The last living bearers of the Story. This could be the last letter I can write before they eliminate my eyesight. Please, God, forgive me for today. I desire vengeance tenfold.

I remember what they did to my family. I have been here for months, and yet it is three days that I am in the shadow of the bowels of this beast of vengeance that swallowed me. I know our God is loving, gracious, and slow to anger.

But on this day, what do I do when my God loves my greatest enemies?

Brothers and sisters, do you love your enemies?

On this difficult day, how, O God, can I preach Your love and grace with mercy to my captors in the shadow of what they did to my family? Can I preach your love and goodness to my captors if I know You can forgive them?

I lift my shackles and chains as their sounds become my musical notes of praise to You as I cling to Your promise to return. I cling to my great hope that God will use me in my final days to reach both our captors and His underground church. It is my hope.

I will send more parts of our Story with each letter. As you read the following pages, you will see our great hope. It may appear that our light is dying, but the shadow proves a still-existing Light. I have many more subversive words hiding in my mind, resisting my captor's colonization, that will join with other flashes of light cutting through our dark night.

Know this, my family: even when they one day fulfill their threat and remove my eyes, I will still see His light. I find some peace when your prayers slash through these weeping walls and through the imprisoned prison guards and then rest on me. They comfort me when I cannot forget what my captors have done.

I have a great secret of a great hope. I do not know where this concentration camp is located, but I do know a significant event happened in this same location. I hear the daily cries of the fellowship in suffering here in my time, penetrating the many walls. But there are other voices from another time that others cannot hear.

Is it possible to see and hear both the silent and audible weeping prayers of others from the distant past in my head? Their prayers hover over me and move into me. They cry out to God in an older form of English and also in a language I am not familiar with. They are suffering with severe cold temperatures, and they do not have enough clothing to stay warm. They are dying in great numbers. They inspire me as they pray for their enemies and for their own people.

I heard them cry out to God, and they prayed for a Pablo after he lost his family and for the remnant hiding from the fearful in power. Did they know that their prayers from the distant past encouraged me for today and tomorrow? How can that be? How could they know about me by name, and what would happen to me, my family, and the subterranean family hundreds of years ago in the past, that I would hear their prayers here today?

All people, even some of us in the remnant, thought the stump from the once-great church was dead among thriving thorns and lifeless ground. But His love in us is a Seed planted in hard ground. Above the ground, under the cover of the eclipsing days with drought and famine, we see what was once a great tree cut down. The axe still stuck in the center of the stump proclaims its triumph.

But underground . . . yes underground, with new seed inside hard ground, love rooted in Him under the stump grows, fertilized by the blood of our Savior that dripped from splintered beams. The roots below the stump descended and established deeper roots with every oppression and persecution and are now ascending and breaking the surface of the hard ground. The great tree that appeared to be cut down is returning.

O God, show us our selfish pursuits of power and control, the corruption of our riches, the surveillance and misuse of artificial intelligence by the collusion of nations, the infanticide, the continued racism, the antisemitism, the pandemics, our youth enslaved by the fear of a false story passed into them, suicide of the young and old, corporations suppressing freedom of speech in the name of protecting the false story by those with evil in their hearts.

Yet I am chief among sinners! Shall I be condemned by others for my present struggles and my regretful past? Do I drown in my sins, regrets, and unforgiveness? Do I remain quiet? Shall you be condemned by your past?

May it never be!

We are no longer condemned by God. Know that my heart aches to see you one more time for a final embrace. I pray you hold the faith through all testing and coming tribulation and know that our Author dwells within His Story in these difficult days. He will not let His created characters overrule the Author who created them in His Story.

Remember the only King with His own blood on His own hands.

I love you, my brothers and sisters.

No king but King Jesus.

Resistance to tyranny is obedience to God.

Walk into the Story that will unfold with each drop staining this letter.

With love,

Pablo

CHAPTER 1

**Near Plymouth, Massachusetts Bay Colony
1750**

A thunder crack in the night above the yelling men and barking dogs split the sky in two. The invisible war, now partially unveiled, moved in a new way on land and in the air. The Dark Light moved within the hunters and their dogs and chased the dying light hidden within her.

She carried what the hunters wanted. She imagined what the monster within the hunters looked like from every previous generation to now. Pinned to the wet sand, she heaved for just one more breath to gather strength to run as she trembled on her back. The men were closing in as the dogs had found her scent in the distance. Random shots echoed her fears. Something hissed through the air by her head and something else by her shoulder.

The pain exploded.

Did I get shot again?

A hand covered her mouth in anticipation. Her muffled scream escaped through her clenched lips and the hand, where the water met the sand under the partial light of the moon penetrating the darkening clouds. Her chest arched forward to reach for the elusive freedom in the air for the next breath. She tried not to bite the hand covering her mouth during the next scream. Blood, seemingly coming from everywhere, mixed with the foam of the water as her dress turned from soiled white to red. The blood in the tide seemed to come from distant shores onto the beautiful but flawed land. Could she get back up to run while seemingly impaled into the cold and wet sand with gunshot wounds?

For the first time, the crying voices moved from inhabiting only her dreams to now while she was awake. They echoed from all directions high and low and intersected in her. She needed to get up and run.

She squeezed the wet sand with both her hands and whimpered through the fingers of the hand covering her mouth. The hands that did not belong to her moved from covering her mouth to pulling on her to rise.

"Even if you have been shot, there is no time. Rise up. We just need to run to the tree, where I pray our help is waiting. We may still have enough time to get away."

The cries from her dreams grew stronger around her as her breathing weakened. More shots from the hunters closing in rang out and silenced the cries.

CHAPTER 2

MO

Near Boston, Massachusetts Bay Colony
1766

The rising late summer sun broke through the oppressive pockets of morning fog. Someday he would understand the voices and cries in his every nightmare. His eyes fixed on his right and left hands. Under the conquering dawn, he stood with the unveiling of a new day on his right hand against the shadow from his master's home on his left.

Mo stood with a shade of color between the daily dawn and dusk. He was darker than the whites but lighter than his fellow slaves. Though they told him he was about sixteen years old and going nowhere, he still tried to dream of his future. He fought against the effects of the dreams with the voices in his head, from distracting him of life away from his master.

But for right now, Mo needed to help little Betsy as she raised both arms and pushed her hands up against Mo's thigh.

Mo caressed her head and squatted down to meet her face to face while she kept her arms up, seeking help. He possessed one mouth and yet from it he did not know whether to smile or curse aloud again. But cursing, and therefore teaching Betsy new words that she would eventually repeat later, would only get Betsy and him in trouble. Perhaps this time he could try to control his emotions.

Breathe. Breathe. Breathe.

Betsy was about five years old, and her older brother, Will, about a year older. How could any-one really know how old anyone was when they did not have birthdays? No one celebrated birthdays. The master did not allow it. How many slaves really wanted to celebrate their births?

"Betsy, who tied your arms like this?"

Betsy did her cute laugh with her dimples smiling with her. Mo was old enough to see the effects of drought on the hard ground of his heart he would have to dig out of. There were days he imagined standing above the big cracks in the ground, and he wondered if someday a larger crack in the ground would swallow and bury him alive.

Her laugh thawed Mo's heart and was the only laugh he heard on most days. He could imagine the cracking in his heart opening wider, vibrating all the way to his ears. It was as if an invisible hand planted something deep inside the crack. Something deep inside where the birds or blazing sun could not steal or scorch. Someday he wanted to have a daughter like Betsy.

Betsy paused, as if waiting for Mo to finish his thoughts. She did not have a father but came to Mo when she needed a father figure. "Papa, Will did it. He found one of the master's cowskins. He always sees the master walking around with this, so he found it and tied me up. We thought it was funny when I could not free myself."

Betsy studied his eyes. She tilted her head. "Are your eyes sad or angry? Papa, you aren't going to get mad again and scare me, are you?"

Mo sighed and made his mouth submit to its master. *Someday I want several kids like Betsy and Will.* "Will just does not know any better. We need to get you free." She was not old enough to fully understand what the cowskins were used for. The grown-ups had so far succeeded in not allowing her to see the weapon used. Mo was not going to be the first one to explain to her the marks left on most backs.

Let her enjoy a few more months of laughter.

"There you go. You are free. Now go and hit your brother when he is not looking. He will think it is funny if you strike him while he is sleeping." Mo smiled when Betsy laughed as she ran away.

Mo stood back up and looked at the cowskin in his hands.

What was he going to do with it? He knew what he wanted to do with it. He wanted to strike his master with his own whip. When sleeping or awake. Mo thought *that* would be funny. But it was not time yet.

The master would whip him if he found him with the strap. If he told the master that the kids were playing with it, they could all get in trouble. If Mo buried it, would the master destroy their slave shack trying to find it? Would he even notice it was missing when he had several other straps waiting to cause permanent injuries?

The pull toward the pit of hell dwelling inside his master yanked on Mo daily. He longed for what pulled on the other side of him. A life away from the work under his owner's shadow with eyes. Away from the slaver's spies. One day they would all die. Perhaps all of this in one day.

His master often laughed, or moved his mouth, into a crooked smile when he said the name he'd given to Mo. Somehow it was a cruel joke that his master had named him Moses when the man had bought him shortly after birth. Mo always wondered if someone had stolen him from good people when he was very young.

The young boy did not know much about the Moses who'd led the slaves to the promised land in the old book he was not allowed to read. His master made sure he did not even know how to read. The master and his men told him they would kill him if he even held that book. They would separate him from what was left of his family—his mother. And she was not even his mother from birth. The woman he called mother was the first one who'd cared for him after his birth mother died after birthing him as a slave. Or was she killed? Or did she run away and leave him? If that was the case, Mo could not hate her, as he would have done the same thing.

That book. He knew if he read that book, they would whip him with the hard cowskin before they killed him.

Why would they not want me to read that book if that same book commands slave owners to take us as slaves, like they claim the book says?

On a hot day when shirts were removed on the hot cotton field, the raised lines on most backs reminded him of slashes in the night. Did the slashes rise up from below, or were they like lightning strikes from above?

Mo stretched his back, as it was still sore from sleeping curled up on the cold ground on another cold night. And it was not even close to winter yet. He was sure the master had blankets to stay warm every cold night.

He closed his eyes and sighed as yelling came from the house again. There was another voice with the master's. Mo mainly learned about what was happening in the world beyond the cotton plantation when the master talked with his slave-master friends. Mo turned his head in all directions and ran to the wall under the open window of the master's house.

The master growled. "I heard about that lawyer Benjamin Kent, who just won the first case to free a slave in a trial against that slave's master. Will our properties whine and win in our corrupt courts to take away our right to own land next? Things are turning upside down. Will the prisoners rule in their prisons and imprison us next?"

"People will wake up to the rising insurrection. We are people of the rule of law, and we brought the slaves to this colony and legally sanctioned slavery well over a hundred years ago. It is not going away anytime soon and will never go away as long as I have work that needs to be done." The master's friend laughed.

"But we are stupid enough to think we can trust slaves. You remember when smallpox arrived in Boston forty-five years ago? That crazy preacher and that doctor convinced everyone that one slave could teach us how to defeat smallpox. And people believed them!"

"His name was Onesimus. Who has heard that name before? But that slave was right—he showed them how to defeat the smallpox. It was the only time I have known a slave to have the intelligence to be right about anything."

"Do not give too much credit. Even a woman can be right once or twice. Look, my woman married me, right?"

They both laughed, before the master stopped and said, "Speaking of the most ignorant of my slaves, one of my boys needs to learn some more."

The master pointed his yell toward the open window. "Moses, come here." With the yell directed well past where Mo crouched, the master clearly did not know Mo was nearby.

The master had so many slaves that he did not know the names of most of them. But he knew Mo's name.

Mo knew his mother would not be happy with his plan. The knife strapped with some of the owner's own cotton was hidden underneath his pants leg and still cold. This was for his mother's freedom. Her life was his. He just needed to remember not to fall on his left hip.

He knew it was proper for him to acknowledge right away that he heard his master yelling and to say he was coming. But on this day, his mouth felt like he had said yes one too many times.

Is today the day for my plan?

"Boy, I told you to come here . . . *now.*" The master laughed again and spoke to his friend. "My breathing property, like my land property, is to be trampled under my feet."

Mo thought of Betsy and how she was now free to run and play. He looked at his hands, still holding the dark-red-stained strap in his hands.

A wind howled from where he stood toward the road away from the only home he knew.

CHAPTER 3

MARY

Near Plymouth, Massachusetts Bay Colony
1750

Mary stood outside her home in the intersection of the arriving dawn and the remnants of the fleeing night. Some people called her a thief, but she gave her life to both sides. She turned her head to her left and gazed in the direction of her fellow Indians. She turned her head to her right and gazed in the direction of her fellow colonists.

Somebody needed to do something. Not doing something would just lead to more war between her peoples. Most days she could find a way to rest in partial peace, living between the two groups. She knew why years ago they'd placed her ancestors in "praying towns" to live between the two sides. The natives who converted to Christianity, the "Praying Indians," were not always trusted by other fellow Indians, but trusted enough to be placed by the colonists to act as a level of protection between them and the native Indians. But usually not trusted enough to be fully assimilated with the colonists.

Mary was a living remnant of the Praying Indians and the old praying towns of years ago. She was still a living reminder of life between the worlds of the Indians, the Christian Indians, and the colonists. She'd thought that when she became a Christian and married a colonist, she would be embraced into the colonial community. But lingering thoughts spread in whispers about her. They thought she was a thief who stole a weak man away from a possible wife in the colony. Still, living between her two peoples seemed to be the best fit.

After another hour and another day at the front of her house, Mary, like a child left alone at home waiting for a loved one to return, decided Adam was not coming home today. The morning light was still missing within the four walls. She walked back inside, wondering if he could somehow be waiting to have breakfast in the shadows under their partially thatched-roof house. The extra chair at the table was still empty.

The same routine the past sixteen months. Years ago her hope for life changed when God told her in a dream she would one day have a child. But now in her early forties, she still waited for her husband to one day come back home and was still without the promised child. Although a few in her community believed that not all women were supposed to have children, many did not. Her husband refused to wait any longer. He'd told her someone would bear his name, and if it wasn't through Mary, it would have to be with someone else.

Peering through a back window, Mary sighed and wiped her eyes, as through the window a young mom breastfed her young one in the saltbox house next door. The home seemed to taunt her. It reminded her that the neighbor's roof was slanted like a box of salt, but her own home was bland and tasteless. One room. The highlight flavor in the decomposing visual meal was the attic loft for her child to one day sleep. She had separated and prepared the area, anticipating her beloved son or daughter, along with the yellow-paged books she grew up with and her house's only rug.

As she stood looking upward for future help and then answered with the regret of another day, she returned back to her present life, balancing both worlds in separate hands. Each world was like a knife in each hand, and the two hands were both trying to grab the knife in the other hand. Mary resisted like a mother separating her two fighting kids.

You are both of the same body. Why can't you both get along?

Her friend Martha walked up from behind. "Mary, have you wasted part of your morning again? He is not coming back."

Though Mary did not turn toward Martha, Mary was familiar with the remorse spreading through her friend.

Martha cleared her throat. "Are you going to follow through with our plan?"

Mary shrugged. "Someone, or something, is trying to pull me from opposite sides. My seams are fraying.

I just don't want to be the cause of bloodshed." She shook her head. "If I am going, then I need to go very soon. I ask God what does He want me to do, and I still have no answer." Mary turned toward Martha, against her better judgment.

Martha pointed her finger at Mary. "You know what you must do. You just don't want to do it."

Mary closed her eyes and took a deep breath. She walked over and took the secret item hidden behind a table and closed her fist. She stepped to the entrance, stopped, and turned toward Martha, still inside.

Mary tilted her head skyward. "Are you happy now? I am going."

Martha laughed. "I will be praying for you . . . because that is what we do."

The remnant of the Praying Indians both laughed.

Mary continued her walk, not knowing what awaited her. It was a beautiful morning to put her life at risk. What was left to live for? She existed with an elusive peace with her two peoples. No more husband. No family. Only two friends. One God. One empty, unfulfilled promise from God.

As she crossed from her home between the two worlds, she moved farther from the colonists and entered the periphery of the Indian village. The familiar outpost guards stopped her.

"Hey, Christian. Have you come back to return something else you took?"

More guards assembled nearby as others kept watchful eyes, looking around the periphery.

Do they actually think I would bring others to come and attack while I distract them? Mary pointed back toward the colonists and then locked eyes. "You know that I do not have any of their, or your, violence."

The main guard stopped smiling. "I know you, Mary. I know that we do not even need to search you. But it is not what you have with you but what is inside of you that is a concern. Who do you serve? Us or them?"

"Neither. Only the same God that you will one day bow down to. You just don't know it yet."

The guards laughed and shook their heads.

"Is your God pleased with your stealing? The same God that your people have killed for? I hear that you now spend time with a slave of theirs," the leader said.

Mary looked at her hand. She swept her brown hip-length hair from her face and moved her fingers, as if clawing at an invisible object. "I cling and hang on with slipping fingers upon my understanding of God's unmerited favor. I do not fully understand. I try to do what is right. Someday you should try serving someone besides yourself."

The leader snickered. "Your husband found a woman. She is now pregnant with his second child. He is happy. She is happy too."

He then laughed again. "He took away all that you had left. It is true justice when the thief finds out she married a thief better than her!"

Betrayed by an audible gasp, she covered her mouth too late. Another guard put his hand on the leader's shoulder and turned toward Mary with downward eyes. Now she knew where her husband went. He really was not coming back. So many months of suppressing the internal rebellion, and at the most inconvenient time, the open and festering wound from the battle exposed her for others to see. She wanted to cover herself in front of these men. She stood straighter as tears dripped off her cheeks. No words could be formed to express the fissure that turned into a clean break in her heart.

The other guard moved his hand from the main guard's shoulder and stepped between the leader and Mary. He pushed the leader away from her. She wanted to strike at them but calmed down when the leader paused.

She still wanted to strike her fellow Indians and colonists to just end it all. She wanted to run from God and His empty promises. Something snapped within her, and she stood with her knees locked. The guard who'd stepped between them moved to the side to reveal the leader still had a smile on his face. His laughing stopped as he flexed his arms and studied her next move in eager anticipation.

Any last remnant of respect for the men slinked away, but she still had the hidden item with her. Like someone falling down a cliffside and holding on to a single rock, she grasped it in her secret pocket like it was the last remnant of what she had left.

CHAPTER 4

CAESAR

Dover, Delaware Colony
1775

Caesar rolled out of bed alone but was accompanied by pain on the left side of his face. He again stood before his mirror, off centered so only the right side of his face peered back at him. His chest thumped in anticipation of his revolutionary plans for the morning. He bathed, dressed, and sat down for his pottage and old, hard biscuits.

In between weary bites of the cold, tough beef in his pottage, the empty chair across the table taunted him. It was pure nonsense to have purchased the second chair, but he'd bought it anyway in open and flagrant rebellion.

Caesar practiced conversation in his head. Then for the first time that day, he spoke aloud. With no fear of being a madman.

"Good morning, Dorothy. My . . . you look most divine . . . No, that is not right . . . You look beautiful . . . You look beautiful this morning. I enjoyed our brief conversation . . . two weeks ago . . . downtown. And I was wondering if . . . perhaps . . . we could eat sometime . . . if you would like to join me for lunch . . . someday . . ."

Caesar buried his head in his hands, avoiding touching the left side of his face. He usually had a busy schedule, but on days like this, would he be able to leave his home and venture outside? He did not like to impose. Even hiding behind a green scarf, he still did not like terrifying people. Especially ones he wanted to impress. Every day it was much safer inside. Curtains drawn. With the empty chair.

Caesar cleared his throat. Today would be the day. He walked over to his choice of scarves. He separated the dozen or so green scarves and picked out a less stained dark-green one. He covered part of his face. He then went to the mirror with only the right side of his face showing. He made some final adjustments, then tucked some strands of hair behind his ear. He walked to the door.

He paused and looked at his right hand on the knob. Did he really want to go outside? Today? To her?

He opened the door partway and placed his right ear between the expanding space of the partially opened door and outside. It did not sound like anyone was near. He placed the right side of his face outside. It was a clear early morning. Cold but clear, with no sign of rain so far. There were people nearby, but they were walking away from his home, so he would be safe if he stepped out.

With few people out and about, Caesar took long steps toward downtown, which reminded him of riding his finest horse and cutting through the air with no concern about his face or his health. But he could not be too early so as to impose even more upon Dorothy with his spontaneous and uninvited visit.

It would be warmer soon, so he could not bundle himself to hide better, as he preferred. Caesar pulled his scarf tighter over the left side of his face and tried to keep his head down. As he turned the corner, a young mother with three children walked toward him.

What is a young mother with three young children doing out at this hour? You should be in the safety of home.

"Good morning," Caesar said as they approached.

The mother and her children looked up at him, and she said, "Good—" and then moved, as if a rat had suddenly appeared on her breakfast table.

She pulled her kids away from him as she positioned herself between her children and Caesar. Caesar's feet were as if stuck in thick mud. As one of the children cried, the mother grouped her children into walking the opposite direction of Caesar as the mother kept her head turned toward him.

After the mother looked down at her crying children, a strange look crossed her face. Perhaps like remorse after dismembering the rat on her table in front of her children.

When she was several strides away, she mouthed *I'm sorry* above the wailing children.

This was not new for Caesar. For the last few years, he'd had almost half his face eaten away by one of humanity's worst adversaries. This battle had increased in ferocity the last few months and repulsed many away from him. Perhaps because most people did not want Caesar's face to act as a mirror in front of *them*, reminding each person of the daily death encroaching and spreading upon each person.

Something was in the air. All could sense that soon no one would be able to hide the face of war, with a soiled, fraying veil soon to be fully removed to reveal the ugly cancer that humans inflicted upon each other. A scarf was no defense against the king. The coming war would separate the loyalists and the rebels, brother against brother, sister against sister.

But this time a woman with wailing children, just trying to survive in the battle of the day, stabbed at his chest in a new way, as if someone twisted the blade. The blade turned and moved within whatever still filled his chest. It was not empty. The blade did not turn into a frozen sword in hard ground. The heart still beat in the opposing fist gripping it.

Caesar stood stuck in the mud. He pulled his scarf tighter. He looked toward his home. He looked toward the direction of Dorothy's home.

Far away.

CHAPTER 5

MO

**Near Boston, Massachusetts Bay Colony
1766**

Mo's legs jerked into a reflexive bending movement as he prepared for what was next after his master yelled for him. The ground seemed to shift, and he put his hands on his legs and bent forward under the weight of the master's command to come. When Mo had his daughter or son one day, he was never going to yell at them like a slave master calling his slaves.

The man's words moved like a pack of hunting dogs unleashed from a dark throne within the house that cast the shadow at night and day. One of the master's cowskin straps that he used for beatings taunted Mo and seemed to pulsate in his right hand. The straps used to break the master's slaves now attempted to seduce Mo into using the knife strapped to his upper leg. *I can free my people here, and I would be a hero of the generations. And even if I died trying, I would be even more of a hero to inspire the Betsys and Wills on every plantation.*

Mo remembered a few years earlier wanting to fight in the French and Indian War, but he was too young to unleash his wrath against the ones who, like his master, enslaved and hunted humans. If he would have been allowed to fight, it would have been a legal way to let his justice loose.

He walked closer to the rear side of the house and hid the strap behind a large bush, to bury or use later. The light of the open road to his right called him. He knew he could run. He knew he could run fast. Could he carry the freedom inside him and outrun men on horses? Or beyond the reach of the sniffing angry dogs? Could he outrun what was fired from a gun?

Mo adjusted the hidden knife and pushed down with his right foot, like driving a stake into the ground, and turned and dragged his feet to his left toward the front of the house. He passed his oldest of friends, Christopher, who reached out and touched Mo's shoulder as he moved.

Additional words from the man inside the house seemed to summon more cloud cover. "I told you to come here. Now."

As Mo approached the open front door, all eyes, like tips of dull knives, jabbed at him. It was as if they expected Mo to do something. Maybe they thought it would amuse them and break the daily monotony. They would soon suffer from what Mo was going to do.

Like the eyes of the master's old beaten-up dogs, the master's men followed with their eyes of wariness as Mo stalked forward. They must have thought, *When was the uncivilized savage going to fully emerge?* They all knew the master was grooming him to one day be in charge of all the slaves, and they also knew Mo would not help his master. Something had to give.

As he walked by the others, he thought of his mother and smiled and whispered to himself, "Be ready . . . be ready . . ."

He was going to enter the master's meeting room, where the master ruled from his throne on high. The last time the master had summoned him into his throne room, he'd insisted that Mo enter and leave while never turning his back to him. He one time even told him to kneel down after entering.

A few feet before Mo entered the room with the opened door, a wide smile covered the master's face. A slithering noise seemed to move from the entrance of the house to the general region of where the master sat. Mo covered his burning nostrils.

Nobody should be smiling while death waits.

As soon as he entered, men who had been leaning against the back wall slammed the door shut. Mo stopped and turned and counted six men. He wondered if they were all related in some way, as they all wore the same smile the master had.

He looked down to the floor, waiting for the thrashing. On the floor, the shadows of the coming hands flared toward him.

He closed his fluttering eyelids. His heart skipped beats. The hands grabbed his shoulders and arms, and someone kicked the back of his leg and made his knees buckle. He yelped and collapsed backward onto the floor.

Familiar clicking noises surrounded him. "Next time you will run when I call you, or you will not run again," the master snarled.

The men pulled him off the floor and threw him into a chair facing the seated master.

The master's teeth clicked, as if anticipating a great meal. "I have had great hope for you. I sense something familiar in you, and you are going to do what I demand. There is a calling over your life."

The master stood and walked to Mo's side as Mo kept his eyes looking forward.

Mo winced when the master put his index finger on Mo's forehead and clicked with his teeth. "I know you because I know how you think."

He leaned closer to Mo and used his hand to turn Mo's head toward him. Mo closed his eyes and could not stop his eyelids from fluttering.

"You have been plotting. Plotting against me. I have removed your mother, and she is in another location. If you ever turn against me, I will end her suffering and increase yours."

Mo kept his eyes closed. He was not going to cry in front of him. His right hand opened and closed. The weapon with the cold edges pressed against his thigh and asked for him.

This is for Mother.

Mo moved his hand nearer to what called him. The other men closed their circle around Mo. Moisture surrounded his neck and encroached on his fore-head. Sweat fled from his forehead down his cheek. The men tightened their circle.

They took away Mom. There is no one left for me. I have nothing to lose.

The door opened, and they pulled ten slaves into the room. Little Betsy's best friend stood with them, with her hands over her mouth as she bent forward then upright several times, trying to stand tall. The master smiled with black teeth and breath that reminded Mo of the corner of the property where they went to relieve themselves. Mo moved slowly to cover his nose with his forearm, as death itself seemed to spew out of the master's mouth with each word.

Mo tried to keep his hand steady as the master's stare cut through any attempt by Mo to divert his eyes to reassure the now sobbing young girl.

"Slave. Now get up and rule over my slaves."

I could never live if my daughter witnessed what Betsy and her friend are going to see in their short lives. How will this little girl view people older than her? How will she view people different from her? How will she live thinking that all people are like these men? How have I lived like that?

Mo raised his shoulder up to wipe his cheek. He tried not to let them see the moisture near his eyes. His legs could not move as he adjusted his posture and moved his right hand toward his left hip. The hidden blade was still cold and demanded a warmer internal environment.

The master walked away from him as he laughed. Guns were in hand, ready for use. Even if Mo was able to pull out the knife, he wasn't sure he could get close enough to the master to kill him without one of the other men killing Mo first. The other slaves would be killed in the ensuing shooting. Betsy could be killed later in the slaver's fury.

There will be a right time. Betsy, one day I will really free you.

Mo raised his head up and turned toward the master. "If I prove to be who you believe me to be, will you return my mother?" Mo's voice cracked.

The master walked toward the back of the room and came behind him and then to Mo's side. "I don't negotiate with my property."

Mo closed his eyes.

"Your mother will live or die based on your actions . . . or my mood. And right now, I have no more patience. Go." He pointed toward the other slaves.

This was not the time for the plan. His mother would need to wait. They pulled him up from the chair, and two men shoved him to the floor. One kick to his stomach made him forget about his mother.

As he lay heaving, searching for the lost air, he found that his time to free the slaves was not there. He was going to the cotton fields again.

***

Mo and his fellow slaves tried to ignore the master's demon walking between them and around the periphery of their section of work in the cotton field. This particular demon hated his life and doing slave duty. He preferred to work under the large trees on a hot day. Alone. And with his alcohol ruling him.

Sometimes an individual slave did such a great job of ignoring the demon's taunts that when the demon did say something relevant, another nearby slave would have to nudge the fellow slave to mentally return back to the body who was working.

Midday, one of the younger slaves asked for water and then collapsed. The others continued staring down at the hard ground and working, as they usually did when someone collapsed, while those nearby helped the one who'd collapsed. Mo told a slave to run and bring water. All the slaves with Mo stopped their work this time. The demon grumbled something with his hands planted on his hips as his face harvested a red crop.

The demon stomped over to the young man assisting the worker on the ground. The demon's entire body trembled as he shook his head. He then switched to nodding. He bent and put the young man in a headlock and forced his face onto the ground. The slave turned his head to breathe and grunted and moaned as he pushed upward to shove the demon off. The demon widened his smile.

The slave's breathing slowed with a higher pitch in gasping. Three of the other slaves ran toward them. The demon snarled with a quick snap of his teeth, like an angry dog scaring off competition from taking his meal.

He paused and smiled. "I have been watching this one. So much complaining. Crying. Why am I alive? To watch over this? I have had enough. Watch his eyes."

The slave closed his eyes and collapsed.

"He'll be fine in a few minutes. I will take care of him. Get back to work. Who else is refusing to work?" the demon said.

One young girl cried out. Two boys looked at her and walked toward the demon.

Mo ran and placed himself between the young men and the demon and raised his hands up. "Stop, my brothers. This is a trap that you will not be able to get out of. If you attack him, your lives are over."

One of the young men continued walking up to Mo and placed his face in front of Mo's. "What lives do we have if we do nothing? Will you continue to rule over breathing dead children working from sunrise to sunset for the master demon and his workers?"

"This is not the right time. Someday we will be free." Mo shook his head.

"Go ahead and kill me," the demon said while laughing. "I have nothing to lose. I'll never own this plantation. Do you think I want to rule over you animals the rest of my life?" The laughing stopped abruptly.

The slave who'd first collapsed sat up. The demon bent toward the slave who had crumbled from the headlock, turned him over, and pulled on his arms to rise up. The slave's chest did not move.

The demon smiled. "Go ahead and kill me before I kill more!" He pulled out a knife from its sheath attached to his belt. "I will tell him how all of you attacked me after I kill you all."

The demon sprang upward and lunged toward one of the young men surrounding him. Mo blinked as the demon's knife reflected into his eyes. He moved to the side to avoid the reflection but could not stop it from seemingly calling his name. The demon's deep guttural tone, like a voice that belonged to someone else, made everyone take one step back. "Someone is trying to stop my reign in my slave. Which one of you is the one I want?"

Mo jumped in between to protect his friends as the demon slashed the knife in front of him. Mo yelped and grabbed his wet right hand. The demon grabbed a young man and squeezed the headlock as the young man verged on passing out. Sixteen years of rage pulled on the fraying leash, and Mo could not stop his body from shaking or his eyes from pulsating and blurring. Mo tackled the demon and the young man to the ground. The young man crumpled. The demon screamed in fear and then in laughter.

Mo straddled him with the demon's knife in Mo's hand, when another young man ran toward them. Mo turned his head toward his right hand. The veins on the back of his hand moved in rhythm to his pounding chest. Christopher came out of nowhere and hit the side of Mo's head and wrestled the knife out of Mo's hand.

With the authority of an older brother, Christopher stopped Mo from retaliating, with only his words. "Not you, Mo. God has a plan for you, and therefore it must be for all of us as well."

The demon laughed. "That same God created men to rule over the animals. You will always be just an animal."

The same slithering noise from the master's house moved toward and stopped underneath the demon. His voice deepened. "I will chase you down like I have with all my other slaves since the garden. I will appoint one of my demons to hunt you down when you think you are free and have escaped. I will be waiting for you." The demon laughed. "Even when this vessel I inhabit dies, I will find another. I will find you. I already know who you are and where you will go. I will find you when you are most tired after trying to sleep with one eye open all the time."

The demon spoke as if right to the eyes of Mo's heart. He spit onto Mo's face. "Slave . . ." He squeezed the young man's neck still in the headlock.

Heat from rage awoke within the confines of its living cage as it rushed with all its power to bust open a now weakened door. Mo's body shook, and the hairs on the back of his arms and neck rose up in surrender, like locks unbolting and releasing a beast inside a bending cage. Mo reached toward his own left hip and pulled out his knife and ended the demon's laughing.

Even the birds flying overhead silenced their cries, with blood on the ground. Everything stopped moving. A stillness in the air weighed down. The young man coughed and heaved for newfound air. Mo knew what the others knew. In the eyes of the master, each of them was now guilty of murder. There was no self-defense claim in the courtroom of the master and his demons.

Mo dropped the knife. He wiped his hands on the dirt and tried to rub out the crimson red. He then wept and stood, shaking his head. Christopher stood with his head down and his mouth wide open.

"I am so sorry. Not for this murderer . . . but for how I have now affected the rest of your lives. I will tell Master what I did. Perhaps he will believe me and let all of you live."

"We have to run," one young slave then said. "We die if we don't run, and if we run, at least there is a chance that a few of us can find free men up north."

Mo shook his head. "There are six of us. We need to hide the body. No time to bury him. We must separate and go in different directions. Tonight, let us meet at Smith's farm. We know where it is from our trips with the master when we would trade, and this time we will trade slavery for freedom. We meet when the moon is at the highest. Stay hidden during daylight."

They dragged the body behind a large bush underneath a large tree, then ran in separate directions.

CHAPTER 6

MARY

**Near Plymouth, Massachusetts Bay Colony
1750**

Mary left the laughing outpost guards and walked toward the chief. Though she had spent much time with the colonists, she still had some favor with her own people as well. But who were her people really?

She passed several women preparing for the day. Some smiled and some tried to look busy. Two young children tapped their mothers' shoulders and pointed to her. Mary waved.

The sky was clear as the smells of her life floated around her. Some were going to have fish. Even unseen offerings of corn and beans floated in and out of her nostrils.

Mary let go of the frozen grip of her hands and stashed her item in a hidden pocket she'd sewed into her dress weeks before in preparation. Some colonial women tied their long hair in a bun, but Mary kept her brown hair long and unencumbered, as she had from her youth. Her fingers ached, and she had a hard time opening and closing her hands as she brushed her hair away from her face. The invisible meals seemed to enter her, and she smiled. She exhaled and breathed in a sometimes forgotten peace.

My food helps me remember the peace that surpasses all understanding.

Over the years, most in the village could see a different spirit within Mary, and there was a certain degree of trust they had for her, even though they had heard rumors of her previous history of thievery. They still kept one eye open on her at all times. If for anything, it was to not allow her to talk about Jesus.

They said He was the white man's God.

How can He be the white man's God when He created every man and woman from every tribe, tongue, and nation?

After several more guards stopped her, and after several deep breaths, they allowed her to enter into the presence of the chief. Inside, the chief walked toward Mary. He was a short but strong man who carried the burden of his people on his strong back. Mary tilted her head down but acknowledged that there was a presence that surrounded the man. The chief emptied the area of his guards within his small, minimalist-styled home, until only Mary remained.

Mary scanned the combination of books and weapons of war he collected, up against the walls of his meeting area. It was a thatched-roof room but had the comfort and intimacy of an old teepee.

"Mary, I hope you have something for me."

Mary had a difficult time moving her right hand to grab what was hidden in her pocket. *Will he take it?* Her hand fisted and seemed to be stuck in her pocket. After a few moments, she was able to free her trembling hand while pulling out the item.

Mary shook her head. "This was not easy. They have trust of me. They . . . should know better."

She handed the paper to the chief. He paused and studied her eyes and then the paper. He fixed his eyes on her again and then lifted the paper upward so he could look at her and the paper side by side from a distance. He smiled. "I will be ready. If this is a trick, much of our and their blood will be shed."

He narrowed his eyes. "I will hold you responsible for this." He pointed to the piece of paper. "You will lie awake at night, alone, with no man to protect you and not knowing if you should close your eyes, for you will not be able to rest knowing what could happen to you in the night. Which night, you will not know. When you will die slowly, you will not know."

Mary closed her eyes for a few moments, and as she walked away, the chief said, "Our people, *your* people, are in debt to you once again. I know you worked hard on this. The Great Spirit is pleased with you and your work. Go and make more right choices."

Mary started her walk home when someone bumped into her and put something in her dress pocket. Only a few people knew about that secret pocket. Mary adjusted her petticoat and gave a knowing smile. As she passed a mother combing her daughter's long dark hair, she felt a great love for her people. Her brothers. Her sisters.

She remembered her childhood when her parents would fight. Her mother would scream at her father that the colonists were taking their land and that they needed to kill the invaders before their own people were completely wiped out. Her father would scream back that the majority of colonists were desiring peace and that the land belonged to God and He would choose who would steward what was His.

As a little girl, she remembered sitting on the ground looking up at her heroes on each side of her as they yelled at each other, forgetting that their trembling daughter was holding herself to stop the shaking between them. She remembered her mother saying to her father, "You know what happened on that island."

Her father shook his head and replied, "You know we have blood on our hands too. Killing people with their family watching, burning down their homes with families trapped inside was not helpful."

Her mother wiped her face. "They burned down our villages, and with our people trapped and screaming their last words for help was not helpful."

Her father extended out his hands. "We all have blood on our hands."

Her mother placed her head in her hands. "But we can't forget what they did to us on that island."

She loved both her parents. She remembered crying alone several times and pacing outside and one moment believing her mother was right, and then moments later believing her father was right.

Years later the sounds of her parents screaming still remained trapped, echoing with no resolution and no way out within her head.

But perhaps the short meeting with the chief today would start something different. She paused her steps. She was not able to face either village as she stood in between them.

I need to get away. I have time today, so I can make that long walk. Several minutes of walking could help clear her mind and distract her from what was going on in her head. She turned and headed to one of her favorite places.

The birds seemed to chirp and sing more than usual, as if trying to cheer her up. They reminded her she was not alone. She spun around to say, "I hear you, and I thank God for each of you." One bird chirped even louder above the others, as if responding. The others escorted her in their morning chorus. Even the birds seemed to worship the Creator among His creation in their outdoor church service.

After a lengthy stroll, she arrived at her sacred place and paused again to take in what was happening and what would one day happen on this spot. Before her a clearing that seemed like a courtyard before entering the area near a tree that reminded her of a throne before its subjects. Alone. Set apart from the others. A European beech tree bigger and taller than the nearest surrounding trees. A perfect view to the area many locals said was the spot where the Pilgrims had landed aboard the *Mayflower*.

She leaned against the beech as she scanned all that was before it. She picked up a small piece of bark that had fallen. She studied it in her hand.

This is my prayer. O Great Spirit, my God, I know You have this area separated and set apart for You. With whatever power I have in You, I dedicate this area as a monument of how You can make even our sinful ways into something great. Even if this tree does not survive, may this area still be a monument of Your faithfulness, even moving through the unfaithful. Your perfect will done by the imperfect.

Then she returned back to leaning on the tree. She placed the small piece of bark on the ground. For the moment she stood between all the many prayers said and answered for all God's children over the years, from the Israelites in the Middle East, to those who came here from Europe, to those forced against their will to come here from Africa, and to those who were native to this land.

There has to be a God, right? But what happened on that island in 1675 I cannot forget. I know the stories.

The voices inside her screamed louder than before.

God, where are You? How can we get back to You above all others?

CHAPTER 7

MO

**Near Boston, Massachusetts Bay Colony
1766**

The sun retreated underground below the horizon as Mo hid behind a large tree at Smith's farm. The scene of Mo and his friends running away after Mo had killed the master's worker replayed in his head. Blood from the beatings in the fields was not new to him, but it was different when one's own hands caused it and were covered in it. If he lived long enough to find a woman who could love him, would he ever be able to tell her what he had done? If he ever had the opportunity to bring into the world a child like Betsy to free others, could he keep the secret from his daughter? With permanent blood on his hands, could he now ever be a good father?

Even in the deepening and expanding eclipse of the day, Mo stepped back and marveled at the tree now shielding him. It dominated the sky. For a time the tree would protect him.

This tree was like an old woman who had seen everything and outlived others. The stories it could tell of what they'd done to each other. It saw family gatherings. *I have no family.* It saw kids climbing up its trunk and branches and playing down below. *Did the children who looked like me ever play like that? I have seen adults whipped at trees. What could this tree tell me? What about all the picnics? Wonderful food I have only seen and never had. Embraces of loved ones. Where are mine?*

There was enough darkness to hide but enough light to search the near horizon. Where were the others? Smith had a large plantation, and one could hide behind the different tree groves. Mo had already waited at least an hour or two, and there was still no sign of the others.

Something stirred in some bushes several feet away. The bushes moved and then stopped. Demons working for the master could easily hide in the dark. Even fellow slaves sometimes could not be trusted, as they sometimes worked for their masters. Who could blame them when they and their families were threatened if they did not help their masters?

A large bird cawed above him as it also retreated from the night. Mo waited several more minutes for any other signs of life. Maybe he'd just imagined the movement.

No, something or someone was nearby. Reminded of an old story he'd heard from a fellow slave, the moving bush could only be more obvious if it had been on fire and speaking to him.

No one approached from up or down the nearby road. It was clear as far as he could tell. He moseyed with light feet in the direction of the bush. The ground seemed harder than when he'd run to the Smith plantation. Still no movement. No signs of any of the others. He bent and crawled toward the bush. Could it be a stray calf needing to be returned to its master? Someone's legs stuck out without movement on the ground off to the side of the bush. Someone was hiding. But the legs were not moving. With the disappearing light, he recognized the sores on the bottom of the feet.

One of the older slaves. Christopher.

"Christopher, are you okay?" Mo did not want to move any closer in hope of avoiding what was coming.

With hesitation and a voice just above a whisper, Christopher spoke. "Mo . . . I knew I would find . . . you . . . God told me . . ."

Mo shook his head. "There is no time for God—we need to move." Mo put his hand on Christopher's shoulder to calm him. "Can you get up?"

Christopher's panting increased. "They shot the rest. I saw dogs chewing on some of them . . . they almost got me . . ."

Mo's tears ran down his face as tracks of cleaner lines ran down Christopher's dirty face.

"You have been shot . . . How did you get here?"

"We initially went in different directions, but the younger ones were scared, so I gathered them and we ran together. I could not leave them on their own. But they slowed me down. What could I do?"

Everything seemed to stop and wait for Christopher. "The master eventually saw us in the distance. Satan within them enraged them so much that they shot at us with no regard. They shot at all of us . . . there were too many dogs." Christopher adjusted his position with a moan. "I was shot first, and they ran away from me . . . They passed me . . . The demons didn't see that I fell in the bushes." Christopher heaved for a big breath. "Somehow . . . the dogs ran by me . . . I think God threw them off . . . He must have wanted . . . me to find you . . . one last time."

Mo closed his eyes and shook his head. He thought of the strange voices in his dreams at night. He cleared his throat. His voice cracked and staggered. "You have been shot . . . This is my fault. I should have just hit the demon and kept him alive. But I could not . . . too much anger." Mo opened his eyes more fully and turned toward the tree. He waited as Christopher gathered more strength.

Christopher held his left side, as if trying to keep something inside him a bit longer. He groaned and exhaled, like he had run a long race. He grabbed Mo's torn shirt to pull him closer and tore it some more. "I have something for you. There is a great Light. God is planting something . . . and generations will be affected by that Seed . . . Carry that Seed of God . . . even if it at first does not seem right . . . Do not follow your heart . . ."

Mo saw the crimson stain on Christopher's side colonize more of his shirt and the land beneath him. His breathing slowed. His eyes fixed on Mo. There was a fire in his unblinking eyes that grew stronger as Christopher's breathing shallowed.

Mo had to turn his head toward the tree. Tears streamed down. Somehow, someway, a thought implanted into his head. *A long time ago, someone was praying at a tree. Praying for me? I can feel the words on me now. Who was she?*

A breeze brushed against his face and departed as Christopher's last exhalation rose from both of them and drifted upward. All his previous words seemingly lifted and floated away to another place that would always be near Mo. Words in a prayer that would descend back down one day. Words that would speak for him one day before a great Light. Christopher stopped talking. He stopped moving. The words blew further away to warm Mo's next memory of Christopher.

There was now no one else for Mo to worry or care about. He knew he would not see his mother again. What was there to live for? Who was there to live for? But what about Betsy? Would the hope of a family, a daughter to bring freedom, be enough to sustain him from the hunt through all generations?

Was that dogs and voices in the distance? No time for mourning. What use was he if they killed him as he wasted time lamenting a friend who'd died?

He bent his head toward his darkening hands. The blood of a murdered friend now mixed with the dried blood of a murderer. What would the God of wrath that the slavers taught, do with a child of His who became a bad seed? When would the angry God send Mo to hell?

Then the nightmares in his head and the life he lived would finally stop.

Chapter 8

KING GEORGE

Buckingham House, England
1774

George had noticed for the last several months a distant digging sound. He stood with his hands on his hips before his great wall. It started as a remote shoveling sound, but over the last few days, it had grown louder. Scraping. Clawing. Digging. Underground. The wall and his people behind it were safe and had never been seriously threatened, with the world's strongest military under his command. The colonized found comfort and security when George took on their burdens for them. The wall provided an enclosure for keeping his wandering children protected under his guard. It was one of the few reasons he could get any sleep at night. His people were safe. He was safe.

But this night was different.

The sound, like the rhythm of ocean water alternating between high tide and low tide, seemed to now be only a few feet away somewhere below ground level as it aimed at moving under him and then through his wall to leave. Was it wolves enticing part of George's herd to leave from the protection of the great Shepherd to sure death on the other side of his wall? George shook his head in his shaking hands.

What madness would infect people to risk their lives and the comfort of my provision?

He had ordered many of his men, men who feared their God, to build a reinforcement wall within the interior of the main wall. He commanded his men to shoot anyone who tried to wander and deceive others to escape to their ruin. His men built extra barriers and protection in front of George with their backs to him, so they did not notice his body trembling and his eyes darting to and fro. How was George to be faithful with the commands of God if those under George's command rebelled against the God dwelling in George?

He wiped his forehead and rubbed his hands on his damp and torn breeches. Then one man, while standing with his hands on the wall, yelled, "They are breaking through to the other side somewhere!"

George collapsed onto the ground. As he lay on his side, he pulled his knees to his chest as some men jumped over him as they ran away from the wall. They abandoned him.

A voice inside of him slithered. *The murderer is deceiving many to leave you. You will be alone with only your thoughts.*

He awoke from his nightmare with a cry into the night in Buckingham House. His wife, Queen Charlotte, placed her hand on his chest.

"You were talking in your sleep. Those nightmares are getting worse. My dear, are you okay?"

The king did not answer. He pushed her hand away and wiped his face and then his hands. He jumped out of bed and paced around the bedroom.

"My nightmare . . . was very real. It used to always be the same. But every day this week it has been different. I am sorry I awoke you, my love."

The queen sat up, facing him. "What is really wrong?"

George paced, as if waiting for marching orders. He stopped and faced away from her. "There is too much unrest. We have fought wars to maintain our way of life. Our way of life is under attack. There are some who are foolish enough, ignorant enough, to rebel against their God and their Motherland."

He then stopped and faced a window. "God will strike down the ungrateful fools." His voice elevated. "Do they not know how God has blessed them?"

Charlotte stepped out of bed and placed her hand on his shoulder as she hugged him from behind. "God is in you. They will all come to know the truth."

George separated from her and walked away, shaking his head. He paused and looked out the window and scanned his kingdom in the nighttime. "But at what cost does truth extract this time? Do we want war between brethren? We finished our war with the French, and we were victorious. But at what cost? What a tremendous financial cost. Lives lost can be replaced, but how will we pay the cost to be free in God's kingdom? Will my commands, like the Coercive Acts, work on the rebellious colonies? What happens when we close their ports and house our soldiers on what they perceive as their soil and in their establishments?"

He paced again and motioned, with his hand, like an axe hitting stubborn wood. "Is this not a cancer that must be cut off before it spreads to others? I fear that others under our submission and influence may want to do what the colonies are doing. At what further cost will I pay for freedom? Do we not know that sometimes the Shepherd must maim wandering sheep to remind the other sheep from wandering into trouble?"

His love's voice raised. "You are more than a Shepherd."

The one appointed by the divine wiped his hands and clenched them into fists. "God Himself indwells in me. Empowers me. I can feel the power running through me. Others who see God in me bow down before me in my castle. I would be wrong to stop them from doing so."

He walked out of the room. It was another night with little to no sleep. It was another night for Charlotte by herself.

The king returned to stick his head into the room. "What was I saying while I was sleeping?"

Queen Charlotte sat with her head bowed. She raised her head toward him. "It was mostly nonsense. You spoke in mumbling sentences, and I could only make out one word."

King George then pivoted and returned to the doorway. Charlotte had her head down again, as if looking for help somewhere on the floor.

"What word was that?"

She remained with her head down and did not look up to say, "Murderer."

George reflexively moved his head backward, as if avoiding an annoying fly. *Murderer? It was just a bad dream. The same dream almost every night.* On his way to an outdoor balcony, he carefully checked for anyone hiding in the night behind a wall, waiting to end the divine right in a king.

Could a murderer somewhere want to kill God in George all over again, like they did with Jesus in a human body? The Dark Light spoke to George about this matter. Jesus had the perfect vengeance ruling inside George, just waiting to enact full justice and revenge upon the modern-day sinners and then rule the world through George. All the enemies, especially the murderer, had to pay for killing an innocent man on the cross hundreds of years ago. Jesus was innocent. He was a lamb slaughtered. The murderer would soon pay.

Then King George remembered who he was and the Dark Light that lived with him.

He could feel someone, or something, standing near. He was not alone. He was never alone.

King George III went into the night like a shepherd, on guard against the wolves while on his high vantage point overseeing his expanding kingdom. He sought what the Dark Light wanted. At least for now, there was unity with the source of his power.

The murderer. He is out there. I must find him.

CHAPTER 9

GEORGE WHITEFIELD

Gloucester, England
1726

He stood near his garden, on the moving line on the ground of the afternoon changing into evening. He tried to harmonize the two sides with his crossed eyes. Something was wrong. Some of his plants were dying. He covered his nose with the bend of his elbow, though most times he did not notice the smell in the small yard.

When his once-again distracted mother allowed him a rare break from work at his parents' tavern, twelve-year-old George Whitefield returned to his garden, holding his favorite books of plays and stories.

It was not actually a tavern but an inn, though everyone just thought of it as a tavern. He tucked the books under his arm and stared at the aftermath of seeds he'd planted in the garden behind his home and parents' business.

He would act out a spontaneous play performing in his head in a given moment and performed for his wilted audience. He made up stories about the night attempting to overtake the day of the garden. He turned his head all around to make sure there was no one else in his staged playhouse. He waved his arms up and down, trying to emphasize each word with each action as he acted outwardly the play in his head, playing inwardly before an audience of one. He practiced saying each word differently to find the best effect on his audience. He was perfect, as no one ever booed him.

Though he had never had an interest in plants months before, he was fascinated with how his garden grew despite its challenges. The edge of the tavern's shadow moved over the section where the planted seeds did not grow as well compared to the seeds on the more lighted side of the makeshift garden.

The dividing edge moved like an expanding wall capturing its subjects behind it as the captives were stuck in the ground, unable to flee. The wall moved forward until it captured the entire yard and then recaptured the yard all over again the following day.

The plants imprisoned on one side of the wall never did as well the plants that were free on the other side. He watered and cared for them equally, but there was always a difference between the two sides. He remained standing on the line.

Human beings also played an important role in the health of the seeds and seedlings. Some of the plants did not grow because many of the patrons of the tavern stumbled and trampled into the backyard to relieve themselves. They often collapsed upon the seedlings until the following morning.

As he stood in place, George remembered all the events he'd witnessed in the tavern and in the backyard. He was ashamed by what his eyes wanted to see.

Men with women not married to each other should not do those things.

But yet curiosity often pulled on him. It was as if one eye wanted to indulge in things he knew he should not indulge in, and the other eye tried to focus on other things. Though other kids made fun of his crossed eyes, most of the time it was not an issue for him. At times it was difficult to focus on one thing without the distraction of something else pulling on him, but he persevered. But something in him, or around him, resisted him and pulled him in the wrong direction during the worst times.

His mother stepped outside and found George. With one hand on her hip and the other pointing a bent and permanently crooked finger at him, she yelled, "Damn you, boy. I should have known you would be back here. No wonder your sins made you cross-eyed. You have one eye on work and the other on your foibles. Get your arse in here. I need help, and there is work to do."

With that his mother disappeared. Like his father had when he'd died, when George was two. Adults had tried to help George grow up over the years, but there was always that emptiness. Escaping to another world through reading and his favorite plays helped plant him in other worlds than the one without a father and with a sometimes absent mother.

The previous night, he'd awoken in tears and his heart pounding for attention when he had a nightmare of his mother dying. In the nightmare, he was even more of an orphan than he'd ever imagined.

George had a minute or two before someone would come out to get him. He turned his head in all directions, and since it was safe, he then spoke to himself, as no one else ever listened. As the youngest of seven children, he was the last one born and the last one heard. He held a captive audience in the small garden.

Alcohol was not always bad, but when people had an invisible leash attached to it, people could do bad things to themselves and others. He did not ever want to turn into one of those people with the leash wrapped around their necks tethered to something living yet invisible.

His work at a tavern and helping desperate people to do improper things could wait. George patted one wilting plant as he scanned his kingdom. "I will see you later, my little planties. I will read you another play, and perhaps you can grow so tall that I can climb one of you and scale over these walls and escape to freedom. Escape to a place where seeds can grow and blossom within a shadow that moves and overtakes."

A hand appeared from the doorway in the corner of his eye. Was it possible to smell a hand when it is several feet away? From the fumes of alcohol, he knew whose hand it belonged to. Fingers of the hand grabbed George's left earlobe and pulled. His mother's boyfriend always smelled like the tavern. "She told you to come here, you useless boy."

George winced and cried out, as he was sure this time that frayed left earlobe would tear off and fall into excrement for the fat rats to nibble on. As the hand pulled him back toward the back door and then inside, he tripped over and landed on top of someone who had collapsed onto the floor just inside of the doorway. George's face touched down on the face of the man, when other hands pulled George off him.

"Move out of the way, boy. Degory is not moving," someone said.

George stood, as if he had fallen on someone's warm excrement. George brushed his clothes, as if brushing something invisible off him. He did not know what to do. He moved out of the way and planted himself against a wall and wondered if he'd almost kissed a dead man with dried vomit in his beard. The other men tried to shake Degory awake, but he was not moving. One person ran off to find a doctor.

George recognized the man not moving on the ground.

I was the last one who gave him the alcohol poison.

CHAPTER 10

MO

Near Boston, Massachusetts Bay Colony
1766

The dream every night summoned him like his master did back home. Like the master's slaves on the plantation, the voices within the dream seeking one voice to free them cried out. In the dream, Mo walked in the dark barefoot, with his feet sloshing in the mud. Why was there water on the ground when it had not rained in months? Nothing grew here. There were no trees or even grass or bushes. Just dark-colored weeds.

Voices crying out moved like the wind above him. A shriek tore through the night sky. He could not see where it came from. The sky did not allow him to even know if there was a star in the sky.

The shriek moved again and pierced through him and made him cover his ears as it passed above him. It was roaming. Searching. Looking. Did it see Mo?

He clawed at his neck, trying to remove the hand tightening around his throat. There was no hand. Mo looked for water. Any water. His tongue stuck to the roof of his mouth. He could not scream, even if he wanted to. The crying voices ceased. But yet he knew there were people around. Or something was. All were hiding.

Mo then remembered his wet feet. *Just a drop will keep me alive a little longer.*

He put a finger on his foot and brought it to his mouth. He spat it out. He wiped his mouth and spat out any residual taste out of his mouth. It was famil-iar. It tasted like whenever someone hit him in the mouth back home.

It was warm.

It was blood.

Mo returned from remembering his nightmare and knelt back down next to Christopher. It was difficult to focus after wandering in the nightmare. He shook his head, as if to wake himself up. He wanted to cry out and join the voices in his dream, but stopped, as it would give away his location to the hunter demons working for their master. "Goodbye, my friend. I am sorry for what I did to you."

Mo placed his hand on Christopher's face as the yelling and barking dogs moved closer. Christopher still had a fire in his eyes, full of love for others up until his last breath, but Mo had something else burning deep inside of him. It ate at him and would consume him if left unchecked. The burning spread inside him like moments before a lit fuse reached the barrel of gunpowder.

What was he going to do now? The key was the dogs. He could easily hide from the men. Water. Yes, water was the key. He remembered men in the past talking about the ocean nearby. They'd never allowed him to see the ocean, and he'd always wondered what that much water looked like. Could he get to the ocean and then reappear farther down the coast to throw off his scent from the dogs?

Mo remembered he could not swim.

Now what? He could run fast. He could climb one of the larger trees. But what help would that be if the men had guns and dogs that could track him down?

Christopher died with his right hand in the right pocket of his pants, like he'd died before he could finish one final act.

Was Christopher hiding a weapon?

Mo moved Christopher's hand from his pocket and noticed something bunched up in his hand.

A *weapon.*

He pulled out folded and slightly crumpled pages.

Whose are these? Christopher did not know how to read or write. None of us could. We were never allowed.

Mo studied the writing. The yelling and barking moved toward him.

Somehow I know this is Christopher's writing. How did he learn how to write?

There was no time. Mo could not read it anyway. Already guilty of killing a demon, chances were that whatever was written on the pages would be just another reason for them to kill Mo. They might even accuse Mo of writing, and that by itself would be certain death. There was nothing that could be said in those words that would save him from what was approaching. The words were of no use for him now. *What a useless weapon.* Mo let go of the pages. He turned one last time toward Christopher before running for his life, or perhaps for the future lives of his children, who would one day hunt the hunters.

Christopher laid with opened lifeless eyes as Mo's eyes widened.

Can they kill me three times? Once for murder, twice for escaping my master, and a third time for these papers? They can only kill me once.

He stuffed the papers into his pocket. For the first time in his life, he carried something different. Saliva gathered in his mouth. He moaned and put his hands on his stomach. He turned his head to throw up, but then the sensation passed. The voices and the dogs in the distance were closing in. If he did not run, they would be upon him in several minutes. It was at least half an hour before he could get to where he thought the ocean was.

His throat tightened like a large serpent slithering around his neck and slowly squeezing. A voice, seemingly searching ahead for the men and their dogs, spoke inside his head. *It's just a matter of time. You are mine.*

He ran. Holding his stomach. Faster than he had ever run. He ran full speed for the first time outside the plantation. He was now farther away from his home at the plantation than he had ever been on his own.

As he ran, he turned behind him and noticed the darker shadows, darker than the night, just appearing behind some trees. Though it would soon approach the dawn hours, they had not spotted him yet.

In the distance, one of the men turned his head side to side. Looking for him. "It's just a matter of time. You are mine," the man yelled.

Mo bent forward as his stomach moved like a fist pounding inside, wanting to get outside. What was wrong? He never had stomachaches. Mo headed for some cover behind an area of thick brush as they had gained ground on him. Then he heard a yell.

"We know you are out there. You know we are closing in. Don't stop. I will let you run. I like this game. An even better excuse to kill you."

Was the voice familiar? It was also unlike any human sound he had heard before. It seemed to come from below ground and into the air above Mo. He continued running and turned one more time behind him. Though it was a mystery to him how they had still not spotted him, they were closing in.

Several minutes went by, when Mo noticed the voices and the barking of the dogs turned the right way and were now closer. They were only about half the distance away, and they were now accurately following him—but they had still not spotted him.

"Look what I have here," another man screamed.

Mo recognized the voice. In the past he'd refused to remember the man's name, as he was a hired "slave breaker." Slave masters hired him to break resistant slaves mentally and physically until they submitted to all their master's demands. He was known to kill slaves in that process if necessary, if for anything, for the purpose of striking fear into other slaves witnessing the breaking.

Mo had no doubt what the slave breaker was capable of. Someone in the distance pulled two moving objects up. He recognized the small outlines and their voices, even though it was the first time he'd heard them scream.

Betsy and her friend.

"For me, slaves are like buying dirt. No cost, for they are everywhere. Speak out your surrender in the next minute, or one of these dies."

Before he could speak, one of them slumped to the ground. The man laughed and dropped the knife. "Too late. Look what you did."

Mo heard a voice in his head. *I am hunting you and your kind through all generations.*

The man howled, then grunted and growled while raising his arms. The man laughed again. His voice deepened and almost slithered. "I am hunting you and your kind through all generations. I will always roam and hunt down my animals."

Mo wiped his eyes and then stood up in the open, no longer trying to hide. But the man still could not see him. *How can that be? It is dark, but I can see them—why can they not see me?*

Another one died because of him. He was not worth all the lost lives. Mo stood still while they moved closer. He remained watching, his disappearing minutes spilling onto the ground like the blood of his brothers and sisters. He did not move.

The men and dogs suddenly stopped, as if they had bumped up against an expanding wall. They moved sideways, looking for an opening, and then ran in a southern direction. Mo ran east toward the ocean.

He paused and thought of yelling and giving himself up to save lives. He stood facing the men as they ran away from him. How did they not see him?

My Betsy. Was she the one killed? If she was not the one killed, what will they do with her?

Mo wiped his face and shook his head and continued running.

A voice above the barking dogs moving away from Mo yelled, "I will find you when you think you have escaped."

CHAPTER 11

MARY

Near Plymouth, Massachusetts Bay Colony 1750

Mary wiped her eyes and walked into her village with her chest pounding. She turned her head behind her. No one was there. She was again guilty of procrastinating and meeting with Martha. Mary knew it. Martha knew it. It was just a matter of time before Martha would want Mary to report to her about the meeting with the chief. Knowing Martha, she was either waiting at home or would be dropping by before Mary could go inside and sit down.

It was time to confront the truth. If she was even thinking about running away, where could she go? Could she give up whatever slight chance her husband, Adam, would come home? He would never find her if she ran away. Would she run away from her only friends, Agnes and Martha? Mary left any ideas of leaving.

Dusk approached. There she was. Martha waited in the distance with her hands on her hips. Was she angry? Would she laugh about the whole thing for the first time? Mary trudged forward.

Martha looked behind Mary and whispered, "Did he take it?"

Mary leaned toward Martha's ear. "The chief is a good man. You knew what was going to happen. I gave him the note. He knows the meeting is in one week." Mary leaned away.

Martha smiled. "And then what happened?"

Mary shook her head and turned away. Away from the choices before her. "I can't win in this. I am not sure we can win this for all our peoples. You and I want the same thing, but I just do not know if this two-part plan of ours is the best way to do this. Everything has to work perfectly, and life does not ever work out perfectly."

Mary paced a few steps and then stopped with her back facing Martha. Was it possible to feel someone's eyes pressing and piercing? "I don't want to talk about it anymore. I need to go see Agnes and make sure she is doing okay. You remember Agnes? She's helping us set her master up? You know, Agnes, the person God told us to work with so her coming child could live in freedom?"

Mary turned to face Martha.

Her friend bent her spine backward and exaggerated with her hands struggling to stay on her hips. "She's huuuge. I have seen large horses seek shelter from the rain underneath her belly. She is just a few weeks before birthing. Of course she is not doing great. And of course I am not going to forget that belly." Martha moaned and groaned and waddled a few steps, as if carrying a fat calf across a large field.

Martha narrowed her eyes. "Is checking up on her the only thing you want to do at her home?"

"Of course. What else would it be?" Mary tilted her head.

Martha smiled. "Well, there is the small matter that Agnes's master is the leader of the colonist community and does not leave his plantation very often. You know, the other side of this difficult attempt at marriage between two peoples. We are like the two last remaining children from a large family still trying to head off an ugly and violent divorce, with both sides of the family waiting to line up their support of each of our competing parents."

Martha held up a hand. "Two questions. Did you know the first divorce in the colonies was just over one hundred years ago? And are you planning to steal more information from his home, with Agnes's help?"

"No. And no. Most people don't realize I was done stealing a long time ago."

Martha put her hand on Mary's shoulder. "You are a descendant of Praying Indians. But everyone still thinks you steal more than you pray. When are you going to tell everyone who you really are?"

"I am not worried about what other people think of me. God is still making me new, even with the dying old patterns. Who would not be bitter with unforgiveness from the history and patterns of brothers and sisters sinning against each other? Does acting out injustice against those who committed injustice make things better? I am not God, so I should not think I can judge like Him."

Mary stepped away and then returned. "There has to be a way I can make things right. People can believe that I am a thief if they want to, but please do not tell anyone else of my search for the truth of who I am. It doesn't need to be complicated, with others not understanding what I am trying to understand."

"You were a Praying Indian before you met Adam. Adam is gone, and I fear Mary is going to return to the old confused Mary that she was before she found God. Rebel. Rebel against who you used to be. I have my own struggles with money, which I have spent foolishly. You know of my financial debt and how I have little patience in waiting for God to finally do something. I still tell Him, 'Get up. Do something.'"

Martha paused to control herself. "Do not give up your pursuit of God. We must leave who we used to be. I see the confusion you have. Satan is trying you. He wants you to fail. To fall back to comfortable old ways."

"But can I trust your God with *all* things? I thought God told me I would be with child and that my child would help to plant the seed that would destroy slavery and bring peace. I wish there was a way for my child, whether a boy or a girl, to now be old enough to one day free people like Agnes and their offspring. Agnes should not be a slave. I cannot have children. My husband left me. I only have Satan left with me, in my dreams, in my nightmares." Mary whirled and gazed toward the sun setting.

Martha moved in front of Mary and wiped Mary's cheeks. "Are you still having that same dream?"

"I will tell you about it when I am able." Mary crossed her arms and turned her head away. *But I do not even want to think about what I hear in the nightmare that waits until I surrender to sleep. The voices follow me during the day. I try to run from them, but they catch me every night in my sleep.*

"We are all still praying for you." Martha pressed a finger on Mary's chest. "Someone you believe in, but do not fully trust, placed you strategically in this location between different peoples. He will show you, as surely as the ocean will meet the sand, where to go and what to carry for Him."

"Agnes has granted me much favor. She is drawn to the Praying Indians. Did you know that she said we have been in her dreams?"

"I did not know that."

"I feel like a liar too. Agnes deserves better. But I cannot tell her all of our plan."

"Just stick with our strategy."

Mary walked away, with her parents arguing in her head about whether they should follow the colonists or their own people.

And then there was that nightmare.

CHAPTER 12

CAESAR

Dover, Delaware Colony
1775

Caesar stood stuck in the mud as the mother with the wailing children moved away from him. People hiding from him because of cancer's scorched-face policy upon his cheek did not bother him as much as it used to. He had empathy for those who were scared of him. It was yet another reason to just stay inside his home with the empty chair.

Why am I out here?

He loved to ride his horse. He was good at that. But sometimes whatever opposed him rode him to where he did not want to go. What opposed him joined forces with fear, and on a daily basis, an almost hourly basis, Caesar attempted to rebel against the greatest force that opposed each man and woman. It utilized the mercenary forces of fear with its spies inside every person and home, searching, roaming, for the weak ones.

But like a horse refusing to be broken by the rider enforcing its will, he fought back against what weighed on him when many others simply complied. He dreamed of reversing the roles and ripping the reins away from what sat on his back and then riding free to then free others. One day the cancer that colonized every heart and mind would be broken. Cast away. And the children would laugh in pure joy in the face of the retreating fear.

But fear, and with it the fear of death, was a powerful foe. He could not think of anyone who'd ever defeated it. That death king ruled with little resistance.

I can do this.

He was Caesar Rodney. He was a colony official and a most valued and trusted official who served his people well. Under the veil of the scarf. War was roaming the land as the beast from the other side of the Atlantic stirred and vented. The king's demons at his beck and call, and if left unchecked they would soon spread a stronger form of the cancer of tyranny across the face of their land. Caesar was to prepare the people for what was coming.

But for now Caesar wanted to stop the crying. The crying children on the outside and his own crying inside. How much time did everyone have when all were on the edge of full-out war? He wanted to be with Dorothy. The woman who could one day occupy that empty chair at home. He refused to stay with regret and feet in mud.

Caesar took that most difficult of all steps and took the next one. He continued walking with his scarf firmly pulled over the left side of his face and with his head and eyes down. He knew feet well. He could identify each person in his neighborhood based on their lack of footwear, or their footwear, and how they moved. There were the fine English-made leather shoes. Boots. Even jackboots that many men wore. There were moccasins. Nicely tanned and not-so-nicely tanned leathers. He even recognized the shoes made from the ten foot workshops. He could even tell who could afford the work from the better cobblers in town. He was walking into the part of town where feet moved with less confidence and where it was more difficult to tell what the shoes ever looked like before the continuation of the living daily death march.

Caesar wanted to stop off at his friend Edward's house for the alcohol-free dosage of strong encouragement that Edward was always willing to add to his own tab. Even before the left side of Caesar's face started losing its war, and even when pain accompanied him every day, Edward was there for Caesar. Edward never remembered having parents and never had any siblings, and he often said that Caesar was like a younger brother to him.

"Good morning, Caesar. You look like a man ready to start a new story on this fine new day!"

"You perceive well, my friend. I grow weary with the fatigue of chains, and today is a new day to be free. I am going to Dorothy's."

"Dorothy! That is great news. Two stories intersecting. I quite enjoy that. I know it must have been difficult to make that choice, but regret is always famished for more. Starve it."

"Tell me more about her one more time, to give me strength."

Edward laughed a deep laugh with his hands holding on for a bumpy ride on a big belly. "Dorothy is a fine woman. But you should know that her husband left her about five years ago and divorced her. She was devastated. She is not the same since. She has not been active in seeking company. She stays at home, like you too many times when you are not working, where it is too safe."

"I am so sorry to hear that. I knew she was alone. Men sometimes make foolish choices."

"And another thing. We all have our personality issues, and you must know that she is quite sensitive to people saying 'pardon me' or 'I am sorry.' She heard so much of that when her husband left her. Carry on."

"I must be careful, for I know I am guilty of that." Caesar paused. "I apologize for that."

"Ha! Stop. You are procrastinating. Go now. She is an early riser. Now is a good time."

"Thank you for your help. You are a valued friend . . . my only real friend. Thank you."

Edward gently pushed him away. Caesar laughed and waved to his friend. He continued his journey with a destination a few more blocks away. He had never been to her house, never met with her before, but he'd marked it in his mind for the last few weeks after following her. He was sorry about that.

Caesar knew he had a couple of hours before he had to leave for a colony meeting. He was not sure when he would be back in town again, as already high tensions between loyalists and rebels were reaching concerning heights.

As he strolled closer to her home, his heart pounded more and almost in rhythm to his shaking hands. His chest warmed and seemed to spread upward toward his face. His face gently pounded and reminded him of a sheet of ice melting away when confronted with a burning sun. The river going from his chest flowed. It seemed to flow all the way to his toes and fingertips. Like summer melting away what opposed it.

The left side of his face throbbed more. It stopped him in his tracks. Standing in the mud, he placed his hand on his face. It felt like someone else's face. That side had not been touched in weeks. Was it his imagination, or did his face cave in more? Was his face pounding with each heartbeat?

Not *now*.

Caesar quietly cried out in pain.

CHAPTER 13

MO

**Near Dover, New Hampshire Colony
1766**

Mo ran at night and walked and hid by day, away from the slaver devils and their demons. It was four days since Christopher had died. Though only about sixteen years old, his mind and body told him he'd aged forty years, wandering from slavery for dozens of miles, hiding, and living every sleep time with the nightmare and the voices.

Why did Christopher have to die? Mo running for his life cost lives. It was Mo's fault that lives were lost because he had killed the demon. All he had left were the torn and dirt-soiled pants, torn shirt that hung with his bones sticking out, and Christopher's papers, which he could not read, still in his pocket.

There seemed to be fewer slaves in the region where he rested. During his exodus, several slaves along the way had told him he was now in New Hampshire. They smuggled food out of their masters' homes to feed him until his next stop. Was it just his imagination, or were there more trees in the northern parts? Even the food seemed to be different from where he came from. Back home he'd watched his master and his family, and the workers who were not slaves, eat like heaven on earth. Salted cod, chowder, fried ham. Fish hash and oatmeal in the mornings. Creamed codfish. But it was the baked beans, wafting through the house, that he could not have that had been the most difficult.

The food in the more northern parts seemed even richer in smells and in taste. His tongue tingled with new experiences formerly withheld during his short life. The new foods were all encouraging and gave him hope, but the food was still from slave masters.

He spoke with slaves who greeted him away from enemy eyes. No one back home had spoken to Mo and his fellow slaves about the outside world. An outside world where Mo imagined people were free to interact with others, the powerful, and the not powerful, all working toward life without chains. The only world he and his fellow slaves had known was when the master or his demons spit out the venom of words comparing them to animals they worked with. But here he heard more about the French and Indian War and of another war that would one day come.

They told him the war took many lives but also cost the British a tremendous financial toll. And even though the British won the war, there were signs that the British were passing on the monetary cost to the colonies. The slaves said their slave masters spoke of one day needing to rebel against the British slave king. Mo's chest throbbed with all the talk about war. Finally, vengeance upon the slavers.

On this particular day, a large slave worked the grounds on the outer edge of what other slaves had told him was the Johnson plantation. He was obviously highly trusted, as there was no white man nearby. Dusk approached, but the air was still burning hot. The slave, a man capable of casting a shadow covering two men, wiped the sweat off his face and hair every few minutes.

Mo approached and talked with the slave, who called himself Henry. At first Mo thought Henry was very light skinned for one of African blood. Even lighter than Mo. He was a head taller and half a body wider than Mo. Henry spoke like he was a house slave, but he could not read Mo's papers. Up close, Mo realized that he was not African. Or was he?

What is he?

Henry returned to the house multiple times that day and returned with food smuggled in his pockets. This happened for two days as Mo gathered strength hiding and resting. Mo knew he would have to leave and continue his wandering.

Henry returned with more food. "You have been running away and running in place for most of your life. When are you going to stop running?"

Mo looked up and down the road at the arrival of another dusk. "Well, for these last few days, I have stopped running. But to answer your question, until I am free."

Henry laughed. "Today there is nowhere to be totally free in this life. At least not for us. Not yet. You could grow up to old age trying to give birth to freedom for others before we are all free. And the slavers think they are free, but they are not free. Even believers will not be totally free until we are with God."

Henry's eyes narrowed, and he stood straighter. "But we continue to pray and seek God, and if He tells us it must be delayed, then it does not mean it is denied. Delayed but not denied. If he asks us to fight, then we fight."

"Tell me again about this war you think is one day coming."

Henry put two fists, knuckles to knuckles, on the left side of his chest. "One hand is a fist. It is the blood-stained hand of the king. The other hand used to be open. It always conformed to the fist. But now the once-opened hand is closing into a fist, pushing back against the other bloody closed fist. As in all wars and all our sins against each other, both hands belong to the same person. Both are born of the same mother and father. The same land of birth. Both hands push against each other, and one will have to open, unless they both fall limp on the ground in a pool of blood."

"You seem to think you know all things. What is the solution?"

"I do not know all things. But this I know: the answer is the Creator, the Father of the one who created the one with the beating heart and the one who should steward the hands."

"But all slaves want to kill their slave masters."

"Oh, most would whisper 'yes.' Does God believe that slaves killing slaves is the solution? That a stronger slave wins over the weaker? Is the solution might makes right?"

Mo wondered how slaves could be free.

"The coming rebels, they will one day want to live apart from the king and his slave-master ways. There will always be loyalists believing in the king. They will proclaim that the king should rule over his colonies, as he does over all his other subjects."

"But they all have slaves. Where can we go? I just want to live my life."

"You are right. Slave masters will be fighting each other. What will happen to us?"

"We cannot fight them all and win. Do I stay out of the fight? Do I join one side?"

"Men slaving their brothers and sisters will bring down God's justice at some point, as God gives us all a chance to make it right before He judges. The slavers do not fully know what they are doing. That does not excuse them, and they will face judgment from God. But without the love of God in their lives, they do not know what they are doing."

Henry moved closer to Mo. "It seems to me that the flawed rebels will be one step closer to what we want. Our way to freedom is if the rebels win their freedom. If the king wins, then masters of slaves and their slaves will have combined and forced their subjects to serve the king, and we will have to serve the slaves of the king. There is one less person above us if the rebels win, is the way I see it."

"I want all the slave masters, on both sides, to die. Then we can live."

"Be careful of what you want. You are a slave master as well, over yourself . . ."

With his blood thumping in his ears, Mo did not hear Henry continue talking. Mo knew he would have vengeance before he was killed, but he knew he could not kill every slave master. And he did not want to side with the slave masters on either side.

Mo paused and raised a finger upward. "If I side with the rebels, then what will happen to me when they lose? We will all hang."

"Yes. Treason against the king. But either I die in the fields working to never be free, or I die fighting for what is a step closer to being right and perhaps our children's children being free. Either way I die."

Some slaves thought there might be a chance for their freedom if the rebels could one day win the coming war. Other slaves sided with loyalists, saying that the disorganized and small-in-number rebels could never have a chance of winning against the most powerful military power in the world and they would be killed fighting for the rebels, either during the war or after when they lost. Some believed that supporting the status quo of slavery to king and country was their best chance of living tolerable lives.

Mo did not want to get caught in the middle of the arguing. He only wanted to be able to live his life as he wanted to live. Mo studied Henry. He was big and strong, yet he remained a slave, with the ability to run for hours before anyone would notice he was gone.

"You are very smart. You are very strong. Why do you remain here?" Mo studied for an answer in Henry's face.

Henry clearly knew it was coming. "For a day like this. You were carried and protected at birth. You and your sister were appointed to do great things for your God. I have prayed to be free one day, and now I have met you. He will tell me what to do next. I am to pray for you, as you will help me and our offspring to be free one day."

Mo stood stunned. *What does that mean? And I have never been told I have a sister. How can he know these things? How will I free others?*

Henry bowed his head and prayed. "Lord, I have done what You have asked me to do. I will continue to wait for You. Now do what You want to do. Free us in Your timing, in Your ways, not our own. King Jesus, rule over us. No king but King Jesus."

Henry turned behind him and then all around him. "Someone is reminding me," he whispered. "Go about five miles down this road, and when you come across the largest tree, look to your right. There is a plantation. We call it Big Large Tree Plantation. It is hidden behind the tree and down a hillside, where they may be able to help you. Do not tell anyone apart from that plantation what I have told you."

"Thank you, Henry. I will not forget what you did for me."

Henry returned to preparing the land. Mo walked away with a weakened vengeance.

The following late afternoon, Mo found the plantation. With the food that Henry gave him, he spent several hours watching the workers on the perimeter. He walked behind trees toward one working alone. The worker looked up and spotted him. The man hiked to him as Mo prepared to fight or run if needed.

"Greetings." The man put out his hand. "My name is Thomas. Who are you?"

"Am I safe here for now?"

"You are safe here."

"A man by the name—someone told me to come here."

"Henry has sent several of us to earn money and live here. You remind me of my brother. He died south of here. You are safe here. Can I introduce you to the master of the plantation?"

"I don't want anything to do with any master."

Thomas nodded and then smiled. "Elias is different." He spoke as if sharing a wonderful secret.

"He lets you call him by his first name?"

Other workers gathered around Thomas and Mo. Thomas pointed to a man walking toward them several feet away. Mo trembled and studied the other men for a hint of what to do. All seemed to be at peace, but Mo's body stiffened and his hands clenched into fists.

What if this Elias is just another demon working for the devil back home?

The man edged closer. Mo positioned himself between the gathered men and freedom to run. The weight of all eyes upon him made his heart pound harder. They had the eyes of people wondering how Mo was going to react to a master approaching. They held no fear in their eyes.

Thomas put his hand on Mo. "You do not have to run again."

Mo turned his head toward Thomas and then toward the man coming. Mo's chest heaved for air, and he pushed Thomas to start running. Thomas stopped him.

Mo pushed him again. "You are trying to trap me. All of you are trying to trick me."

Thomas moved closer to Mo. "It is different here. You do not have to run. Here you are free to run if that is your choice."

"You know they are after me. The master will think that I have come to steal or to set you as rebels against him," Mo whispered, and looked side to side.

Thomas smiled with the other men. "It is not like that here. Here we can choose to be paid as workers. We just have to make it look like we are slaves when strangers are nearby."

The man was inching closer. Mo put his right hand to cover his chest. He looked at the surrounding men and women to see if they could hear the fist pounding the inside of his heart, trying to get away.

The man reached the group. He was a large man but short. Big body. Big smile. Big bald head. He came closer as the others moved aside for a clear pathway. He focused on Mo's eyes.

"You have a wonderful name," Elias said with a big smile. "Many come here looking for home. We are near Dover, New Hampshire."

Mo's eyes widened. His tongue was stuck to the roof of his mouth. Was there water nearby? He looked downward, as he could not look him in the eye.

"Mo, you are welcome to stay. But if you stay, you will need to work. I pay an honest man's wage, even if the man is not always honest."

"I always try to be honest." Mo looked him in the eyes for the first time.

"Yes, I know." Elias narrowed his eyes. "But something consumes you."

Elias turned his head toward the men. "Speaking of consuming, it is dinner time. Let us eat." Elias patted his stomach, and it did not sound empty.

It was Mo's first full hot meal in a long time—since the last time he'd eaten his master's scraps and leftovers. At the big table, there was enough food to eat a second time. There was what they identified as turkey, potatoes from the Irish, turnips, roast pork, pea soup, and salmon pie. These were all new flavors he had never seen or tasted. Unrequited past pleasant odors were now met with a full mouth and full stomach.

After the meal, Elias asked Mo to stay to talk with him in a different room. As Mo waddled and held his stomach, he burped. *Is that okay here?* He entered the room. It seemed that every bit of wall space was filled with shelves of books.

With his mouth stuck open, he said, "Sir, I do not believe I have ever seen so many books. What do they say?"

Elias laughed. "I wish I could say. Like many conversations with many different dear friends, I have forgotten what some of the books spoke to me. But most of them, they are now in me. They have helped shape me. I have an interest in theology. The study of God."

Why would anyone want to study God? The same God who is why I am running for my life.

Elias looked into Mo. "You are free here. You are tired. You will dream dreams. Though you cannot read, God has been teaching you in ways that you will understand what He is saying. What you believed were random thoughts in your days and nights were words from the Author of the Story you live in. We have much to talk about. You have seen much in your short life, and there is more to come. Go and rest, and we will talk again tomorrow."

Mo shifted his stance. He wiped his forehead. *I don't want to sleep. No more nightmares.*

CHAPTER 14

MO

**Near Dover, New Hampshire Colony
1766**

The dream visited him again. In the dream Mo tilted his head upward, thinking about his future child. He closed his eyes during the short respite. Perhaps a future daughter to change the world? Maybe a son? His chest warmed.

The dream continued as voices cried out under the midnight moon and Mo had to fully open his eyes. The same voices as before. But this time was different. Outlines of birds screeched in the sky and moved in all directions. The screeching birds hunted for something down below where Mo stood looking upward for help. A large bird, the only one not screeching, grabbed him by its talons. It was the largest bird and the only one of its kind in the sky. Mo was flying! Piercing the sky and its dark clouds caused Mo to cover his burning nostrils. The effects of something dead covered the entire land. He grabbed the talons with the strongest grip possible. He did not want to fall into the unseen abyss where he came from.

Dozens of the screeching birds tried to attack the larger bird as it carried him. But the birds missed when they tried to bring down the large bird carrying Mo. As if an invisible hand surrounded the bird and deflected the attacks. Slashes of light cut through the sky and gave Mo moments of clear vision down below. Human and animal bodies scattered across the barren land. Burned trees and what used to be life covered the land with no water. He turned his head in all directions to where the voices came from. Then something happened to the bird carrying him. In the next moment, he was down below and tied up. What had happened? Mo screamed out as a sharp pain penetrated his bare back. The slave breaker was just getting started.

Mo jumped out of the dream and sat up in bed, holding his back. The dream inflicted pain this time. He placed his hand on his back, and it burned without any raised markings. It was predawn. It was time to move on in the cover of the dark before the light arrived. Already dressed in the previous day's clothes, his only clothes, he grabbed Christopher's folded papers off to the side of the bed and put them in his pocket. He poked his head out the doorway of a bedroom in Elias's house. He took his first step down the hallway toward the back door. The cold doorknob almost stung his hand.

"Good morning, young man."

Mo did not even have to turn his head. He stood with the door ajar and both feet still inside.

"Before you go for a nice early morning walk, why don't you come over here and keep me company to ease me into another day."

Mo closed the door and moved toward Elias. He sat across from him at his table, with the only candle in the room lit between them reflecting off Elias's head.

Elias shared the widest smile Mo had ever seen. Elias lifted his head and his shining eyes toward Mo. "Mmmm. I always like to start with one of our fine fresh biscuits. Here, try one."

Mo was so full from his previous meal that he did not think he was hungry. His dinner stomach was full, but his biscuit stomach was empty. And it was simply too much to resist as Elias closed his eyes, his right hand now empty and his left hand rubbing his own well-cared for stomach.

There was also the matter of Mo not having packed any food for the journey. He needed to get full when the next meal was not known. He grabbed the biscuit and tasted a bit of heaven.

"With biscuits this good, why do you not believe in a good God?" Elias laughed as he took a bite of another biscuit.

Mo smiled and then looked away from Elias toward the front door. "After that first biscuit, I moved a step closer to believing." Elias laughed. "But it is a loooong journey. Maybe you should give me a second biscuit just to make sure."

Elias laughed again with his hands on his belly and slid the bowl of biscuits toward him. After a few moments, Elias spoke. "I sense that you have to experience more than a few biscuits?"

Mo lifted a half-eaten biscuit up to pause the conversation as he chewed on the other two and a half biscuits in his mouth. "There are times I think about believing in God. But God said I should be a slave. That us from Africa are animals and are property to be owned. It's in the Bible. That's what the Christian masters say."

Elias shook his head. "Perhaps Satan does not want you to know the truth. There is actually only one Story, but slavers twist the one Story into their own convenient and profitable story. Slavers do not tell of the one true Story above their own false story." Elias probed deeper into Mo's eyes. "Do you not resist when other people tell you who you are above what you say about yourself, especially when they do not even know you? Will you believe what God says about you or what man says about you? Should we not listen to God above what others say about God? Should we not listen to Christ before Christians? Christ before non-Christians?"

Mo shrugged, like a little boy asked what his name was and not old enough to answer. He stood and walked to a desk and picked up a written page. The words reminded him of marks he'd drawn in the dirt with other kids when he was younger. The lines pointed to all the different directions he wanted to run away.

Mo pointed to the page. "Can I ask, what is this?"

Elias rose from his chair and meandered toward Mo. "That is a letter I hope to send soon. I am almost done with it."

"It says something very important, doesn't it?" Mo asked as he placed it back on the desk.

Elias smiled as his face blushed. "It is a letter to my son and daughter."

Mo bowed his head. "I am sorry. I did not act right in asking about your personal things."

"Actually, this letter has something to do with you."

"Me?"

Elias motioned for him to sit down. "Do you mind if I read to you my letter to my adult children?"

Mo shook his head and sat down.

Calvin and Beth,

What a grand play with a grand stage we live in. What an honor and privilege to live the role as your father and to share wonderful times on life's stage with you both. I am a man blessed by God.

It is two years since I saw your faces. Too long to not embrace my son and daughter. A friend recently informed me of a new hope in finding you both. I am sending this message with him, and I have asked him not to disclose your locations to me. I want to respect your last wish that I not see you again. Forgive me for communicating one last time. I pray that you will forgive a father's last wish.

I think of you both every day. I have hope with each sunrise that you will come through the front door that I spent the night staring at. I have many things I am proud of in raising you. But I regret rejecting the Lord during most of your years here in this house. I live with the regret of those lost years where I did not communicate the love and liberty of God.

Did this affect your belief of the king ruling over all of us and God?

Can I communicate with you one last time?

He who kidnaps a man, whether he sells him or he is found in his possession, shall surely be put to death.
—Exodus 21:16

Let them construct a sanctuary for Me, that I may dwell among them.
—Exodus 25:8

For the first time, I must share with you some of my backstory. When your mother and I were raising both of you, I made a sanctuary in my heart for me to dwell and rule above God and all others. I then made our home a dwelling place for me to rule above all others. I ruled accordingly. For this, I ask your forgiveness.

Our king across the Atlantic made a sanctuary in his heart for himself to dwell and rule above God and all others. From his self-created throne room in his heart, he attempts to coerce us in the colonies to make a dwelling place for him and his rulership in our own land. Our king is making us pay for his military adventures and taxes us without representation and our consent.

I will state what is self-evident. I did not always water and feed the growing seedlings of our relationships. I sometimes mandated my laws and exerted my unyielding rulership over you in selfish, controlling ways.

But we cannot rule above God.

The master puppeteer, our Adversary to whom we have ceded control, hides behind the curtain and pulls on our strings as he deceives us into believing we are free. The master puppeteer acts as king to rule over all his colonized puppets to exercise his rule when we believe we are exercising our own. As slaves, we then unknowingly enslave others for the master slave owner.

Who can save us from this unending generational cycle?

Our family backstory tells us where we are today. God performed great miracles to demonstrate that He alone is God, as He freed the Israelites from their oppressors in Egypt. As the verses above state, He gave instructions on how He was to live with them, and with God in their midst, it was not right that one kidnaps his brother or sister to sell or possess.

Today, God still desires to be the One on the throne in our hearts, in our homes, in our land. And it is still wrong to kidnap to sell or possess.

Today, my heart breaks like a father who had his children kidnapped from him.

My heart breaks again in a new location to tell you that your mother died a few months ago. I found her asleep after she never woke up. She was at rest. I had no way of communicating with you our tremendous loss until a friend disclosed to me he knew where you were.

I miss her. I miss you both. I miss her smile in yours. Where now are the remnants of your mother that were at one time displayed to me daily through both of you? I walk into your quiet bedrooms. I remember years before, your mother feeding you from herself when you were crying and not sleeping through the night. I remember seeing you read and play. It was in each of your rooms that you told me of your love for your future spouses, Anna and James. I remember you each taking your belongings to move in with your wife, your husband, the bearers of the fruit of my grandchildren. And how grand they are. After your mother's death, I sat in each of your rooms and wept and remembered her. I remembered you. I have no visible living reminders of the ones I love most.

I must tell you I have been ill. The doctor suspects that I may have a slow-moving cancer. We do not know how much time I have left.

So now we stand onstage of this great Story. For me, my final act. We are separated from the good Creator King and ruled by a lesser created king. We are separated from each other because we have different perspectives on whether to follow or oppose the created King George.

Will we ever be free to live the vision of our brothers and sisters who escaped Egypt? Will we ever be free to live the vision of those who escaped England to come to our shores? Or will we live the vision of the slavers who brought slaves, ripped apart from their families, to our shores? What about the people who are native to this land before us? We are the children of these choices.

The sides will soon fight each other. War is coming. Many have forgotten the God who started life in this land. And yet the Father still desires to dwell with us.

If I shall be labeled a "rebel," then that is who I am. I have seen houses divided. I see what is coming. You see what is coming. Death is roaming our land, waiting to ignite the weapon of division. War will be upon us. Will you not return home for a visit and for us to be together one more time before war separates and divides us permanently?

I have sent this letter to express the value God has for all of His children and the great love I have in my heart for both of you. I pray that this is not goodbye, as I long to see my son and daughter, a free man, a free woman, seek freedom for others.

I now have a different heart in my chest than the one you saw selfishly displayed. There is a different sanctuary for our Father to dwell in. There is a new Ruler in my heart and in this house. The despot is gone.

You are always welcome here, as I will always love you.

Can we talk once again?

These are my last wishes.

I love you, my son.

I love you, my daughter.

Your father,

Elias

Elias put the letter down. "I wrote this months ago. I have not been able to send it. It was not time."

Elias stepped closer to Mo. "Now I know it is time."

"I am sorry that you are dying. People here love you. I cannot remember ever having a father. I don't remember my mother, as I was told she died birthing me. I wonder if your children realize what it is like to not ever have a father? You love your son and daughter. I am sorry for your loss."

Elias tipped his head. "I have been waiting. I knew you would one day come."

Mo narrowed his eyes. "I cannot stay here. I will not be ruled by a master."

Elias smiled. "That is why you were brought here. To learn a new Master."

"I am your fellow man but not your slave."

"Those are words within you to pass on to your offspring in future generations. You are right. I have enough problems fighting slavery off within myself than to want a slave to own. May God strike me down if I ever harbored such a thought." Elias tilted his head down. He sighed. "I believe I descended from a slave a few generations ago. Are we all not related at some point? Is not God our Father?"

Elias turned away from Mo. He sighed again. "And my children rejected that truth."

Mo remembered the demon killing Mo's friends because Mo had killed a demon. He remembered Christians telling him about the wrath of God and how sinners would burn in hell.

Do I even want this God? I do not want Elias to read my letter.

Mo cleared his throat.

Would I even want this God even if He wanted me?

Elias strode closer to Mo, locked eyes, and seemed to scan Mo's entire life. "We live in very precarious times. There are questions to be asked. Is there One who is above the king? If there is no one above the king, then the king will rule as if he is God. It is either a created king or the Creator King. I cannot imagine a way for all to be free unless there is a God that the king, and all kings, must submit to."

Elias paused and looked deeper into Mo. "Someone informed me that you killed someone."

Who is this man? This is not a man like I have ever known before. The walls seemed to close in. Trapped. Again. By another master.

Are his henchman going to walk through the door?

Mo turned his head in every direction. No one else was in the room yet.

They said he was different. That was a lie. His men are coming.

The door was just up ahead. There was early light entering through the windows in the room.

My mom. My Betsy. All the others. My future children. Somebody has to pay for all the murders and slavery. I cannot allow there to be no cost.

He also wanted to hear more from Elias. A man of peace.

But he needed to run, or he might lose control.

Chapter 15

KING GEORGE

Buckingham House, England
1774

It was another night and another fight. King George III left his faithful wife, Queen Charlotte, in the bedroom, to sleep elsewhere. Thoughts attacked like cannons firing images into the mind scape and landing inside his head. Who could stop the bombs from attacking him? Who could hear him internally crying out for help with each bomb landing?

This time he spoke to the coming dream of the night, telling the cannons to stop. Though the explosions were louder, there were momentary pauses that gave him hope that lasted only until another explosion of images flashed before his mind's eye.

After several hours of praying for sleep, he fell asleep while sitting in the library room of his castle until something woke him. He raised his arms up and covered his head with the echo of another volley of cannon fire.

But another sound overtook the explosions in the dream. He was now awake, and the sound started in the darkest corner of the library room and slithered across the floor toward him. King George grabbed both armrests and squeezed until the color escaped his hands. He could only point his head straight ahead, as he did not want what slithered to know it was discovered. It moved until it was under his chair. The slithering stopped. *Is something touching my feet?* He widened his eyes and attempted to utilize the vision given to him by the Dark Light without moving his head. He did not want what was below him to know that George was aware of the presence by moving his head to examine what was below him. Whatever was below him was not visible. It was of another realm.

Not again.

He took a deep breath and turned his head in all directions. Doubting his supernatural abilities, he placed his right hand on his chest and bent to look under his chair. What was on his bare feet? He recoiled his feet, as if they were too close to a flame. *What is that?* There was a strange dark color on his toes.

He jumped. *Did it just move?! This wasn't here yesterday.*

He scratched his chin, and something was different. As if it were somebody else's hand or chin. Did he touch someone else in the room? Was there a growth of some sort on his face? Ignoring his feet, he ran to the nearest mirror. The same dark color on his toes was on his chin.

With his chest pounding and his head throbbing, he ran back to the bedroom, holding his face, and stood above his sleeping queen. "There is something on me. What is it?" he yelled as he pointed to his feet and chin.

The queen jerked her head up and abruptly opened her eyes. Lost in another land, she propped up on an elbow and shook her head, as if shaking the sleep off, and then sat up, trying to make sense. The king stood above her, waiting for an answer. After rubbing her eyes, she moved him near a candlelight to take a better look.

She narrowed her eyes and tilted her head up and down at him. "There is nothing there. Everything looks normal to me."

The king ran to the nearest full-length mirror and rubbed his fingers on his feet and his chin. *Am I standing in someone else's body? This is not me.* The dark coloring invaded him and resisted his rule.

He pointed to his toes and his chin, "You can't see this?"

"I don't see what you see. It looks normal to me." Charlotte covered her mouth. She narrowed her eyes and studied him. She winced, as if in pain.

She stood and put her hands on his shoulders and embraced him. "You worry me. You get these episodes because you are not sleeping well. We need to find a way to get you rest."

The king trembled and then opened his eyes. "They told us about the murderer that seeks to resist our rule through the generations. Satan indwells in the individuals he desires. Who does he live in during our present days? The murderer is out there somewhere plotting to end the divine right of kings. He resists God, who dwells in me. Do you think this burden of God in me is easy? I would rather just live in peace where no one fights me. It would be easier if I was not king and just a regular useful idiot like everyone else."

The king moved away from the queen and paced away and then toward her. "But I must do what God wants me to do. We need to kill the murderer before he kills everything we have and love. The ungrateful Israelites are rebelling against their God. The sheep are trying to kill the Shepherd. They think they can kill God and rule over their garden."

Charlotte, with her mouth wide open, shook her head. She hugged him again.

King George trembled. "The colonies. Can't they see we need their money to support them? Is it wrong for a father to rightly demand that his adult children, who still live in his home, pay their fair share? To protect them?" The king smiled and looked at his open hand, as if examining the finest blade in the kingdom. He moved behind Charlotte and shifted the open hand toward her, as if measuring the first swift and deep cut.

All fears of what was on his body disappeared.

The enemy only understands power. Coercion by the threat of death. "All I have to do is find the one.

The murderer that is hunting me. Then all the others will fall into line afterward. I just need to amputate the cancer to save the body."

Charlotte moved her eyes without moving her head as she followed the king's hands behind her head.

The king did not know what the Dark Light was going to do next. *Stop hiding in the Dark Light. Just make yourself fully known. Get it over with. Where will you take me next? You know I do not like it when you do this.*

The king stopped with his hands in midair behind the queen. His voice changed, as if another man's voice took over. "I need to remind the rebellious toddler colonies the cost of rebellion."

Surely we cannot turn against our own. Right? Please say no.

King George, as if breathing and with his arms pulsating in another person's body, watched his hand close into a grip holding the invisible sword.

His hand moved across Charlotte's throat.

CHAPTER 16

GEORGE WHITEFIELD

Oxford, England
1732

Seventeen-year-old George Whitefield stood with one foot past and one foot still behind the main entrance of the campus of Pembroke College in Oxford. His mother could no longer reconcile her son's desire for education and the theater and continuing to work full time at the tavern. George wished his father could step down from heaven and take his hand to guide him. Though he still had a mother, coming to Pembroke was somehow going to help orphans like him.

He had never stepped so far from home. He also realized his memory of the recurring nightmare did not stay at home and had followed him.

In the dream it was dark. He stood in wet dirt. Parts of what looked like pieces of brick crumbled in his hands. A loud screeching noise pierced the night and his ears as he let go of what was in his hands to cover his ears.

He was barefoot, and the soil covered his feet. Even with the screeching passing over him and now fading, he still heard a violent voice. "Where are you?"

It was a familiar question from the Bible, but these words seemed to be stolen from the original Author. Though the sound seemed to come from everywhere at once, the voice moved more clearly from one direction. A light flashed across the sky and momentarily illuminated the land, and the footprints near him seemed to run away from where he stood. The ground trembled under him, but he did not know if it was from other feet running away or the powerful rumblings from the single voice now moving toward him.

George Whitefield lost his balance from the shifting earth and tripped over something and fell. The trembling in the ground worsened. It seemed to move outward from the direction of the voice, like a coming wave in the ocean, soon to submerge an unanchored drifting vessel. He had tripped on something sticking out of the ground and had fallen on something partially underground and partially on the surface. The dirt under him rose and fell like the ground was breathing. Something, or someone, moaned in pain underneath him.

Degory, the drunk I served alcohol to, is crying from the grave! He seeks vengeance against me!

He pushed off the breathing ground and stood up. He pivoted his head from the field that buried the moaning voice to where the strongest part of the voice came from. He bent and touched the ground like someone saying goodbye to a dying loved one.

George ran toward the voice.

He shook his head and returned from remembering his dream as many young people rushed past him. They all went in different directions, like bees leaving the hive. Who were the bees serving? Where were they going? What were they carrying to and from college?

He turned behind him as a young man and his mother argued. George tried not to stare but could not help himself.

The mother shook her finger at the boy. "We have been looking for you all day. Your father and I have been worried. Why did you leave?"

The boy turned to his mother and revealed a large bruise on the left side of his face. "You know why I left. You know why I must leave."

"If you just did what we asked of you, you would be able to earn your own money one day," the mother responded with a shaking voice as she took his hand.

The boy replied while ripping his hand out of his mother's. "I don't want what you both want . . . and you both can't force me . . ."

The mother slapped the boy's face, causing him to hold his left cheek.

"I will not be forced. I am old enough. I am fifteen years old, and I am my own man."

"You are ungrateful and rebel against all that is good. We have given everything, and this is why you shame us?"

The young boy then ran away. The mother looked at George. "What are you looking at? Stay out of this. You are too young and too selfish to know what is good. Go home if you know what is good for you."

She stomped off in the direction of where her son ran. Where was the father? The boy acted like he did not want his parents. How could anyone *want* to be an orphan? *She has no chance of catching him in this moment, but she knows she has the power of the purse. She will wait until the opportune time.*

George shook his head as the mother and son left. Nearby, two boys were fighting. Others tried to separate them.

What is going on?

George whispered to no one around him. "Why am I here? I do not belong here. I am already cross-eyed, and now I am trying to look at who I am and who I cannot be at the same time. I am not worthy . . . but I believe You called me here."

The boys' fighting then spilled over to where George was lost in thought. One boy pushed the other, and the boy fell up against George's lower legs, and George lost his balance and fell face first on top of the boy.

Is he breathing?

The boy locked eyes with George, inches away from his face. The boy spoke in a voice George did not expect. "Hey, slaver. You have blood on your hands, and you will one day be a slaver."

He smiled and pushed George off him. "Nobody

wants you. That is why your parents left you to be an orphan. But you are mine."

The boys continued fighting as George sat up while stunned on the ground. The boys fought and moved away.

George staggered back to his feet, holding the side of his face. He turned toward the main entrance. He wiped the blood off his cheek. He wiggled a loose tooth.

He remembered falling on Degory's dead body when he was younger. He had never been so close to death before. Memories of the smell of Degory's still-opened mouth reminded him of the last drink he served to Degory before he'd died. Or was he murdered?

George looked at his hands and wondered what they would do next. George took a step farther into campus and toward the awaiting danger.

The awaiting voice.

CHAPTER 17

MO

Near Dover, New Hampshire Colony
1774

Mo sat with his head turned toward the conversation in a corner of the dining room, out of view. Elias and a friend of his, another plantation owner who also hid from prying eyes that they paid their "slaves," talked and seemed to summarize what Mo had suspected for the last few years.

Britain was disappearing into an ocean of debt with their military adventures. The British empire believed it was justified to make the colonies pay for the adventures and to pay their fair share of expenses.

Elias and his friend spoke about how British soldiers had fired upon colonists in the Boston Massacre. The proclamation "No taxation without representation" infiltrated and echoed more throughout the land. In frustration, the colonists had destroyed hundreds of chests of tea in the Boston Tea Party in 1773, and the British Parliament responded with what they termed the "Coercive Acts." The colonists termed it the "Intolerable Acts." The king closed Boston's port and forced the colonists to house British troops. These acts were to punish, deter further rebellion, and to further restore British authority with corresponding decreased sovereignty of the colonies. In response, the Continental Congress of the colonies agreed to unite, and would support the colony of Massachusetts if Britain attacked her.

The presence of war hovered over the rebelling colonies from the Atlantic back to the Motherland.

Mo, now twenty-four years old, remained in the corner, out of the arena of discussion. Mo had worked with Elias for eight years. As Elias's health slowly deteriorated over the years, he gave Mo special charge over his horses, cows, and pigs. People marveled at how the animals followed Mo and his orders.

Someone with dragging feet paced outside the house. Elias and his friend continued talking into the early dawn hours as Mo slipped out the back door.

Mo's best friend, Henry, motioned for him. Mo walked toward Henry.

Henry put his hands on Mo's shoulders. "Elias is not always going to be around. I have been praying, Mo. We have been talking long enough. Enough of the hate you have for so many slave masters who are slaves themselves. It will soon be time to fight. You need to choose a side in the coming war, or it will choose for you."

Mo ran his hand through his closely trimmed hair. "I still do not understand that I have to make a choice. I am better here. I get into a fight every now and then, but I do not know what I would do if I was away from here with all the slavery and slave masters out there."

"When my master died, they let me freely choose to leave the other plantation. I was born here in New Hampshire. Though my skin is light in color, I still have Africa in my blood. You are the same as me. But others like us should also have that same right to live and work. Your future children should be able to choose. The war is in you. It is also coming to you."

Mo turned to walk back to the house.

Henry ran and stood before him. "All men and women are flawed. With the king, you cannot choose another leader. You have to serve him. He is not good. With the flawed rebels, they will at least bring us a step closer to what we need."

"Where, when in history, has a perfect leader served his people perfectly?"

Henry paused. Mo snickered and pushed past Henry to continue toward the house.

"Jesus," Henry said with no fear.

Mo stopped in his tracks and cursed aloud. He did not turn around but marched to the house.

Henry spoke to Mo's back. "That is why I love that name. It is not a curse word. He is the only reason I am able to not hate. Love is the only force that can stop the sin, vengeance, and unforgiveness pattern."

Mo's face warmed, as he fisted his hands and strode faster.

Slavers use that name as they beat and whip their slaves. I will not obey that name.

Elias years before had decided to no longer have slaves. He'd told Mo that most of his close friends did not agree with him but loved him enough to not report him. A very small number of friends agreed with him and also outwardly appeared to have slaves but were secretly paying families of African blood and giving them freedom to leave if they desired.

Mo was a free man working for Elias. He was one of the few who'd escaped to a pocket of more free men and women than farther south. Even on Elias's plantation, some of Elias's mix of workers hated Mo for being too light in skin color and not being enough African. Out of habit, he still hid his hair.

Work was hard. His pay was fair. He was without special privileges above the others. Elias was good and treated him well but expected hard work and things to be done his way. Some workers left, but most desired fair pay and hard work, and they stayed and helped their families prosper.

Elias's friend left, and Elias stopped Mo as he went to his room to prepare for work. Elias pointed Mo toward his study. They sat down to talk about some concerns Elias had.

"Mo, I had another complaint from a worker about your temper."

"I didn't hit him hard this time. It wasn't my fault that he tripped and broke his arm." Mo folded his arms and turned his head away.

"I was not there. I heard conflicting reports on who was the aggressor. I can only give the benefit of doubt to you because I know you are a good man. But the anger . . . it still has its grip around your leash."

Mo's neck tightened as he clinched his fist. His hand was sore.

Elias walked toward Mo. "I do not know what you know. What you have seen and what you live with. Perhaps there will be a day when you can share this with me to lighten your load. But I do know some of the effects of slavery. I lost my son and daughter because of it . . . Do you remember? The cost hit you and your people much, much harder, but the sin of slavery affected me as well."

"I remember." Mo kept his eyes on the back door.

"I sent that letter to them eight years ago, and I never heard anything from them. Are they still alive? I can only give the issue to God. The burden is on Him to help me however He sees fit. I have done all I can. It is the same with your anger and unforgiveness. You are not able to control the fury by yourself. Let me repeat—you cannot do it. You must be transformed. The vengeance inside you is not yours to execute."

Mo laughed. "Eight years ago I would have probably tried to do something stupid to you with what you just said to me. But now it is somewhat different . . . But I still want to hit somebody . . ." Mo fisted his hands and grunted.

Elias fisted his hands and grunted afterward. They both laughed.

Elias then stopped laughing. "You know that the battle for supremacy is both within us and is the same battle outside of us. Is the revolutionary battle outside of you calling you from the revolutionary battle inside?"

Mo knew what he was asking. *We all have our chains. Those in chains put additional chains on others. We all serve the master of death, who chases us until we can no longer run.*

The thickening cloud of war hovered over the land, and soon it would be at the front and back doors. There was no true neutrality. And even if one was able to somehow remain neutral, the effects of the war on each person would never be neutral.

Mo shrugged. "Which side would I fight for? If I fight for the rebels and they lose, the king will hang us all. If I fight for the king and they lose, would not the vengeance of the rebels kill all the loyalists? Would there not still be slaves no matter who wins?"

"Vengeance is a powerful thing that we cannot handle. That is why the Scriptures tell us vengeance is God's"

"Both sides believe in the slavery of my people."

"You have not told me your full story, but I know what my eyes see and I know the common sins of slave masters. Some say that you can fight on either side and win your freedom. But would they actually live by their promise, I do not know. You are light skinned. Covering your head, and under certain circumstances, you might pass as . . . Did someone violate your mother?"

Mo burst out of his chair with both hands trying to stay open. He stood searching the room. He looked at the back of his hands throbbing and pulsating. *What do I do with these?*

He was unable to hide his fists in his pockets. The rage in his hands was too big to hide in small pockets. He knew he had to open his hands. He trembled more as he waited for his fists to unclench.

I want to be free. To return and kill those who killed me and Mother.

Mo bent his head down. Rebelling against all his efforts to suppress, his body still trembled. On the floor, Elias's shadow moved toward his own as Elias put his hand on his shoulder. Mo at first flinched away from the hand, but then his hands opened.

Tears ran down Mo's eyes as Elias spoke. "Only the love of God can change us. Only the love of God can rule over vengeance."

"What side do I fight for? With you as the only exception I know, white men want to rule over us."

"Beware of those who desire to divide us against each other. They always want power and control. If a white man tells another that they should fight against the African because he is African, that is wrong. If an African tells another African to fight against the white man because he is white, that is wrong. If God is our Father, then we are all brothers and sisters. Though Satan wants to divide us against each other, it should not be white or black or any other group above others. Since what happened at the garden, who should ultimately decide what is right and wrong?"

Mo closed his eyes as his blood pounded in his arms. Elias then talked softer, as if to emphasize something he had been wanting to say for years.

"Power and control apart from God corrupts because only God can and should hold ultimate power and control. A character in a story created by his author has no ultimate authority over the author who created him. That is not the character's role. It is the author of the story that determines the roles each of his created characters are to have. Though He is gracious to allow us an immense amount of freedom in our roles, and He will make this clear to you."

The pounding then went to his legs. Mo ran to the doorway and stopped.

"With the present and future founders of a new nation, the perfect God uses the best imperfect men and women available to Him to accomplish His perfect will. God is extending an invitation to you." Elias bent his head, as if in prayer.

Mo turned his head toward Elias and then in the direction of where he came from. *Somebody needs to pay.*

"The human hunt continues," Elias said. "Satan tries to chase us down. But there is another. You cannot run away from God. You actually want *Him* to hunt you down."

Mo stood motionless at the doorway.

CHAPTER 18

KING GEORGE

Buckingham House, England
1775

King George III tried to escape into sleep. A presence followed him from the awake realm and was stronger with his defenses down in the dream realm. The king's power in the dream realm was that of a mere peasant. The dream placed him nearby someone, or something, digging. It was nearby the wall where his bed's wood-crafted headboard stood. Could something beneath his power actually breach his defenses past the world's foremost military while in his white silk-laden bed lined with the finest of purple bed curtains?

The queen was still asleep, as she was not privy to experiencing the spiritual realm like the king could. *What was that noise?* He sat up to figure out where the digging was coming from. But the sound stopped.

The king awoke nervous about a special meeting with Parliament scheduled later. He walked softly into the bathroom to begin the day early. In his mirror the spot on his chin was larger than the previous day. Urgently lifting his silk sleepwear, he saw the dark markings on his toes had risen to below his knees. He did not bother Charlotte, as he already knew she would not be able to see the marking.

"What does this mean? Is it overtaking me?" the king said to himself.

In the mirror something moved in his eyes. *What was that?* He leaned closer. Another pair of closed eyes were deeply immersed inside of his own open eyes. He blinked to clear his vision. He moved closer to the mirror, and the eyes inside his eyes then opened, like a serpent's mouth opening for the kill. The king cursed aloud and jerked from the mirror, closing his eyes and raising his arms to cover his face, like he had seen a horrific crime. He bent down, like he was avoiding a sword swinging at his head.

Sitting on the floor, he uncovered his eyes and looked up and down, scanning himself. His eyes worked like they normally did. His awareness of his internal sense of being was normal. He pushed himself off the floor onto one bended knee. "What . . . what was that? Who are you?"

He turned his head to scan all around himself. Something awakened. Something moved under his skin, like a snake slithering underneath the sheets of a bed at night. Or like gentle waves rolling onto a beach. George gasped and covered his quivering mouth.

It reminded him of the first ceremony with the strange Dark Light years before. An older cousin taught him about it and told him that it had visited George's parents years before. The cousin told him about how it came upon anyone who sought power and control in their lives.

A good priest once told him that the Dark Light shape-shifted and cloaked itself into many forms. He'd said it hid inside the lust of one wanting what was not his. It hid in the liar and his lie when he attempted to protect his own power and control. It hid in a slaver and impaired his vision to see the slave as a brother or sister. It hid in the slave to not see the slaver as a brother or sister. It hid in unrepentant and unforgiven sin that divided brothers and sisters and clouded visibility to see others as brothers and sisters instead of the power and control mindset of pitting group against group.

King George did not much care for that particular priest, and he did not care about those other things. He only cared about how the Dark Light helped the ruling class rule over the sheep and the special power it gave in the family line of kings and queens.

George had participated with his cousin in one of the cutting rituals, and the Dark Light power had entered into him. He grew up scared to use the Dark Light within him, as he feared that if he opened the door for the strong man, the strong man would rip the door out of George's hands and enter inside fully unhindered.

What would God think about him using it? Was it just another way that God moved, like his cousin said? Or was it like witchcraft and the occult, like the priest said? Why should he listen to a priest anyway, after what a priest did to him when he was too young to fight back?

Years later when he was older, living in royalty but in a valley of doubt and powerlessness, he'd participated in another ceremony and asked the Dark Light for help. For power. He'd grabbed it like a hungry stray rabid dog taking meat from an invisible hand. Something within him was released and roamed free as he watched in tightening chains.

Those extra eyes had to have something to do with the invisible invited guest now unafraid to reveal himself and who now refused to leave.

He trembled so hard he thought the floor vibrated. He wanted to run. He stood and avoided the mirror. As he walked away, a fleeting peace left the room. He would not be alone to face Parliament. He would have help in these difficult days.

Why was he concerned with what others said about him? Lies. Why was he concerned about his empire starting to disintegrate, starting with the rebels in the colonies on the other side of the Atlantic? They were ungrateful, spoiled children biting the hand that fed them. He was the most powerful man leading the most powerful nation with the most powerful military in the world.

In meetings, when others would enter his presence, they were to bow three times and never to turn their backs to him. They had to remain standing. Who would commit treason against the king when punishments like being drawn and quartered would occur? This could include being hanged, but the rope would be cut right before death. The king's men then cut the rebel's stomach open, and the rebel would watch in horror as the king's men lit the rebel's intestines on fire. Then they decapitated the rebel, and the body could be quartered and the parts placed in strategic locations as a warning to others.

Related family members of the deceased would lose what they owned and would never be able to own land or a business, and they would be burned alive if they, too, were found guilty of treason.

The Shepherd must save his sheep from the wolf.

The king had some quiet time before the meeting. The eyes within had full access to move about inside him. He wiped his forehead and hands, thinking about the eyes within, the Dark Light, exploring every part of his mind and body to learn his weaknesses, desires, and appetites.

The king held on to his faith that he would not be alone in his greatest hour of need. His empire was on the edge. One push either way would determine the Motherland's fate and his with it. Someone had to stop the one who came to kill him.

The king was not alone. He had supporters in Parliament. And he had the Dark Light. He needed it. He despised it.

King George entered, with his chest pushed out, to face both Houses of Parliament after arriving from his luxurious coach. He commanded full submission, wearing a royal robe of crimson to accompany his diamond-studded crown.

No one else can see the markings.

After preliminary discussion, it was now time for what all had come for.

The Shepherd will rise.

The colonies were rebelling. War started in Lexington and Concord in the colony of Massachusetts. The rebels fought valiantly at the Battle of Bunker Hill, and though Britain won that battle, it came with a heavy and extensive cost. With the king scanning the room, what was the king going to do?

I will find you, murderer. The king started by reviewing how the colonies in North America were misled by dangerous men while forgetting their allegiance for which they owed.

"... we have thought fit ... to suppress such rebellion, and to bring the traitors to justice ... and ... to disclose and make known all traitorous conspiracies and attempts against us, our crown and dignity ... and to disclose and make known all treasons and traitorous conspiracies which they shall know to be against us, our crown and dignity ... *God* save the *king*."

The king finished in minutes in what seemed to him was just a few seconds. He smiled as the cheers echoed through the chambers. All there knew the beast of justice was formally released. The rebellious children would be forced to concede all powers to the Motherland. Traitors would be hanged. Burned. Their weak and disorganized factions of an army would be obliterated. The traitors called the Continental Congress would all hang begging for the mercy of death.

As the king looked down toward his feet and lower legs as bodily servants, he smiled. *They have no ability to know the Dark Light will spread across the Atlantic, hunting each rebel into their homes and destroying their bodies and souls.*

The world's most powerful man had just unleashed another wave of the world's most powerful army from the world's most powerful nation. Wave after wave of the power of the Dark Light roaming inside him was now released to hunt across the Atlantic.

CHAPTER 19

CAESAR

Dover, Delaware Colony
1775

The night rider dropped things, and as each item hit the hard ground, a flash, like a distant comet, streaked across the sky. Though the night was overcoming the sky, flashes increased as more items hit the ground. Like cannon fire in a battle.

The rider stopped his horse to look at the fires across the sky but then turned his head toward the horrific shrieking moving nearby and overhead.

Something awakened.

The shrieking shadows moved through the night. Hundreds of them. They were looking. Looking for something. The rider summoned his snarling horse, and they sprinted through the dark and continued dropping the items. The shrieking shadows in the sky then turned their attention to the rider.

At a distance, Caesar Rodney stood moving his head with the rider and wanted to help. He could only watch. The rider looked like he had been riding for years. He stood on his horse's back in full gallop and scanned the land around him and then jumped and landed with his hands on the reins and his feet in the stirrups! The rider protected and carried something in his arm. He turned his head, as if looking for someone. With a momentary flash in the sky, the rider turned his head toward Caesar at the exact moment he locked eyes with him. Like an invisible sword so sharp that Caesar did not even know about the cut, the rider's eyes pierced through him. The rider's eyes guided Caesar's eyes to the horse standing next to him.

Where did this horse come from?

Caesar turned his head toward the horse next to him and then to the ground surrounding him and then back to the horse. Voices, screams, cried out from the ground. He sensed that he would die a slow death if he rode the horse beyond where he was standing. He was safer remaining where he was.

More voices cried out.

They called him.

Caesar climbed onto the horse and remained still as his horse turned her head back toward him. His face throbbed as she moved her head from looking back at him to pointing her head forward three times, with the last time accompanied by a snort. Some of the moving shadows changed their attention and shrieked louder as they moved toward him in this present darkness.

Caesar stepped out of the memory of the dream and stood in front of a door. The wave of pain stopped. He stood with his hand raised as he remembered the strange dream he had every night. He had forgotten about the dream until he raised his hand to knock on Dorothy's door.

He pulled back his shaking hand and placed it back into his pocket. His hand did not shake in his pocket. He pulled out his hand and watched it shake as he adjusted his scarf. He knocked on her door. When he stopped knocking, there was still a knocking sound. Was it his heart? Or was it his knees?

Someone opened the door partway, without Caesar knowing if it was Dorothy behind the door.

A woman's voice escaped. "May I assist you?"

"Dorothy?"

"Yes. May I ask who you are?"

"This is Caesar. We met the other day . . . down-town . . . I am the one with the scarf."

"Oh yes. Caesar." The door opened fully. "Please come in."

Caesar wanted to finish everything and jump with his arms in the air and then walk home a victor. But he wasn't finished. He stepped inside, and she closed the door. He scanned the room. There was a man's coat and scarf with a covering of dust on them draped over a chair. There were a pair of men's faded and worn fine English leather shoes under a small table, with cobwebs connecting the shoes.

Dorothy followed Caesar's eyes, skimming the room with a weariness that hinted that she was too tired to explain the still-remaining items in her home.

He pulled his scarf tighter. "I am sorry if I have inconvenienced you. Sometimes I prefer to be undisturbed in the safety of my home . . . I'm sorry . . . not that you are like me."

Dorothy looked at him as if he had sneaked a peek at her diary. Her eyes widened, as if she had discovered the name of her husband's mistress for the first time.

"Do you know my husband? Do you work for him?"

Caesar coughed to clear his throat. He pulled his scar tighter around his face. *Did she see my cancer? Perhaps she was scared of what was underneath the cancer.*

He lifted his hands in front of his shoulders in surrender. "No. I do not know your husband."

"Are you here to take away what I have left? I will not give you back his belongings. His last remaining money . . . it is all I have . . ." She moved a step toward the door.

"I . . . it is not mine to take . . ." Caesar slumped forward as they both said "I am sorry" at the same time. Caesar said "Pardon me" and remembered what his friend Edward had said about Dorothy.

She opened her mouth, and it remained open, as did Caesar's. As they stared at each other with mirrored faces, they both laughed.

They both sat down and shared coffee, crumpets, and conversation.

Dorothy acted like she tried to remember how to entertain a guest in her home. She quickly warmed to the idea of sharing with a friend. Perhaps a good friend.

"So Mr. Rodney, how is it you have time to be here? I have heard that you serve in the Continental Congress, you are an associate justice of our Delaware Supreme Court, you were a member of the state assembly and a high sheriff, and captain of a militia."

Caesar's face warmed, and he experienced the color of lovely red in a most inopportune time. He was certain it reflected Dorothy's color theme of her home. "I do distract myself with things that are both conveniently important and distracting."

She tilted her head with eyes attempting to penetrate. "Distracting from what?"

"Well, if you have not noticed, my face." *What am I doing? I never talk about this with anyone.* "My pain. I almost had to go back home a few minutes ago. But the wave of pain abated. I continue to search for a cure for my cancer."

They conversed about many things. Life regrets. Victories. Losses. Confronting the days that they lived. The coming war swirling around them.

Dorothy glanced toward the front door.

Caesar haltingly said, "I am sorry . . ." and then shut his mouth. "If you need me to leave, I will leave."

She continued staring toward the door without blinking. "My husband left me a few years ago. He walked right through that door . . . changed everything he left behind after that. I still do not have the energy to remove his things from our home."

She returned her gaze back to Caesar. "He was very upset that many here were resisting him. He was a loyalist to the king with the war against the French and continued to be a loyalist until his last day here. Some did not like him for his views. I do not like oppressive kings." She sighed and turned her head away from Caesar. "We had other differences. He found another woman who shared his views. Since then, I hide my views. I hide everything. Perhaps I would still have a husband if I had submitted to the king as well."

Mr. Rodney caught himself before he said he was sorry. "This has been a very fine hour with you. Perhaps we could both escape our chains and meet again?"

She smiled and nodded. Caesar attempted to memorize her face. How she spoke. Her mannerisms. The sadness in her eyes forever singed in his mind. He had a sense of loyalty to her. Her beauty.

Her eyes, with a growing ember of their time together, contrasted the dusk on her face, revealing a loyalty to her loyalist husband. But in their time together, their heads were as if well above the darkening clouds. They shared the shining well above the hard land and waited for a good rain to come and cleanse everything back to where it once was. For a time they shared their pain and some joy above the looming war casting a great shadow over the land.

Chapter 20

MARY

**Near Plymouth, Massachusetts Bay Colony
1750**

Mary was in a dark place in her dream. The ground was wet. It was warm. Like warm water thick enough to make mud. Every once in a while, a streak of light crossed the distant sky. Strange noises emanated from the streaks of light.

She jerked her foot upward when she thought she stepped on something that moved. She seemed to awaken or alert others as voices beneath her spoke, but not clearly.

Then something entered her ear and cascaded deep inside her from about fifty feet away. This noise was different. She moved closer to it. Then she fig-ured it out.

This one was different. It was a singular voice.

Her knees buckled.

What was that? Mary stopped remembering her dream and continued walking with weighted dusk approaching upon her. She was about a mile away from where her friend Agnes lived nearer to

Plymouth. She had to move on the perimeter of the colonist village as she approached the plantation where Agnes lived. Mary avoided moving through town if she did not have to. Even after all this time, and the degree of trust she and others had, she was still not at ease walking through town as an Indian in the approaching darkness. She also wanted to avoid being stopped by people wanting to know if her husband had returned home.

She knew the secrets taught by her people on how to blend in and how to navigate the night. Sounds, quiet walking on different parts of her feet, and knowing when to stop and move in differing shades of dark and light, and other patterns of the upcoming night, guided her past most others without knowing she'd infiltrated through their personal spaces. She would soon enter Agnes's master's plantation with no serious effort. It also helped that he usually went to bed shortly after nightfall.

A commotion of some sort moved nearby. It was out of her view. It moved toward her. She sprinted off the side of the road and hid. As she crouched behind a large bush, something moved across the road ahead of her. A man with a rifle hid behind a tree. He saw Mary and motioned for her to return to where she came from. Mary shook her head no. The man became more adamant with his hand motions, and when Mary continued to shake her head no, the man pointed to other areas near the road. Other heads and rifles moved from behind bushes.

Mary did not feel threatened, for if they were going to harm her, they would have already done so without giving her a warning. The commotion she heard down the road grew closer.

These were not hunters. *They are going to attack someone.*

With tensions already present between the colonists, the Indians, and those for and opposing the king and the French, Mary did not want to be in the middle of an attack on someone. She did not want to be a witness or an assumed accessory to another atrocity.

Someday soon there would be a war between the British and the French, and she knew some Indian tribes would choose one side and some would choose the other side. War was coming.

The men approaching down the road might think I am a scout for those hiding behind trees. They might think I drew them here into a trap. They will kill me . . . and they will end up killing our plans with Agnes.

Mary glanced her head up and down the road.

It was too late to run. They would spot her. The large sound approaching was new to her. It could not be a man. It sounded like an entire village was walking fast toward her. In perfect rhythm. Then around the bend. They were wearing red.

Redcoats are coming. They know there are some who resist them and the king and support the French. Force is always their answer.

She had never seen so many together at once. There must have been at least 150 men.

The ground trembled. As the redcoats passed in front of her, shots rang out from behind trees and bushes. The redcoats never saw it coming. The colonists behind the trees did not fight like the redcoats. They'd learned, and fought like her people. The redcoats regrouped and formed a line and marched toward Mary's side of the road.

They are coming right at me!

Most of the men behind the trees and bushes stayed and continued firing at the redcoats, but several ran with Mary away from the soon-to-come gunfire. A volley of fire came. While Mary was lying down, she saw branches and small trees fall. Men cried out. A young man's cracking voice near her cried out. Then she heard the same voice weeping. The voice was so near. Right near her a man was lying face up. Mary bent down to see if she could help, and the man tried to say something to her. But his words were warbled, like someone with a foot pushing on his mouth.

He coughed. "Moth . . . er . . . help . . . me," and then he coughed more. Blood ran out of his mouth. Then his eyes did not blink and his face did not move.

Mary knew another volley was coming and dove to the ground. A wave of whistling and tearing passed overhead, seeking its target. More branches and small trees fell. This time there was no more voice. Mary knew she had time to run before they fired another volley. And she ran.

She wept as she ran. In her head, she heard the voices of her parents. One said, "We have to make peace with them," and the other voice said, "We remember what they did, and we must make war."

She then heard a new voice in her head. Like from a flawed king with his blood-stained hands wrapped around the throat of a rebellious child.

I will find you.

Mary stopped running. Collapsed. She curled up into a ball and rocked to calm herself enough to then try to run again. *Which side am I on? Where do I run?*

The redcoats were moving, but her legs could not move.

CHAPTER 21

GEORGE WHITEFIELD

Oxford, England
1732

Orphans on the streets preferred to sleep in the shadows, away from the passing adults, for safety, but when hunger struck, they moved to the sidewalks and streets. During the day, they came out looking for food. As George walked to Pembroke College on an unusually bright and sunny morning after the fog rolled in, most of the orphan boys were out of the shadows and enjoying the reclusive sun on their faces.

George went up to one of the boys living in a hidden alley. The other boys had not hesitated to ask for food from George on previous days, but this one particular boy always stood behind the others and often missed out on the food. The other boys nearby gathered around the orphan boy George had chosen.

George pulled out food from the worn pocket of his fraying breeches and handed the food first to the boy who stood behind the others and then to the rest. Parents abandoned or rejected these boys for various reasons, including poverty, enslaved to their alcohol, and inability to physically provide, or sometimes the boys ran away so they did not have to work long days to support their family. George knew about the parents who were slaves with invisible chains, as he'd served many of them in his youth in his parents' inn, or what some called their favorite tavern. George smiled when the unintelligible "Thank you" was drowned in food.

As he walked away from the boys, something dark from George's youth re-tightened the invisible rope around his neck that sometimes went slack. When George tried to do more good to free his throat for better breathing, the rope sometimes pulled tighter in its own whims.

Later that same morning, George Whitefield walked to work past the golden-colored stone buildings with every tower and steeple pointing upward. He walked into the dining hall and through other students and coworkers unaware of his entrance. Did anyone know his name?

He picked up a towel and went to the side where the workers interacted with the students. Students less than ten feet away from him complained about the food, knowing that George, one of the workers, was nearby. George was like a moth on the wall waiting to find a light to go to, as everyone in the dining room hall ignored the moth until it was convenient to smash him against the wall.

He pulled out a drinking glass from the pile of clean dishes. He tried to clean a persistent stain of some sort. He used a fingernail to scratch it off, but it was too hard. From the corner of George's eye stood a group of the wealthiest students. Each with two wealthy parents at home, pleased with themselves that they had sent their offspring to Pembroke College. Each of the students smiled and laughed as they studied the failing servitor trying to serve.

I can't get this clean.

He knew some of the rich boys had rich parents who despised both those living on the streets and those a mere step above on the economic ladder. They laughed again, and they were not going to leave him alone. They were children of parents comfortably unaware on their mountains of money and what life was like in the lower valleys. George wanted to live on the mountain and with two parents.

One of the taller students glided up to him, like a plantation owner getting ready to hit a rogue sheep who'd strayed once again. Or perhaps like a plantation owner stomping toward a slave not serving to the master's standards. As the student bent to look down his own nose at George, he said, "Hey, boy, why can't you take out that stain?"

The boy pointed at a stain on George's shirt. When George bent his head down, the boy poked George in the eye. He then pulled on the tenuous threads and tore George's shirt. "No wonder the stain remains. You have to remove it for the glass to be clean. Remove yourself and go back to the tavern you were born in so that we can be rid of you, for you are of no good use here. This is a place for those with real families and a sound mind."

The student's friends laughed, and one said, "I would buy you some clothes, but the torn clothes you have are a good reminder of who you are. You do not belong here."

One student laughed and went up to him and said "Maybe this will help" and threw water from a glass at his face. The other students laughed again. He then said, "When you leave this place, then the stain will be gone."

After the students in the group left and George wiped his face, two young men came to talk with him. They both were similar in age, the same well-groomed brownish hair, and lean builds shorter than George.

"My name is John, and this is my brother, Charles. We started a student club here and would like to invite you to come to one of our meetings."

"I have heard of the Wesleys' 'Holy Club.' You must really think I need it."

John spoke again and pointed to himself, his brother, and everyone else in the spacious room. "We all need it. Who could not benefit from being more holy before a holy God?"

Charles nodded and turned his head toward the boys walking out the dining hall. "As sinful as those rich boys were with you, though poor in humility, they were right. We can't remove the stains."

Over the next few months and years, George learned much from the Wesleys, about life as a student, and about Jesus. At times the Dark Light would recede as he sought holiness. But at other times, even when exercising great spiritual discipline, someone, or something, pulled harder on the tightening rope.

George, at times, convinced himself that he had eased his conscience by doing what he was supposed to do. It was now 1735, and he was twenty-one years old and did everything he thought the Bible instructed, from eating bland food, fasting, meditating, and praying with every word in his Scripture readings. He convinced himself that he had kept the beast of guilt hidden and out of sight on a short leash. But with continued attempts at hiding and shortening the leash of guilt, something pulled harder on the rope around his own neck.

I am supposed to be free in You, but I am not free.

One night in his room after completing his Bible studies and meditation, he surprised himself with a moan he had never heard before. He turned his head to see who else was in the room. That sound could not have come from him. But no one else was in the room. He collapsed onto his bed. Hidden in his room, there was no one to see his limp body and loss of breath. He was exhausted with eating from the tree of the knowledge of good and evil. Shifting onto his side, he sobbed, convulsed, and pulled his knees up to his chest, like a little boy hunted down by a childhood monster and without any parents around for protection. He was alone. There was no one to hold his hand to help him understand the assault that punished him in the day and robbed him of sleep in the night. Like a baby in the womb, he wanted to stay curled up, protected within the room. He knew if he survived the next few minutes and let go of his knees, his hands, now unoccupied, would soon destroy something. He would strike something or someone.

"I am not good enough! I cannot do this!"

The invisible blood on his hands called to him. Judged him. His sins! His future sins! His enslavement to his sins and his sins that enslaved others. His enslavement with trying to be good enough. His past sins of knowingly giving alcohol to men who should not have been given more alcohol. He'd seen some in the tavern not enslaved to alcohol and others slowly die every day. He'd seen someone die before his eyes with stains of George's own hands on the dead man's last glass. He knew he should have not served him. He could not free his hands to cover his ears. The voices crying out!

George screamed out loud. "Where are You, God? I am here, but where are You?"

George's body convulsed again. Then he entered into a vision. He fought as if he were floating on the ocean. He tried to pull back on the reins of the ocean, to pull back the waves of a storm carrying him to the pounded beach. He could not stop the ocean, and the waves rode him. There were rocks up ahead. He tried to protect himself from the coming rocks as the waves carried him, but he could not swim against the power of the ocean. He tried to push the waves of water back toward the ocean.

The vision continued as a singular wave picked him up and pushed him toward the largest rock on the coastline. There was broken wood floating below the great rock. This rock had broken all other vessels that had challenged it. And now George was a living vessel carried toward death and moments away from crashing against the immovable rock.

"What more must I do? I have done all that You have asked . . . and yet You want more? Who are You?"

As the vision hurled him into the air toward the large rock, all sense of time slowed. While in the air plummeting toward the rock, there was a partial view of someone's hand writing in a book. The book! He instantly recognized the book filled with words that could change the world! It was an old Bible carried to shores aboard a ship years before! A dead man can rise! The orphan has a Father! The slave has a Redeemer! It was not his own hand that wrote the book. The book was not his story to control and script his own way. It was the work of Someone else. He had to follow the Author of his faith. It was His Story, and He moved through those willing and unwilling.

Why am I alive? What do I live for? Who do I live for?

He was weak. He was unable to follow the words as they were intended. He failed every day. Hundreds of times every day.

The words on a page of the book moved. They throbbed. In the rhythm of a heartbeat that was not his own.

He did not know His heart.

Then the vision crashed George against the giant rock. A crack reverberated inside him, like a splintered beam breaking inside him. The rock broke him. After hitting the rock, he slid down and the ocean yanked him back toward itself.

The ocean grabbed his legs and pulled him toward the ocean floor as it took him away further. Like a little boy lifting his arms to be taken up into his father's arms, he could only raise his open hands above the disappearing surface of the water.

George then opened his eyes in a new way upon his bed. It was as if he was already awake, but his other eyes within him opened for the first time. The vision finished. His body relaxed. He breathed better. His muscles ached in every part of his body.

But he was breathing. He was alive.

He laughed aloud. He leaped and jumped up and down on his bed.

He had a Father.

He was out of the womb for a second time in his life.

The leash broke.

All debts were already forgiven. Paid, though not by his own merits.

The chains were gone.

He could not control the Author. It was not his story. The Author could do what He wanted to do, but He wanted to work through George Whitefield, even with all his flaws. It was His Story, and George had a role.

The Dark Light receded further than it ever had and could only wait for another opportune time.

CHAPTER 22

MO

**Gowanus Heights, New York Colony
1776**

Mo's heart raced as he turned away from the two men pummeling each other on the ground. He forced his eyes to scan the campsite to study the assembled men. Mo was a soldier like the other men, but Mo was fighting a different fight. How could the men fighting the king they claimed was attempting to enslave them, not see that some in the rebel Continental Army were also guilty of enslaving? How could they not see that their leaders proclaiming liberty themselves did not practice what they preached? Yet he could not tell them that he was once a slave and now desired to fight. They would never allow him to fight alongside them if they knew who he was.

Mo adjusted his hat over the edges of his hairline and propped his weapon against a nearby tree to set aside the temptation. Mo's eyelids fluttered as he tried to keep his eyes closed to the idiots fighting before him. On this cool morning, the temperature within and around Mo rose. Or was it just inside him?

He loosened what was left of his plantation work-shirt collar to give more room for his pounding neck and the heat within. Most of the men wore their work shirts from home for their fighting uniform.

At the moment, it was a mistake that Elias had spoken to various people in power to find a place in one of the Pennsylvania regiments in the Continental Army for Mo to "enact God's will." Elias's last words to Mo as he left were, "Keep your hat on, your head straight, and your eyes off yourself. Fix your eyes on the Light of the world, and He will guide you."

George Washington had selected Thomas Mifflin as brigadier general, one of George Washington's most trusted of men. Mifflin was an honest man to counter the corruption ravaging the army. Mo had heard that Mifflin was raised as a pacifist Quaker but presently left no doubt that there would be no rivals to his leadership.

But two men were fighting each other just feet away from Mo. Where was the general? What good was a group of ill, and ill-prepared men, soon to fight a superior force, when they were rolling around the ground fighting *themselves*?

Soldiers gathered around the rolling men and took sides. Some bet future food rations as wagers of who would rise victoriously. One of the fighting men yelled to the other a term that any slave would find repulsive. Mo's right hand clenched as he stomped closer to the fighting duo. Many of the gathered started chanting the same word. Mo pushed his way closer to the fight and, when he was within range, kicked the one on the ground who'd uttered the word.

The others surrounding Mo and the fighting men yelled more and louder, and two men from the crowd pushed Mo down, while others kicked him. Mo had ruined their game. As many as ten different men kicked and punched Mo as he lay on his side with his hands and arms protecting his head. He tried to rock himself between blows while trying to keep his hat on.

When the men thought he'd had enough, with generations flowing in his blood, Mo rose and attacked those who'd beat him. All ten of them at the same time. After the third time he got up, the men stopped fighting, as Mo chose death at their hands over surrendering.

Mifflin pushed men aside with his angry arms and cursing words. "What are you doing? You are idiots! Either you submit to the king, who wants to kill you, or me."

All fighting stopped as he continued. "Which is it?"

When no one answered he asked again. "WHICH IS IT?"

He bent to pull Mo off the ground with but a single finger and thumb pulling on Mo's earlobe. Mo pressed his hat against his own head, but judging by Mifflin's expression, the general had seen the edges of Mo's exposed hair.

With the hand still attached to his earlobe, Mo pulled his hat back into place as the fights distracted the men with their various wounds.

If he had doubts before, he now knows I am part African.

Mifflin paused. His eyes penetrated through Mo. He twisted Mo's earlobe and scanned his fighting men and spoke with a combination of full authority and almost gentle instruction. "I need every man here to fight the one who seeks to hang you. I don't care if you are rich, poor, or whatever additional mistakes your mother and father were that brought you into this world—I don't care. Who is with me?"

All the men yelled in agreement.

Mifflin spat near Mo's feet and yelled to all the men as his eyes fixed on Mo. "Get back to work." Mifflin twisted and then let go of Mo's ear.

Mo turned his back and pushed others away to create a path.

Mifflin walked to Mo and spun him toward him as spittle flew out of his mouth. He sprayed Mo as he tried to whisper one inch from his face. "You best not disappoint me. If you get into another fight, I will kick you where the lies leave you. You'll be picking up parts of your teeth before I would ever allow you to serve against the king. Do you understand?"

Mo could only look down, for he knew if he looked at the commander's eyes, he would not be able to control himself. He could only mutter a "Yes."

"Elias is a good man. I trust him, but I lost any trust I had for you."

The commander looked at a small bit of hair protruding outside of Mo's hat. "Your life balances on an edge of a cliff while looking down. Will you be able to allow God living in you to do what *He* wants to do? You think you escaped slavery, but you are still a slave."

Mifflin looked around the camp and whispered, "God knows we need help. But do you know that *you* need help?"

Mo could only look away.

"Look at me." Through the corner of Mo's eye, he noted the commander spoke with life in his eyes.

Mo tilted his head toward him but could not point his eyes straight at his.

The commander then said, "Perhaps a flawed man should not point his finger at flawed men . . . and yet God still uses us to do what is right." Mifflin pushed him away.

Mo staggered to his weapon propped against the tree and then to the other side of the camp. *Maybe it is time to run again?* He reached again for his weapon and then paused. He screamed into both hands covering his mouth. His chest heaved, as if he was resisting birthing something that he would not regret later. He stopped heaving as he looked up at a tree's outline with the rising sun behind it.

I have a plan.

CHAPTER 23

MARY

Near Plymouth, Massachusetts Bay Colony
1750

The redcoats separated and searched for all the men who'd tried to ambush them as dusk entered the day. Some of those who'd been hiding behind trees had escaped. Mary trembled on the ground underneath thick brush. Footsteps moved near her, and someone even somehow ran over her without stopping. After several minutes, the heavy footsteps returned back to the main road.

At a distance back on the road, cries for mercy were answered with bayonets. Mary had never heard grown men cry like little boys before.

She stayed lying on her side. She tried to control her trembling so she would not make noises with the covering and surrounding brush. She prayed for protection, as her legs were still not able to move enough to run. After several minutes when the crying stopped and the heavy footsteps moved farther away, her ability to move her legs returned.

Mary sat up to tune her ears and lift her head above her surroundings. Though most of the light of day was not present, a dark presence pressed on her. It had weighed on her during the shooting. She covered her nose to pause from what wafted throughout. All of this was so strong that she would not have been surprised to hear the footsteps of the king himself roaming the area.

I need to run.

Everyone was gone. Once-moving humans before the attack now lay motionless. The presence moved with the redcoats to search another area. Mary pushed up and walked back to the road. In the distance, the redcoats marched toward both of her peoples.

Mary faced where the redcoats were heading, and her back faced where she'd been heading toward Agnes's home before she was caught in the crossfire.

Should I run toward them? I know secret pathways where I can pass the redcoats and warn my people in each of my two villages. If I only have time to warn one group, which one do I warn?

But what about Agnes?

Was not the plan for Agnes more important than what would happen in the next several minutes with the redcoats?

She shook her head and walked toward the direction of the redcoats. Her legs moved like they were in thick mud. She could not run.

God, what are You doing to my legs?

She tried to run, but her feet felt like tree trunks. A woman praying at a tree flashed in and then out of her mind. The woman was not at the tree near Plymouth at the clearing but somewhere else Mary did not recognize. The dark-skinned woman was not dressed like an Indian or a colonist.

She physically could not move away from the road through the familiar paths she knew to pass the redcoats, even if she wanted to. After several minutes she remained in the middle of the road. People screamed and gunshots echoed in the distance. It was too late. Her heart pounded like a drum of war. Her parents' voices yelled in her head. War was ahead of her. In her. It was in the air and penetrating through the ground. And war in the future was still coming. Mary was paralyzed in the mud. There was nothing she could do.

She tried rocking herself.

God working through Agnes is our hope.

Something unlocked in her, and she pivoted and ran away from the redcoats. The voices of her parents went with her, but that did not stop her attempt at running away from her parents' voices, like when she had run away from home.

This time she was running to help her friend Agnes. Was Agnes okay? The best chance to determine if Agnes was okay was to now move in the cover of night.

Mary did not encounter a single person, as most hid from the redcoats and other possible skirmishes.

The light of the moon guided her until she arrived at the plantation.

I know they are looking for Agnes. Satan is trying to stop our plan. What if they killed Agnes? Then what would we do? The most important part of our plan would be destroyed.

Mary let out a sigh of relief. Agnes paced back and forth away and toward the house. Mary smiled, with Agnes now okay and the master asleep.

Mary did a native bird call as she waved a hand above a bush.

Agnes held her stomach as she walked and moaned and knelt to hide with Mary.

Mary put her hand on Agnes's shoulder. "I know this sounds like I am a crazy woman, but I was worried that somehow the king found out about our plan. I am telling you that he is after you. I thank God you are okay."

Agnes wiped Mary's forehead.

Mary studied her moonlit eyes. "How are you feeling? A little while ago I was reminded that we are in the crossfire and mercy of leaders that do not fully represent us. I am telling you, war is coming with the French, and after that someday people will revolt against the king."

"What took you so long to get here?"

"I saw redcoats! They were nearby. I saw a group attack them, and I was caught in the middle of the ambush. I saw some of the colonists attack the redcoats."

Mary paused to catch her breath as Agnes tilted her head. "Did you hear what I just said? I saw some of the colonists attack the redcoats. They attacked the most powerful army in the world. I do not understand why, but I believe it foreshadowed the future." Mary shook her head. "They have learned from my people. They fought like my people. That is the only way they could ever defeat them. I can feel it deep within me. I think it spills over into my dreams."

A noise from the house stopped Mary. When she was satisfied that they would be okay, she continued. "There is coming war between my people, the colonists, the French, and the British. The king is ruled by and wants vengeance, but he does not know the trap up ahead. I tried not to pay attention before in their affairs, but now I know—war is coming, Agnes . . . Parts of it are already here. I saw what it will look like just a little while ago."

"Will we be better off with the Indians, the French, the king, or the colonists?" Agnes bent her head, as if bracing herself for a troubling answer.

"What side is God on?" Mary shrugged her shoulders.

Agnes rolled her eyes. "I have no idea. Does God pick sides, or does He want love, truth, and justice above the tribes of man? He can't be happy seeing his children, brothers, and sisters killing each other."

Agnes held her stomach. "I don't know how many more times I can do this, Mary. I know we need to discuss plans. I know we need to share the latest information. We know the role I will play. We need to move on our plan soon if I am going to be able to help." Agnes's eyes widened as she shook her head. "This baby is going to change things, and he does not heed our plans."

Mary laughed and then stopped immediately. "Any more word on the missing slave?"

Agnes lifted her head up toward the dark sky. She turned her head in different directions, as if looking for something moving above her. "No. I think he is far away, and we will never find him. I have a difficult time predicting what my master will do. To this day he still confuses me. Perhaps because I have African blood in me and he is European and Indian, I have a hard time understanding his ways."

She paused and laughed. "Why do I still call him my master when God is my Master? I am confused as I try to figure out which side I support today. To him, he only sees one of his African-blooded slaves got pregnant and one of his other slaves is missing. He never asked what happened with my pregnancy, because he only cares that I am pregnant and it interferes with my work, and one of his slaves escaped."

"He refuses to see me. He only likes some Indians, but not all," Mary said." Even Praying Indians. Since I cannot meet with him, I will give this to you. Are you ready for this?"

"What is it?"

"God is on the move. The chief is tired of the fighting. Give this note to the one who calls himself your master, because the chief wants to meet with him. Can you believe it? All our prayers will be answered. The chief wants peace with the head of the colonists!"

Agnes took the note with her, eyes still fixed on Mary. She shook her head and covered her face with her arm. "I cannot believe this. You were right, Mary, for us to just keep praying."

Mary held on to the other note someone had sneaked into her pocket earlier. The plan was moving forward. "Regarding the second part of our arrangement, someone at the village put information into my pocket about what will happen for you during the coming meeting between the leaders. Me and Martha did not want anyone hurt above all things, with the meeting and with our part of the plan during the meeting. With the master out for hours with the chief, that is our best opportunity for no one to get hurt."

"Do you think the meeting that you, me, and Martha want will actually happen between the chief and the master?"

"This is our best chance for our people and you. The master here never leaves this plantation, and he has his spies everywhere. He knows that he has the men and resources to capture any missing slave within a short time. That is why I wonder if that missing slave is already dead. The master would be gone for a few hours with this coming meeting. You will keep the master's wife preoccupied, and we are gathering the resources to take advantage of those hours. This plan of ours, our futures, your baby's future, depends on all of us making this work. Then one day you can return to take away the rest of the slaves here."

Mary then stared off into the night, with the corner of her eye on Agnes.

Agnes blinked her eyes in her attempt to see Mary's face. "Mary, what is really going on? What is happening?"

"I was just remembering a dream I have been having. Almost every night for months now. I wish I knew what it was about."

"I don't have dreams."

"Do you still sense that your master is scared of something?"

"He is scared of his wife. His wife's family is very wealthy—they have dozens of slaves—and his wife's father does not like him. The father-in-law hates him so much that if the father-in-law thinks that the master is not treating his daughter well, he will not pass on his wealth to a rebellious son-in-law, even if it means the wealth does not go to his daughter."

Agnes moved closer to Mary. "The master wants that money. His wife knows that. She does not much care for the money and the slaves that come with it. She thinks that the money gained by slavery is cursed. She treats me well most of the time. He already has power with all his political connections, but he does not have great wealth. If he does any wrong before his wife and his father-in-law, he loses what he wants most. She uses this as power over him."

"I guess everyone has a master?"

"The master has a master. He hates his wife. She is his master." Agnes smiled and nodded her head.

"Agnes, you better get back before he or his spies discover you out here. You need to be alive if our plan is to happen. If all goes well, I am convinced God is going to use you to free many other slaves. God has told me himself. Now that I know you are okay, I will continue to prepare. Do you think your master has any idea what we are going to do?"

"I do not believe he realizes how everything will soon change." Agnes silhouetted with the moonlight.

As Agnes stood, Mary lifted her head. The outline of Agnes's stomach reminded her of a major desire in her own life. Mary's future child that God promised her before her husband had left her. The night shadow casted itself over the outline of Agnes's stomach and covered over Mary.

Something pulled at Mary's heart, in a direction that scared her. A direction she did not want to go. It was too dark in that place. She tried not to look at Agnes's stomach. She tried to forget about broken promises and all the lies.

What if I had that child? Mary hit herself on the side of her head as Agnes scanned the surroundings. *My life would be more complete knowing that someone I loved would never leave me. And I could rest knowing that I raised up someone who would bring all our peoples together, like God told me.*

CHAPTER 24

MO

Gowanus Heights, New York Colony
1776

The storm was coming. Mo and Henry, who'd come with him from Elias's place, along with his new friend Augustine, talked about what they were witnessing a few miles away. Mo was amused, standing in the middle between Augustine cursing God, whom he claimed to not believe in, and Henry's strong faith responses.

Rumors spread amongst the men that there was no way General George Washington could know where the British were going to strike. New York? Long Island? Would an attack on Long Island be merely a distraction of a far larger attack upon New York, which was likely their ultimate goal? If New York City was taken, the rest of the divided colonies would fall.

Whisperings between the two men on each side of Mo included rumors that General Washington had split his vastly outnumbered troops between New York and Long Island, not knowing where the invasion of the tyranny of hell would start. Those same rumors also included that the British had already landed somewhere on Long Island. Mo tried to ignore the hair on the back of his neck reaching up like hands trying to surrender.

It was a tense and expectant night in August as Mo and his friends stood on trembling ground miles away from the city. Something strange was happening in the sky above New York City. Even in the dark of the evening hours, it was not hard to see something perhaps even more ominous than the thousands of British soldiers soon to attack them.

There. It seemed to stand still. A large storm cloud. It was virtually motionless above the city. Waiting. Seemingly searching the surrounding skies and periphery of the city in preparation, or a prelude, to something. The lone cloud built in intensity. No one had ever seen a cloud that black in color taking residence and lying in wait over a city before.

It seemed that all nine thousand men present in the Continental Army, in the Gowanus Heights region, stopped any work, conversation, or sleep as their eyes focused on the sky above their city. Now all eyes and mouths stuck open, and no one else spoke. Then Augustine walked away and fell to his knees, facing the unprotected city.

It was difficult for Mo to move his eyes from the storm building above the city to Augustine. Augustine swayed back and forth, alternately bowing his head to the ground and raising his head up to the heavens. Augustine, as if just inches away, emanated rumblings from the innermost part of himself.

"I confess. I have sinned. I am Sodom and Gomorrah. Spare all around me, for it is I that you seek. Please have mercy on us. I know You exist. I know I have conveniently said You do not exist so that I could delude myself into believing I am king of my own kingdom . . . I am sorry. Forgive me. No more slavery. No more selfish convenience."

Mo turned his head away from Augustine toward the cloud, as it seemed to respond with an even deeper darkened color. Lights flashed within the cloud, as if lighted beings fought against other beings and the lighted ones cast out the others and they now fell and struck the ground below. The cloud expelled fire from the sky and created fire on the trembling ground below.

Augustine increased the intensity of his swaying and rocking.

Mo shook his head. "I don't want any part of a God if he is going to be killing us over here. At least without God, I was still alive."

Someone near him said, "I do not know if that is God doing that over the city or is it God allowing this to happen? But this I know—God is waking us to remember He is God and we are not. It looks like I am not the only one who He's awakened."

Another lightning bolt shot out from the cloud to the city below. Sounds echoed and carried through the still air, as if the city was only feet away. Cries of pain and for help traveled from the city. Mo heard a single woman scream for help in finding her children after an explosion. A child screamed for a mother. The storm billowed above the city, and at times the thunder became one continuous sound. Flashes of light became longer episodes of sunlight at night. The smell of sulfur filled the air with the sky attack.

I am glad I am not over there because—

Lightning struck the ground about one hundred feet from Mo and his friends. All three were knocked down when the ground rumbled and moved under them. Cries next to Mo echoed behind the smoke where the lightning had struck. Broken cries and broken pleas for help pierced through the wall of smoke.

After Mo came to, he staggered into standing and ran to try to help Henry and Augustine. Those men were okay, and the three moved toward the men gathered in another area where lightning had struck. A group of men already there covered their eyes and noses as they turned away. Three men vomited off to the side.

When Mo and Augustine and Henry reached the area, they discovered that two of their fellow soldiers were almost completely gone, with only smoking residual parts left. The tips of their swords and coins on them had melted into reminders.

They are gone.

Some of the surrounding men confessed their sins to God. Some cried for mercy. Mo tilted his head toward the sky. Some men surrounding the smoking residue of their friends lifted up fists to the sky and cursed. More lightning strikes hit the city.

We stand still when we should fight. When will we fight?

Mo needed to hit something. Anything. He looked at the men crying and begging for their lives. He lifted his face upward again and swung his fists. Hoping that somehow one fist would land on the invisible Father, who inflicted His will.

When his arms became too tired to lift, Mo bent forward, weeping, trying to bend far enough to increase space for his pounding heart and throbbing lungs to move.

He struggled to remain standing. With his hands pushing off his thighs, he straightened. *Enough. I will not bow down to anyone or anything.*

CHAPTER 25

KING GEORGE

Buckingham House, England
1775

After another sleepless night, it was time to win the day. King George III stood at the mirror he swore he would never look at again. He attempted to control the power pumping in his head and chest and flowing into the iron fists seemingly out of his control. He held the hands up toward the morning light as the veins on the back of his hands expanded and then contracted. He flinched when his right hand turned toward him. *Who are you?*

For a few moments, the hand resisted the king. *I rule over you. You do not rule over me.*

The last moment of rebellion passed, and he turned his hand away from himself.

He picked up the newspaper screaming at him from across the room. The news confirmed the verbal reports he'd heard from others in Plymouth, watching the great ship *Charming Nancy* yards away in the water as it arrived from the colonies on the other side of his Atlantic.

Families sometimes traveled with their husbands and fathers, accompanying them in civilizing new lands. Colonizing. Families and friends at the dock waited for their conquering heroes to return home. They waited to hear reports of how the rebels had fled in disorganized panic when confronted by a superior army in size, order, and discipline. God judge the ungrateful colonies and God save the king.

But even as *Charming Nancy* was still a distance away silhouetted by the setting sun, those waiting at the dock covered their noses and walked farther away from the water. The article stated that some of the waiting friends and families had become ill, as something horrific on the ship fired in volleys of odor and attacked those waiting at the dock. Perhaps wafting in the air was the remnants of a rebel body left on board to remind the living of the dead?

As the vessel docked, the invisible warning emanated from the ship and cleared more off the dock.

The odor came from the ship itself.

The splintered beams cried out.

Or was the odor from those who were inside? What was happening?

Even with all of those on board standing next to each other, there were too many people missing from the initial idealized painted artwork in everyone's head. Then the figures in the romanticized painting moved. One by one they walked out or were assisted or carried out, with missing arms. Missing legs. They looked starved. Defeated. Families stood incomplete. Young children comforted their sobbing mothers. There were too many empty spaces between those on the ship.

But they were winning the war, right?

Hushed broken conversations spread through the air amongst the gathering. Many whispered stories while they shook their heads. The soldiers did not tell stories of the rebel cowards running away. They told stories of the disorganized rebels in war, vastly outnumbered, farmers and young boys. They . . . they'd looked through the redcoats without blinking and with no regard for their own lives at Bunker Hill.

The king threw the paper down.

Something crawled at his legs and his face. *I will not open my eyes. I will fight the insurrection against me.*

But it grew stronger. It was almost like something, or someone, was pulling his eyelids upward to the heavens. The soreness in his chest multiplied and pounded more. He could always find some semblance of peace in knowing he had the most powerful military force ever assembled in the history of shepherds leading their lost and rebellious sheep.

They will bow down. Like my children. Like my servants. Like hands follow their master.

He opened his eyes because he *wanted* to open his eyes. He avoided the mirror but lifted his eyelids just wide enough. The dark markings were higher up on his legs.

He hesitated and then reached out to hold on to the nearby table. He closed his eyes again and trembled. He took a few steps away from a direct view into the mirror. He slowly opened his eyes again. In the mirror, the eyes within his eyes were already open and the spot on his chin had spread to cover most of his mouth before he slammed his eyes shut.

The king jumped away from the mirror, like an adult moving his face from a childhood monster that followed him from his childhood. He swiped at the air as if some unseen animal tried to jump on him. He ran out of the room and to a nearby table to look for a book. The book that was by the one-foot-high cross he made with garden branches and vines as a youth.

It is still here.

He blew on the cover to remove the superficial layer of nonuse. He picked up the book. He no longer felt alone.

The floor of the entire room swayed, like a massive ship opposed by a great storm. He attempted to regain his lost balance, when his right hand knocked down his cross as he fell.

On the floor, pain seared into his right hand. He reflexively placed his left hand on his right and felt something on his hands. A cut.

The book remained closed, but for the moment, it was as if his chest were splayed open.

"The rebellious little children are descendants of Cain, sinning and killing Abel. The descendants of Abel are missing limbs from their savage attacks. I see what is happening to my legs. They are trying to take what is mine. But you told me you would protect me."

The king wiped his eyes. He screamed as he shook his fists.

"You gave me power. To protect my sheep. I am your image here on earth. I am the Authority. That is your promise. That is my blood covenant that I made with you in my youth." He paused as his heaving chest became heavier.

"Do you remember? You give me power, and I will take back what was yours before you were cast out of heaven. I will continue to conquer Eden and take it back after it was taken away from you. The rebels who oppose me oppose you. Starting with the murderer, and then the subversive leaders and their disciples who occupy my promised land across the Atlantic—they will die by my right hand. I will spread my rule. I will force others to spread my will. This is the Great Commission . . . my Great Commission."

CHAPTER 26

GEORGE WHITEFIELD

Georgia Colony
1740

George Whitefield stood in the open field with his hands extended out in silent prayer. He compared his hands and then tilted his head toward the field before him, made perfect for planting and harvesting.

My life is testimony to all that God has done to bring me here.

Studying George, the owner of the field spoke hesitantly. "I have heard a lot about you. I understand you were a bit of a celebrity back home and are now developing quite the following here on the other side of the Atlantic."

Whitefield closed his hands and then opened them. "I still do not fully understand what He has done. I am a flawed light submitting under the rulership of the perfect Light."

The man playfully bowed down. "Ordained at age twenty-two is what I hear. Preaching like an actor. No script. Yelling. Crying. Swinging your arms. Acting in God's play. You ride your horse thousands of miles and thousands of times just to preach to the lost. You with the brilliant voice that can carry a mile or two and can fill a field like this one is what I hear."

George pointed his finger to the man. "I am made in the image of the same God who created you."

The man pointed to the field and waved his arms, as if surrendering. "I have read about you, and I could never be you. I am a rule follower. Make a rule, and I follow it. That is not what you did. Many of the other preachers, they did not like your demonstrative ways moving in power. They do not like your audience collapsing, convulsing, screaming. They want all the power. Like our king. And you ride anywhere just to preach to the common person?"

George pointed his finger upward. "That is where we err. We do not have any real power, so it is not ours to keep or claim."

The man pointed his finger at George. "I heard they tried to tell you how to preach, where to preach, and where not to preach. The preacher kings did not want you around."

"There are many who do not like me. Sometimes I do not like me . . . but I must tell all about the One who saved me. I want orphans to know they have a Father. That is why we are building an orphanage that is near here and near to my heart."

The man laughed and shook his head. "So you just went on preaching! Banned from preaching indoors, you took it outside. I heard you preached to eight thousand people at once one time. With that golden voice, they all heard each word, as if God Himself was standing right next to each person, whispering their sins and His love into their ear. People collapsing and convulsing on the ground. And even worse, you started preaching to the rejected. The coal miners! The drunkards. The regular people who would never go into a church for fear of fire and brimstone destroying their favorite taverns!"

Whitefield laughed. "Careful. You're talking about my hometown now!"

The man laughed again. He paused and shrugged his shoulders. "You started an orphanage? Why are you doing that for those rejected?"

"There is something roaming our land, and it is coming, and we as a people have to be prepared. I see it coming to destroy and separate families by redefining the meaning of family, friends, our way of life. We need to know our Father to survive what is coming. If I can play a role in that, then I must. I do not know how much longer I have."

The man walked closer to George Whitefield, too close in the eyes of most social graces. "But . . . you preach to the negroes. The slaves!? Why does a preacher who has slaves at his orphanage want to preach to the animals we use as slaves?"

George sighed, closed his eyes, and lowered his chin. He lifted his head and gazed into the man's narrowed eyes just one foot away.

He did not say a word. Something moved and had

its way inside of George, and he knew his own eyes unveiled what was rising within him.

The landowner's eyes widened. He reacted as if he saw a threatening monster dwelling inside of George, attempting to implant itself into others. His mouth dropped open like a future unspoken secret was revealed. He shook his head and backed up. He turned and walked away, shaking his head. The man stopped in his tracks. He did not turn his head but spoke into the wind ahead of him. "Good God, you know exactly what you are doing . . ." and continued walking away.

Movement caught the corner of George's eye. Something near the largest sugar maple tree in the area, its trunk and leaves seemingly pointing away from the soiled ground the landowner thought he owned. George followed the top of the tree to the beautiful and full branches providing shade for those seeking it.

A head popped up along the side of the massive trunk, just underneath the lowest branch. The eyes watched the landowner walk away. When it was safe, a dark-skinned boy hiding behind the large tree stepped away from it, turning his head from side to side. He walked up to George.

The brown of his clear eyes reflected the morning light back into George's face. "My master let me come to hear you speak today. He can be a good man. I left early. They say that you have the tongue of angels speaking of God. May I request a prayer from you?"

George marveled at the boy in front of him, no older than a young teenager. Short but strong and lean, with hands that looked like they had spent a lifetime in the cotton fields. "Certainly. What is your name?"

"They gave me the name of Robert and—"

A girl stepped out of the shadow from behind the same tree. "My name is Alice."

George laughed. She was about the same age as Robert. Also short, with short hair and still with brightness in her eyes. George had the impression these two were lifelong friends who toiled in the fields together. He extended his hand to hers and then asked as she approached, "Have you been saved by the living God?"

"We do not know what that means," Robert said. "Many do not want us to know what you know. We cannot read. We cannot read the book that crossed the Atlantic in the ship to come here. We know there is a God, but no one has told us what it means to be saved."

George curled his index finger to summon. "Come closer, for I believe God has something great for you."

They gathered, and Whitefield spoke as if his God whispered into his ear to then speak to two of His children. George told them of his past relentless efforts to be right with God and his surrender to a God who was the only one good enough to make him good enough. They confessed their sins and believed that their Savior Jesus died for their sins, and they committed their lives to Him.

Whitefield paused, smiled, and put his arms around them. "There is even more here. Seek God for repudiation or confirmation of what I am about to say, for I believe He says that there will be one who comes through you, and he will be a free man to free others. He will be known as an 'African wonder.'"

The two young ones smiled as they reflected the glint in their eyes to each other. There was a love between the two that George had never seen in two young adults. Actually, George had never seen love like that with anyone before. There was a union that foreshadowed a union to one day come. Born anew and one day to give birth anew.

The landowner yelled something from a distance. He had his hand on his hip while cursing. He pulled something out from behind him and stomped toward George. He again broke normal social graces with a pointed gun about one foot from George's head. The man spoke through gritted teeth. "You can't do that around here. You have slaves, and yet you are now trespassing and planting a bad and destructive seed into the slaves on my ground. You cannot teach the animals how to rule over their master's farm."

A screeching noise crossed the sky, and George raised his head to find the demonic birds of prey. He knew that no one else heard the birds crisscrossing above them.

George found great peace in ignoring the gun inches from his face and aimed his eyes into the man. The man blinked.

"If you kill me," George said, "I go to my Jesus. But your stiff knees and stiff neck will bend like never before, and you will tremble uncontrollably with your jaw unhinged before the Almighty's throne. Not even the sound of your last gasp will escape from His presence. My concern is not for the weak weapon in your hands that holds no power over me, but for your soul. When you are judged for your sins and the eyes of the Almighty slay you, where will *you* go?"

The man blinked with his mouth stuck open, as if an invisible hand drew an invisible line before George. He looked how a man would look like if he had been told he would drop dead if he took one more step.

George did not blink and remained with his eyes fixed upon the man. "This is your field. If you tell me to leave, I will leave. But you should think twice about attempting to take away what belongs to God."

The man jerked his gun toward himself and ran away from George.

George stood with his head downcast. Other pairs of feet belonging to slaves gathered around him, and George said, "Some will be crushed by the rock. Some will run to it."

George knew his God's presence dwelled within him at all times. But somehow he also knew that God desired to dwell in the slave and slave owner as well. George knew from his Father that the slave owner had repeatedly rejected God and His desires and would now be left to fulfill his own desire.

George knew the slave owner, horrified at what God was going to do with the young couple and other slaves, would flee to another one of his fields and injure one of his slaves. He would then enter into his own home and stand in front of his confused wife and kill himself.

George wiped his face. He prayed for the landowner, the slaves, and the man's family. His devastated wife. All the young and adult orphans with and without parents. A pain sliced into new tissue in his own heart. As if he experienced what the slave owner and his slaves felt at the same time.

So many slaves. Who am I that God should use me?

Someone in the small gathering prayed, "Our Lord God. Your Story tells us that you will use any man, woman, anytime, anywhere, any way, to do what you want to be done. Move in us and move now!"

Shaking his head after the prayer, George scanned the empty field and wondered why God had chosen George Whitefield to be here for such a time as this. He prayed for a great harvest in preparation to confront the hunter of humans roaming the land.

And preparation for what was coming to his country.

CHAPTER 27

CAESAR

State House, Pennsylvania Colony
1776

It had been a few months since Caesar first went to Dorothy's home. Since that time they'd shared wonderful dinners and walks. It had been a few weeks since the last time he'd seen her. The time on his pocket watch was known to not always be accurate, but it still recorded time. And it was time to confront his limited time left.

The treatments had all failed. There was no doctor or treatment in the colonies that could heal Caesar's facial cancer. Under the tyranny of death's rule and reign, the pain colonized part of his face and, in a mad power attempt, it tried to rule over all parts of his body and mind. Despite his best defenses and his best speeches to himself, cancer captured more and more of his face. There was no hope.

Was all that remained was to die a slow and painful death? Was the only option left to defeat the tyranny was to die and kill it with him? Even that was not a defeat but a draw and cancer would still continue to rule in other individuals.

He sensed colleagues staring at him in the state House. He did not want pity. Just a reprieve from the pain and the weight of death sitting on him day and night. Was there no one who could ease the weight and take the pain? His downcast face was even more downcast when some of his friends in the Continental Congress approached him.

The first colleague stood with his hands on Caesar's shoulders. "Fighting at Lexington and Concord. Bunker Hill. Moores Creek. Caesar, we truly appreciate you being here. We have been on the move from Carpenter's Hall and now here in the Pennsylvania State House. Philadelphia knows us well. Where will we hide next? There will be a day when there is no more running."

He paused and focused even more intently into Caesar's eyes. "We know you well. But you should not be here. Know that we accept you as you are." He motioned to those beside him in the grand room. "We speak to you again. We know of a doctor and treatments back across the Atlantic that can possibly heal you. You know about this treatment. You must confront this before it is too late. We have nothing to offer you here."

Caesar nodded and placed his hand on his colleague's arm. "I have heard of these treatments. They are perhaps my last hope."

Another brother and colleague placed a hand on Caesar's shoulder. "What are you doing here? You should have crossed the Atlantic months ago. We thank you for your loyalty. We do not take that for granted. But you should have listened to us. We think we can get you there in secret, or as secret as possible." He leaned closer to Caesar. "We know people that can take care of you when you arrive. We can create papers that state you are a loyalist to the king. You can have a new identity. They may not know any difference. You need to find that doctor and get that treatment. They have medicines, ointments that can help you. Be healed. Then come back home and continue to court Dorothy as a healthy man. A healthy and faithful husband for her."

Caesar shrugged his shoulders. "Are there things more important than my cancer?"

The colleague pointed to the door. "Our blood brothers and sisters fled oppression over one hundred fifty years ago and risked everything to come here. Go and sail from what freedom we have left here, and go and face your oppressor and get your healing right under the nose of the king looking down on us. Before it is too late. You must at least try, with our help."

Caesar pulled on his scarf and studied the shoes on the floor near him. There were no new shoes. Most were well worn and torn. But here with his brothers, he did not know all of them primarily by their shoes. He knew them face to face, and no one here looked away from him. "A few minutes ago, I received word that my people in Delaware summoned me to return home. As general of the rebel Delaware militia, those seeking liberty beckon. They call me to serve and stop the most recent uprising. I will think again on your thoughts."

Another colleague walked into the conversation. "We have things covered for you here. If the vote for independence *ever* comes up"—he shook his head and rolled his eyes—"there are still two delegates here for your Delaware that can decide the vote. Thomas and George can vote for Delaware for you. The last few minutes I heard, they may now be one minded on the issue of loyalty to the king. If they both vote the same way, your vote would not matter anyway."

Caesar looked to a window and shook his head. *Who can resist the king?* He closed his eyes and cleared his throat. "Do not remind me."

"Their two votes will outnumber your one vote, so Delaware is already decided. It may not be possible to have our desired unanimous vote from all the colonies to declare independence. Though you should have left long ago, listen to us as we tell you again— you should leave here before it is too late."

"I know you are right. Thank you for speaking a difficult truth. But first I must return home to continue our fight to cut out at least a small portion of the cancer of the king spreading on our land."

As he stepped outside, the left side of his face pounded again. It throbbed. Like wave after wave of the king's ships landing on shore, the cancer captured more of his life with each beat of Caesar's heart. Having worse pain now was not a good sign.

The pain is already worse even before I have started riding home. I will have to go slow so that I can survive the pounding. Can I trust that they will be able to quell the riot, for I will surely be late upon my arrival. Will there still be a militia to come home to?

Caesar made his way for perhaps his final return to Delaware. His home. His people. Dorothy. And the empty chair at his table.

Caesar pulled the scarf tighter for the long and bumpy ride.

CHAPTER 28

MARY

Near Plymouth, Massachusetts Bay Colony
1750

Mary heard that the redcoats she had encountered on the road had killed three people as they searched for someone they said was aiding and spying for the French. With both the French and the British vying for the same land and with her people in the middle of them, foreshadowing of a future war was not hard to imagine and only confirmed what she expected. Rumors spread that someone in the village tipped them off. Mary was thankful that more murders did not occur. It would have inflamed even more the tenuous relationships between the French, British, Indians, Praying Indians, loyalists, rebels, and even more.

Mary and Martha sat together resting from a busy day. With the violence of the previous day, Mary silently prayed to God that He would protect Agnes. War would one day come soon, and the lives of many were going to be a cost of freedom and treason. Though Agnes did not voice her fears, Mary knew it was a race against time for both their plan for the leaders and their plan with Agnes to work. But Mary sensed there was something else threatening both of their plans, and she needed to know what that was.

Mary remembered the dream she'd had the previous night. The same one that had visited almost every night for the last few months. She was in a dark place. Every now and then, a streak of light crossed the sky and then hit the ground. Flashes of light showed a rider on a white horse dropping things on the ground. Ear-piercing screeching searched in the sky. But it was the singular voice, a cry really, in the distance that made her take notice. When the voice cried out, the screeching noises seemed distracted from the rider and attempted to locate the source of the voice. They ignored all the voices of pain emanating from the ground and all around.

But Mary could not.

At times she searched through the night to see if she was stepping on uneven ground. Every once in a while, enough light streaked across the sky and there was a momentary glimpse of the hard ground.

But that voice.

The singular voice was separate and away from the other crying voices. It was dangerous. It was deemed a threat in the night.

Mary left the dream and returned back to Martha. The voice in the night from the dream echoed in her head. *There is a voice here I must heed. I need to stay here to help both my peoples and Martha.*

Martha squirmed in place, seated on the ground. Dusk joined them.

Mary described the dream to her. "I just don't know what it means. I believe it is from God." Mary eyed the squirmy Martha. "What is it? What is going on with you?"

Martha covered her mouth, as if attempting to keep her lips sealed over an explosion in her mouth. She wiggled more and rose to try and move in circles in what appeared to be an attempt at distracting herself.

Mary narrowed her eyes. "What is it?"

"I . . . I have to go to the bathroom . . ."

Mary pointed away. "Well, then go."

Martha took a step and then stopped. "Well . . . that is not entirely true . . . I have to tell you something first, as I am worried about you."

"Say what you need to say."

Martha closed her eyes and appeared to be summoning any last reserves of strength. She kept her eyes closed. "I found out something last night. I have my reliable and unreliable sources. The source that spoke to me last night is not always reliable, but yet the news kept me awake. The father of Agnes's baby is coming back. Some say he is violent. He is coming back for Agnes."

Mary stood and moved closer to Martha. "What? I know they had their issues. Is he coming back to kill her?"

"The situation is worse than we thought before.

Something is wrong with him. He may even want the child dead as well."

Mary grabbed her shoulders and shook her. "What?"

Martha paused and seemed to summon more strength. "The attacker said he would fly in the air like a bird of prey and steal life away when she was not looking."

Mary narrowed her eyes and then shook her head in her hands. "Well, that complicates things. We are getting close to our plans for the leaders and with Agnes, and now there is someone who wants to kill Agnes?"

Martha shifted her weight away and then back toward Mary. "Look, I know you want to be here. A bridge of peace between your two peoples. But you need to be with Agnes. You need to protect her even more, now that she is not only almost nine months pregnant but there is someone seeking vengeance upon her."

Mary could not answer, as she could only stare off toward the village.

"Mary, you have done what you needed to do here. The plan is in place. It is in the hands of God now, and being here now makes no difference, especially if Agnes's life is at stake."

Our plan is in motion. The leader of the colonists and the leader of the Indians will both be near here responding to the same message given to them in two days. Martha can facilitate the first part here, as I am with Agnes at her home for the second part. We need

Agnes even more than temporary peace here. We can do both at the same time.

Mary nodded in agreement. "You are right, Martha. Things are moving faster than we thought. I need to make sure Agnes is all right. All is lost if Agnes is killed or taken away. She is absolutely needed. Now go to the bathroom."

Martha jumped up and down, like she was running out of time. She sighed and raised her arms up in the air. She inhaled and exaggerated her next breath. "Thank you for seeing the light. You need to pack your belongings and go to Agnes now. He may be on his way, or he may already be there waiting for the right time."

What would I do without my friend Agnes? What would I do without my friend Martha? Everything would fall apart. The dream that You gave to me. God, what are You now telling me?

CHAPTER 29

KING GEORGE

Buckingham House, England
1775

The king was trying to catch his breath. He felt power while he punched and swiped at the air. A cathartic release moved through his body as he imagined tearing an enemy apart. But the dark markings on King George III continued to infiltrate his body. It included more of his face and did not seem content with a status quo. It wanted more and more of what was his. It would not submit to the divine right and might of the king.

I just need to cut it off.

Could the king wrap his iron fist around the handle of his sword calling him from the corner of the room?

The king shook his head and raised a fist. *They mutilated my soldiers. I will not let them mutilate me.*

He searched the empty room but knew he was not alone. He knew he was in there. In the next room. With the door that the king left open. Where the king kept his books, proclaiming his intellect and spirituality to all who entered. The king stepped into his castle's library. There he was. The back of his head more prominent than his own in the king's chair, with the chair pointed away from King George. George pointed his head down as he stood behind the one in the chair. The door slammed shut behind him.

George could not move away. His feet could not move. *The trap is sprung. Is he the murderer I have been hunting?*

With his feet stuck on the floor, George twisted his body, trying to reach for the closed door. He tried to turn the knob, but the door would not open. It was as if an invisible strong man leaned on it while the king waited for what was coming next.

Then the voice on the throne made itself known, though the face was still a mystery.

He knew the voice. It sounded like his own voice within his own head but with an additional overlord. It was like another mind using George's throat outside of George's body. It then changed to the sound of what he remembered was his father's voice before he died when George was a teenager.

"All of your ancestors. So much sinful pride. I need to kill the murderer who comes to defeat me. Fortunately, the most powerful of my tools left the door wide open. You invited me inside. It is strictly a legal issue. I entered with all legal authority. I own this house. I am enjoying my stay. I think I want to stay awhile." He laughed. "Can the former owner expel the legal squatter when the former owner gave all rights to the squatter?"

Sweat dripped down his back one drop at a time. George tried the door again. The knob did not even move. What was inside was staying inside. The man with the voice reclined back on the chair with his hands behind his head and with his feet on the nearest shelf, still facing away from George as he tilted his head toward some of George's Bibles. George almost jumped as the sensation of hands wrapped around his legs. Without even looking down, something moved farther up his lower legs. He did not allow any movement of his face or any sound from his lips to escape. His dead father still demanded silence.

George noticed that with the being, that man in the room, if George kept his eyes shut, the recurring nightmare dream dominated his thoughts. If he kept his eyes open, the ever-present being dominated the room from the being's mobile throne.

The being echoed a familiar and curious laugh. "Eventually you will close your eyes. Let me tell you what you will see."

George's eyelids were like someone trying to push the sun against setting. They fluttered with resistance but eventually complied and submitted. It was dark. The being stopped talking. But it was not quiet. The stranger's voice changed from being outside George's head to inside his head, speaking through George's own inner voice.

Your kind failed me before. I gave your people every chance to stop this from spreading from this side of the Atlantic. That ship that left here in 1620 and the detestable ship from Africa before that, only survived because His hand protected them from me. The Seed that became the Carpenter became His Seed of His people in the Mayflower and that ship of slaves. He protected the one in the throne room and the little one I could not break. Their poisonous Seed in the blood is now in the colonies that are rebelling against me. I want the murderer. He seeks to end you. You must kill him and any possible offspring before he kills you . . . or I will find someone else in power to occupy.

George involuntarily trembled and instinctively kept his eyes closed. Then a bright light flashed in the room through his darkened eyes. He opened his eyes against the resistance. He picked up something cold in his hand. His own hand now held a knife that he somehow knew was sitting next to him on one of his fine French crafted tables.

You must kill him.

His eyelids pushed downward again, and he could not force them back up. The dream again. Images passed before his eyes. How bright the flash was! The screeching shadows were visible only because it was even darker than the dark night. The shadows were on the hunt.

George knew his own life was tied to the life of that light. In his dream he tried covering his eyes but also tried to keep his eyes on it, for he could not let it escape from him.

Charlotte's life depended on George. All his children's lives depended on him as well. His entire kingdom rested on his shoulders.

I will destroy the murderer.

"Play the violin," the one seated in his chair whispered.

George's arms moved, and his legs unlocked to obey. He opened his eyes. He tilted his head toward the floor and watched his feet move to a song developing in his head and pushing to be born. He walked to the book, squeezed it with a death grip, and threw it on the floor. There it sat in the middle of the floor, like a hunted prey surrounded by the hunters.

He grabbed his violin. He walked around the book like a wolf circling and surrounding its defenseless prey. He played as he had never played before. The notes had a power as they flew into the air to come crashing down. The king cried, as his fingers had never moved that way before. He was created for that moment. The song gestating in his head released and birthed itself through sobs of joy and into the air. His hands perfectly submitted to their master.

The one in the chair laughed.

CHAPTER 30

MO

**Gowanus Heights, New York Colony
1776**

Was it time to fight yet?

Mo remembered his dream. The screeching shadows swooping through the sky. The flashes of light clawing through the dark and tearing the vast veiled fabric.

He remembered the larger bird carrying him. Then his hands and feet were bound down below on the hard ground. The sharp edge of a cowskin whip cut through the skin on his bare back. He cried out in pain. The whip cut again. He tried to raise his hands. There were holes in his wrists! There were stripes of torn flesh hanging on his back. These were not his stripes. This was not his back. This was not his body. He screamed in pain. Then the body flashed back to his own body in the dream.

The crying voices echoed from the sky. Voices cried upward toward the heavens and broke through the hard ground of multiple layers and from multiple generations of dried blood buried underground.

There was a great light before him. Who could answer the cries?

Mo put a stop to the remembering of his dream. He stood against the darkening sky as the large-city-sized fist of a storm cloud hovered and then circled around and back. The peak of the storm lasted about three hours. Mo wanted to fight, but how could he fight against a storm? Augustine begged Mo to get right with God before the storm swung back toward them.

The cloud circled again, like one large unified group of birds of prey ready to fight for corpses. Then someone or something answered their prayers. It stopped.

It was now the early dawn, and after a few hours, all signs of the storm attack were gone. It was a beautiful early morning with no noticeable clouds in the sky. The sky was in peace, as if nothing had happened.

Mo stood at a high ridge and lifted his hands. Thinking about what Augustine had said during the peak of the storm attack hours before, Mo did not want to "get right with God" but only wanted to take the neck of an enemy and twist it with his bare hands.

When would they fight? There was still war, and the enemy was ready to set foot for the full invasion. Rumblings among the men circulated that General Washington had divided his troops between New York City and Gowanus Heights on Long Island. Men were assembled at a higher ridge to defend the coming invasion.

Mo moved closer to leaders after a scout ran up with an updated report. It was estimated that over twenty thousand British troops, more than double the number of soldiers belonging to the Continental Army at Gowanus Heights, had already landed at Gravesend Bay in Long Island and were moving toward them. The scout also reported his concern that they could be flanked unopposed on their left through Jamaica Pass. Mo also knew his men had the water of the bay and British ships moving behind them to cut off the only escape if the Continental Army had to retreat from frontal and flank attacks.

Mo stood scanning over the ridge. *What do I have to lose? I know what is coming. I am ready to execute my plan.*

The voices from his dream cried for someone to do something. The voices needed someone to rise and act for those seeking justice. Who could possibly end the cries in the night?

If everyone else was too fearful to pay the cost, then Mo was ready to fight and be that hero. New embers kindled in his chest, and heated rage blew air to spread the building small flame in a famine-stricken heart land. A battle raged within, and soon he was going to expel it out of him to strike this blood-soiled land. Inside him, with clear skies above and vengeance in the air, the rolling thunder rumbled and lightning struck within as he breathed in the sweet air.

CHAPTER 31

MARY

**Near Plymouth, Massachusetts Bay Colony
1750**

Mary remembered the story that broke her parents' hearts. It broke hers too.

In 1631 the Reverend John Eliot left England to go to Boston. He learned the language of the local Massachusett Indians and preached Jesus amongst them. Leaders established Natick as the first Praying Indian village with the first Praying Indian church. Eliot was the apostle to the Indians. In 1663 they reached a great milestone, as they printed the first Bible in the Western Hemisphere, and it was in their native language.

In 1675 Chief Metacom, also known as King Philip, along with other tribes, led an uprising against the colonists. Many were killed and tortured on both sides. Many homes and towns were attacked and destroyed.

As Mary remembered the story, she stood motionless from a distance, looking at the home of Agnes's master. She did not try to hide herself. She stood lost in the stories from her parents.

Deer Island.

Out of fear the colonists removed the Praying Indians from their surrounding villages around Boston. They stood at the dock, holding on to their Bibles. No food. No extra clothing in the cold temperatures. Against Reverend Eliot's attempts to stop the authorities, colonists moved the Praying Indians because of their fears of them joining the rebellion. He tried to comfort them as the colonists took them to Deer Island in Boston Harbor.

The Praying Indians were trapped on Deer Island from 1675 to 1676. They were left unprotected in the miserable temperatures. Other Praying Indians from other villages were added to those imprisoned.

The reverend attempted to save their lives by taking supplies to his beloved, but colonists capsized his boat. King Philip was eventually killed. Through the Reverend Eliot's and others own financial sacrifices, Eliot eventually personally freed the Praying Indians from Deer Island.

Mary's parents told her that over five hundred women, children, and men were forced to relocate onto Deer Island, and only about a third survived. The few survivors returned home to the loss of their personal properties. Everything was taken away. Remnants of the Praying Indians located to Natick.

They stole our people. They stole our homes. Our fields. They tore apart and stole our families. They took everything away.

Mary stood with the voices of her parents in her head.

"We must raise Mary with the truth. They spilled our blood. They stole what we once had. They almost killed all of us. We must take back what is ours."

"No, we must raise her with the truth of the for- giveness and grace of the sovereign God. We all have blood on our hands."

It was now evening, and Mary stood with her feet sticking in the mud of yesterday's rain. She took a step forward and then back. Her repeating dream supplanted her parents' fading voices and made itself known. She remained standing still.

In her dream she stood exposed, looking up at the screeching darker shadows moving in the sky. The shadows looked for someone. The voices beneath her feet alternated between moans and screams. Then the singular voice again.

How can I hear one whispering voice above the screaming at my feet and in the skies?

In the dream she walked closer to the whisper. The dark shadows, as if now alerted, adjusted their move- ments in the sky to Mary's movement. She stopped, and the dark shadows then moved in a different direc- tion. She took several steps closer to the whisper, and the shadows readjusted their movements back in her direction. Then the whisper paused.

The dark shadows, as if confused, moved farther away. When Mary then restarted her walking toward where the whispering occurred, the dark shadows did not follow her. Mary was concerned that she would accidentally trip over whoever had whispered, for it was difficult to see.

The whisper cut through the night. "To the Great Spirit." It was the first time she heard actual words instead of unclear moaning. Then a flash in the sky moved, as if a star fell from the sky, to where the voice was. With the momentary flash, like lightning across the sky, she saw an outline of a broken cross. The dark shadows were alerted. They readjusted their movement toward her.

In another quick flash, she saw a cross readjusted and propped up by a woman praying on her knees. The location was on an island. Somehow she knew it was Deer Island! The woman's broken prayer cut through the night and her sobbing.

"O God, Your will be done, in Your way, in Your time. Flow through the broken who choose You and through those who reject You. Resist Satan, who hunts us, and have Your way on this land."

Then Mary left the dream. She bent her head down toward her feet in the mud. She pivoted her head back and forth between Agnes and both her peoples. She scanned the surrounding area for any sign of the coming murderer. Or perhaps he had already killed Agnes? She moved toward Agnes's master's house.

CHAPTER 32

CAESAR

**From Philadelphia to Dover, Delaware Colony
1776**

Even with the slower ride, he tried holding his head while attempting to control the reins. Sometimes the pain and blurriness slowed things further. When he paused, his face still vibrated. Though painful to the touch, Caesar debated whether holding the left side of his face on his ride back to Delaware from Pennsylvania was better or if it made things worse.

The first time he moaned, he turned his head, thinking someone else was with him. But it was just him and his horse. This was going to take longer than his previous rides, with not being able to fully exercise his riding skills at maximum speed. It gave him extra time to think.

He practiced imagining the chair in front of him occupied back home.

He whispered to take his mind off the long ride. "Good morning, my lovely Dorothy. I want to remind you that marrying you has been as important for my freedom as any work I have done."

He cleared his throat and continued. "I am used to working toward goals. Goals to bring freedom for all of us. But if I ever forget my love for you, will you stomp on my foot until I awake?"

One day they would be married. He imagined her laughing and blushing like before. He smiled, thinking of her expressions and inability to hide her embarrassment. Dorothy said she loved the most handsome man she knew. Caesar paused the pain with a smile.

His thoughts returned back to the Continental Congress meeting he had left a few hours before. How could there ever be any unanimous agreement on voting for independence, as some of the foolish desired? How could representatives from thirteen different factions ever unanimously agree on any-thing? If they could not all agree on what to eat, how could they possibly agree on whether to commit treason against their king and know that they would be tortured and then killed? And their families with them? He evaluated all the arguments for and against independence from their homeland.

Years before, they were given the freedom to leave and start a new home in the name of the king. They'd prospered more than anyone could have imagined. They likely had one of the highest, if not the high-est, standard of living in the world. Why would the wealthy now throw everything away in a prevent-able war when they had everything they wanted? Did they want more prosperity? What more could they have? Would they look like spoiled rich children rebelling against the very parents who enabled them to be wealthy?

And yet independence was not about being wealthier. It was about being free from the hounding and oppressive iron fist of the king. Was it right for him to oppressively tax those who had no representation in Parliament? Taxation without representation? Was it right that the king attempted to make them worship through the religion of the king above the God of the holy Scriptures?

Caesar shook his head and grunted. They were equal to those back in the homeland and were not to be treated like domesticated lap cats forced to cough up fur balls of their most innermost dreams and money to fund the military adventures of their fat-cat king. They were children of God above being the king's petulant, rebellious children.

At least he was free to ride home without the scarf covering his facial cancer. There was no one he would scare. Could love for Dorothy give him the strength to travel back to Britain to claim his healing from cancer? Free from cancer. Free to court Dorothy after his healing.

Caesar knew his fellow constituents were right. He needed to see the doctor as soon as possible. The hourglass was emptying every moment. It was the greatest of inconveniences that the only doctor who could save him was in the land of the king inflicting more pain on his people than the cancer on Caesar's face ever could. Even if he were to leave for England that night, in the best scenario, with just the travel time alone, it would be weeks before he could even start treatments.

Though he had avoided any mirrors or reflective surfaces for months, Caesar could feel it spreading on his face. It had started as a small spot and had grown to covering most of the left side of his face.

The heart of the lonely night was approaching, but the stories of attacks on riders the last few months accompanied him. He picked up speed. He was not alone. For a moment, his heart raced as he thought of an evening attack. As he reached for the left side of his face, he heard something in the bushes to his right. He overcorrected and lost his balance. It was too late to grab the reins. Caesar fell off onto his left side and hit his left cheek on a rock. He yelled in pain and yelled again as he reflexively grabbed the left side of his face. He cursed as he rolled onto his back.

My horse!

Caesar tried to look up the road but could not turn his head. He would not make it back home in a timely manner if his horse ran off.

How can I return to vote if I am needed?

The horse ran several feet and then stopped. She almost seemed to pause to think, as her mane remained unmoved, pointing straight ahead. Caesar blinked his eyes. *What is she doing?* The horse grunted and pointed ahead, then raised and lifted a front leg up and down, as if marching in place with one leg. With off and on blurred vision, Caesar wiped his face. The blurriness returned soon after. He wiped his face again.

The horse stood still several feet away. She could freely choose to run and live her independence away from the tyrant who'd fallen off her back. Or was she a loyalist and would remain with the familiar one, who was a heavy burden on her back? She turned her head toward Caesar, and even at night her deep-brown eyes seemed to want to say something. She tilted her nose toward the hard ground and then lifted her head upward.

Caesar laughed and turned his whole body to look up the road. The horse stood there. Looking at him. Waiting for him. As if someone had the horse by her reins.

If the mare was speaking, she was saying, "Get up, ugly."

Caesar smiled. He checked his arms and legs. Everything still seemed to be intact. No obvious broken limbs. He looked down at his hands. Blood. He wiped his hand on his face. Pain. Blood.

Caesar staggered to a bent position. With shaking arms, he pushed off his knees and straightened. He looked back to where he'd heard the noise in the bushes. All was clear. Except his sometimes blurry vision.

He wiped his eyes and walked to his waiting rude horse. He wrapped an arm around her head and spoke into her left ear. "I want you to know I will return back to the state House when I finish quieting the riot back home. I will tell my friends I need to leave. Back to my homeland. And over there I will then get a *real* horse." Caesar laughed at her grunt and stroked her mane.

He pulled himself up on her back and paused. He turned his head up the road and then behind him down the road.

Will I finish what I need to do before I run out of time?

CHAPTER 33

GEORGE WHITEFIELD

Somewhere in New England
1748

George Whitefield's heart raced like the horse he was riding. A fear of death grew as the shrieking and growling in the shadows became louder. A darker shadow within the shadow floated toward him. Something was moving closer this time. The presence was nearing. His nostrils burned, and he gagged as it gained on him. He dared not look behind him, as he knew he would lose a step or two.

It was gaining on him. The presence was almost upon him. The hairs on the back of George's spine raised in anticipation as it reached toward him. It would grab him in seconds.

George could not resist and tuned his head back. A large open hand moved with him as it separated the distance between him on his racing horse and the Dark Light following. The Dark Light shot out toward George and wounded the hand as it attempted to reach him. George tried to cover his ears as the screeching increased.

Whose hand is that? Where did it come from?
George awoke gasping for air.

He had ridden most of the previous day. He'd preached to thousands of people who'd taken time off work to listen to him—free men and women, slaves, the poor and rich—and collapsed onto the bed provided by a servant of God somewhere in New England. He was thankful for all the people providing food to eat and places to sleep. People in the colonies, for the most part, were gracious for the preacher on horseback, as he had already traveled thousands of miles over the last several years.

There was no more sleep coming. He thought of his wife, Elizabeth, his bride of seven years, not traveling with him. He thought of his only child. Elizabeth and George had wanted to make sure their son could somehow know he was loved and not alone as they'd held him weeks after he was born, while he'd died in their arms.

George scrambled out of bed and went to the dining area. All members of the household were still asleep. He sat and prayed and thanked God for the previous day and gave thanks ahead of time in great anticipation of the present day. There were reports that tens of thousands of people expected to hear him speak of the God who'd freed him. The same God who wanted to free all who would declare that God was God. He wanted all to know the good Father.

Though he rested at the table, he was still not free from his heart racing. He tried to calm down by praying for his Bethesda Orphan House in Georgia. He needed more people to donate wherever he preached, to save all the children without parents. Someone had to be the living demonstration of the Father acting as their father.

Will I live long enough to save the children?

His torn nightshirt moved in rhythm to an unseen war beat. With his cross eyes and trembling hands, he tried to harmonize the light from the candle next to him and the shadow that his body made onto his letter. The same letter he had been composing the previous weeks when he was able to rest and write.

Someone was chasing him. Or something. His life required God protecting him. But who was hunting him down?

Something moved by a door behind him. He turned, but nothing out of the ordinary was there. He consoled himself into believing that once again it was just his active dramatic imagination. Like actors with the theater in their blood acting in real life.

Something slithered behind him. It seemed to slide on the floor and then paused when he turned his head. It slid again, and he rose and walked to the area. A sound of shock escaped his lips, and George jumped back—someone crouched behind an oak table away from the glowing candle.

The young man took in rapid deep breaths, as if he had been running. He stared at George like he did not know what he or George would do next.

"Young man," George said, "I have never seen you before. Who are you? Why are you hiding?"

The young man closed his eyes, clearly attempting to summon all energy for what would come next. He then whispered, "I . . . nee . . . need . . . help . . . You help meee . . . me?"

"I cannot help you escape, if that is what you have done." George turned his head toward the back door just a few feet away and then toward the front door on the other side of the living room entrance.

The young man stood. *Something is in this young man and needs to come out.* He did not turn his head in any other direction than the direction of George's eyes. His tongue was freed but for a moment. "But God has given you authority and ability to free us."

The young man's eyes widened, and he turned his head back and forth, as if someone else in the room spoke those words. He took a deep breath. "You know sl . . . slavery . . . you . . . willll . . . free many more . . . why not . . . not . . . why not . . . me. . . me?"

New noises stirred outside the front door. George jumped to the door, stopped and paused, and then opened it, and through the beginning dawn, a man walked toward the door with a gun.

He found me. Is he the one hunting me? Not now, O Lord God. I still need to speak for my orphans.

Summoning the God of the universe and peace, George kept the door open while remaining in the doorway, with his heart now racing and wanting to run. "Is there something I can help you with?"

"Hey, I recognize you. You are that George Whitefield they described in all the newspapers I have read and been hearing about."

George was not sure if he felt more at ease or at unease. "Yes I am."

The man continued walking toward him. "Preacher man, I am sorry to bother you, but I am looking for Richard, the owner of this house."

"Richard and his family invited me to stay for the night," George whispered. "He is still asleep. What brings you here at this early hour?"

The man stopped a few feet from George. His eyes narrowed as he first scanned the area and then focused on George. "I am looking for an escaped slave. Have you seen a negro?"

George pointed toward the inside of the house. "Do you want me to awaken Richard?"

The man frowned. "No. I don't need him to find the slave. But you did not answer my question. Have you seen the negro?"

Whitefield scanned the area behind the hunter. "I will keep my eyes open. There is one location where, if I was going to hide, I would hide there. Do you want me to take you there?"

The man looked at George with his head tilted. "Show me now."

George started to walk and then stopped, walked back to the door that was still open, and looked inside before he closed it. "If this slave is still running around, I do not want him coming inside."

Whitefield closed the door and walked the man toward the barn. With the gun.

Is this the end, Lord? I will go where You tell me.

The man then lifted the gun and pointed it toward George. Off to the side, George saw three slaves tied together. George stopped walking. "Is there something wrong?"

With the gun still pointed at George, the man pointed with his left hand toward the men tied up. "I already found these three. Now just looking for the youngest brother."

There was something else there with them. A presence. Not God's presence. The hairs on his spine rose. The presence reminded him of when he'd preached in his last two revivals. It seemed to travel through the air and sometimes slithered on the ground. It moved and gathered in strength and concentrated inside the man holding the gun. Like someone throwing dirt and preparing the coming feeding of an awaiting grave.

The man narrowed his eyes as he pointed to George. His eyes narrowed even farther. "You are preaching to the slaves. You should not do that. Are you preaching against the king as well?"

George's eyes crossed even farther. "I preach to all of God's children. Perhaps you should come later—"

"—but you are planting ideas that will eventually overthrow our way of life if you are not stopped." The man lifted the gun up to underneath George's chin. "You don't want to do that, do you?"

Before George could answer, the man slithered his next words. "I know you have slaves at your orphanage in an attempt to save money caring for those orphans of yours. You know as well as I do how important it is to keep the animals on leash. Don't you?"

George smiled. "I do wonder if I am double minded on this issue. But I am more single minded on my Jesus. If you kill me, I will worship Jesus. If you don't kill me, I will worship Jesus. You are no threat to me."

The man pushed the gun against George's chin and then stomped off toward the tied-up brothers and then hit one of them with the heel of his gun. The man laughed as he saw pieces of teeth missing in the slave's mouth. George reflexively raised his fist but quickly retracted it.

Do I end my life for them? Do I save my own to save others later? Tell me, God.

George stood without moving. The man spoke in a different voice than before. It had a deeper tone, and the voice slithered like a speaking snake. "We will hunt the murderer down, and we will find him. Something blocks me from seeing if you are that murderer. A two-faced old preacher with limited time is no threat to me. You are like one of these captured slaves always trying to escape, and in a short time you will bend your knees. You speak out of both sides of your mouth, and your double-mindedness will slowly over take you. Sleep with one eye open."

"I sleep with both eyes closed," George said as he remembered the nightmares from when his eyes were closed. With the gun still pointed at him, George stepped away and marched back to the house, wincing in anticipation of the creation of a hot hole in his back. He reached the door, turned back toward the smiling man with his captured. He turned away from the man and toward the door. While keeping his back toward the man, George wiped his brow and his hands, reached for the doorknob, and stopped.

George prayed for the young man. He knew he was gone. On the run. In his mind, cries of babies echoed from a faraway place into his thoughts. He thought of the Old Testament and Moses's mother giving birth to Moses. He thought of the New Testament and Mary giving birth to Jesus.

Now was the time to finish the letter.

I do not know how much time I have left.

The hunter of humans still hunts today and is getting closer.

Chapter 34

GEORGE WHITEFIELD

Somewhere in New England
1748

Other than a small amount of writing, George did not move much from the chair in the last hour. He stared at the partially finished letter. His heart still raced from the gun pushing on his chin. The lone candle beside him flickering and revealing upon the letter he held.

He was a slave owner. He thought differently than most other slave masters. Slaves were God's offspring, and he loved them. He loved the slave masters too, as they also were God's offspring. He loved his country. He loved his orphans. He loved the children in the future.

It was time to finish his letter. Not another letter to his Elizabeth. Not another letter to share with his adopted children at the orphanage. But a letter to a people not yet born.

> Dear Children of the Blessing,
> I send greetings and pray you will receive the love of God upon you. Obedience to the Father

bestows incredible blessings and rejection of His love reminds us of His incredible grace. How patient is our Father!

When I rode to this location yesterday, I could feel someone following me. I stopped and hid with my horse behind some large trees. But no one came on the empty road behind me. Even while hiding behind the trees, I looked behind me. But I was alone.

I was tired but I did not want to rest my eyes. For the nightmare would then find me again.

My Lord God, why have You put that voice in that dream? I know You have planted it in my head and it makes itself known when I am asleep. I can hear it now. I am surrounded by dark skies. There are occasional flashes of light in the sky. Things fly in the air, like birds seeking their prey. They are looking for something. And then I stop and I hear it. Voices cry out, but I hear one voice above the other voices. A single voice. It is a cry. The shadows darker than the darkness move toward the voice, and there is nothing to hide it or protect it.

I desire to stop the flying shadows, but I cannot because something is chasing me. I cannot fully commit to the protection of the voice, as I am hounded as well. I run for my life. Where are You, God?

Shortly after I awoke this early morning, a man walked toward me with a gun. What chased me in my dream indwelled in the man and found me. God was my only defense. In my dream today, a hand intervened between me and what was hunting me. In my wakefulness, I could only trust that the hand of my Father was with me. Oh how we need to be saved from what is hunting us!

In sleep and when I am awake, God gives me the trumpet of war to proclaim war against the searching and screeching demons of Satan. Who is truly king? I do not know when the wars are coming, but this I must ask: Is the king our God, or is God our king? Is government our God, or is God our government?

Children of the blessing, if you succumb to the former, how much pain must occur before you conclude the later?

If you live the former, then Satan will deceive and distract us to fight our brothers and sisters. But the king is not God. Government is not God. If we fail, then the king of today, and the kings of future tomorrows, will release their wrath upon who he sees as his rebellious children.

I think of the Israelites. I hold on to their story. God, are You not the Author of their story and ours? I can hear Moses now!

When you have eaten and are satisfied, you shall bless the Lord your God for the good land He has given you. Beware that you do not

forget the Lord your God by not keeping His commandments and His ordinances and His statutes which I am commanding you today; otherwise, when you have eaten and are satisfied, and have built good houses and lived in them, and when your herds and your flocks multiply, and your silver and gold multiply, and all that you have multiplies, then your heart will become proud and you will forget the Lord your God who brought you out from the land of Egypt, out of the house of slavery.
−Deuteronomy 8:10–14

See, I have set before you today life and prosperity, and death and adversity; in that I command you today to love the Lord your God, to walk in His ways and to keep His commandments and His statutes and His judgments, that you may live and multiply, and that the Lord your God may bless you in the land where you are entering to possess it.
But if your heart turns away and you will not obey, but are drawn away and worship other gods and serve them, I declare to you today that you shall surely perish. You will not prolong your days in the land where you are crossing the Jordan to enter and possess it.
I call heaven and earth to witnesses against you today, that I have set before you life and death, the blessing and the curse. So choose life in

order that you may live, you and your descendants, by loving the Lord your God, by obeying His voice, and by holding fast to Him . . .
—Deuteronomy 30:15–20

Though I know that both these sets of verses were written by God moving through Moses for the Israelites, I must say there is a similar pattern that we can study back then that is for us today and for future tomorrows.

People of the blessing in the distant future from my time, remember these verses as the colonies you once studied believed in the God of these words. Or perhaps that knowledge is censored in your contemporary textbooks?

I proclaim that many in your day must be saved from their sins to then save their country. War is coming. These words tell us the only way we can win the coming war. If we love our Father, then we will obey Him. We can be saved from our sins and the total loss of war that is coming. We must choose our Father above all others who attempt to steal us away in deceit.

I speak to you now from years past to you in your present. I am to remind, or perhaps enlighten for the first time, you as a people not yet born. I am a voice of the present, speaking to the future children of the blessing, and speaking from your past for your future.

I am speaking to you, the children of the blessing. It is not I but God speaking through a flawed vessel imparting the will and heart of the perfect Father who is not bound by our limits of time.

Children of the blessing, remember these verses. Do not forget the Father who created you, birthed you, the One who has prospered you, protected you. Do not forget His love, for another awaits your destruction if you separate yourself from your Creator, like a wild animal waiting for you to separate from your help.

Children of the blessing, remember the warning pattern of Scripture for those who separate themselves from their Father and wander. From Adam and Eve onward, to each individual, to every country since. I am chief among sinners. Learn from my failures. Current and past.

I plead with you, remember your Father regarding all these things.

Or you will raise up powerless gods to replace God in vain and in violence.

There are wars coming between brothers and sisters on our homeland. Children of the blessing, how you have prospered from the blood of the flawed in the past that will flow for your present freedom. Men and women will give their lives for you to give yours, not for you to forget the source of everything given to you.

Do not forget the source of the blessings! And when you wander too far, know the Father's *voice that is calling you back to Him. Heed that voice. All other voices of division pulling you away from your Father cannot save you and aim to destroy you. When you are deceived against one another, remember that if God is our Father, then you are my brother. You are my sister.*

Be saved at the feet of your Lord Jesus Christ! Bow down your proud head. Bend your proud stiff knees. Recline in His rest. You are nothing without your Lord God. Will you forget, deny, and resent all the blood spilled for you?

Lord God, take my imperfections and make me perfect enough to fulfill your desires. Use me. Send me.

Your servant,
George Whitefield

A distant gunshot outside seemed to pierce through George. He placed his hand on his racing heart. *My children at the orphanage.* His children. He stopped his writing and leaned forward in his chair. He then reentered into prayer.

Protect me long enough to pass on what You have placed in me.

Though the day began with a beautiful sunrise, would the sun one day set on his future beautiful new country?

CHAPTER 35

KING GEORGE

Buckingham House, England
1775

With new energy fueling his plan against the murderer chasing him, King George III was drying off after stepping out of his bath, when Queen Charlotte spoke to him from the adjoining bedroom. George stared down at his legs and noticed the dark markings were above his knees for the first time. *Will the markings stop after I kill the murderer?*

"I am having nightmares about what is happening in the colonies," Charlotte said.

George refused to look in the mirror, but he rubbed his face and knew the markings had moved from his chin and mouth and were slowly moving up toward his forehead. Charlotte was in the distant background.

"What would happen if they successfully rebelled against their king?" she continued. "Their homeland? They have everything they could want, and they, like little spoiled children who have spent their inheritance, now they want even more?"

George walked to the mirror but stood outside of its view. *You will not control me.*

As he stepped closer to the mirror, Charlotte, still in the other room, said, "What would your grandfather do?"

What would Grandfather do?

George covered his mouth and bent over in pain, out of view from the mirror and Charlotte. He held his chest as he struggled to breathe. If he looked in the mirror, would he see something stabbing his chest?

"Are you there?" Charlotte asked. "Are you listening to me?"

George tried to reclaim control and respond to Charlotte but only lost more of his remaining breath. He closed his eyes and tried to stand tall and inhale, as that usually regained his regality.

Charlotte's footsteps approached, so he overcame wanting to bend forward and winced while standing with his chest out, attempting to push out what penetrated it. He reached for some water, but he spilled it when it failed to enter through an unyielding mouth.

Charlotte appeared at the doorway. "Are you all right?"

George tried again and swallowed what water was able to enter and then coughed. Charlotte waited with a look of concern.

"I am sorry. I am fine, as I was trying to drink some water and swallowed wrong."

Charlotte walked away, clearly satisfied with his answer. George wiped his mouth and stared at the space beside himself.

I know you are here. What do you want?

Then the one with the eyes inside his eyes spoke through his thoughts. George trembled.

Through all my generations of willing vessels, I have now prepared you to save your people.

Different images appeared in his thoughts. He remembered, when he was young, his grandfather ruling as a good king should. King George II. He was likely to be the last British king to ever fight on the battlefield—he'd fought the French. The grandson had seen his grandfather's enemies try to take the life out of his grandfather. He'd been crucified multiple times by his enemies. Those seeking his power. His wealth.

His grandfather had been seduced into having multiple mistresses by the enemies of him and his bride. King George II and his wife, Caroline, had both fought smallpox as he'd stood defiantly by his wife's side while she almost died. Something surrounded and tormented him to the end. The Motherland's savior died in 1760.

They killed him. Even back then the murderer killed him.

George remembered his grandfather's last words for him.

"Do not fail your family and the crown of the empire."

Then he heard the voice of the other eyes within him.

He is coming after you.

King George III yelled to send the message to all rooms. "I will have glory for the crown."

Charlotte came running back toward George. "My love, your grandfather would be proud of you. You are a good king. You deal with the rebellious children as any good parent would. You deal with severity when frank rebellion is breaking out. Children should not rule over parents. Sheep should not rule over the shepherd. Prisoners do not rule over the magistrates. The slave does not rule over his master. Satan does not rule over the God of the universe."

She gathered George in a trembling hug. "We are living in the blessings of God. We are the children of His blessing. He desires us to steward and maintain this way of life He has given us for the world. You are preserving the kingdom of God."

"I have sent my three best generals to subdue the colonies. Howe. Clinton. Burgoyne. I have the Hessians. Some of the most feared fighting forces of all. The wrath of God goes with all of them. Many ropes will not be slack. Many will be quartered. I will execute the wrath of God to save His kingdom."

Charlotte had a smile on her face, but George could see a slight hint of concern in her eyes.

Dark Light, I know what you are doing to me. If I do nothing, you will kill me. But what if I obey you, what then will happen to us? Do you already have another appointed if I fail?

Then George heard the one with the eyes speak inside of him. He walked and hugged his violin.

You will surround the murderer like a rope surrounds a neck.

George smiled as he played his violin.

Chapter 36

MO

**Gowanus Heights, New York Colony
1776**

All those people are losing family just like I have.

Mo stood with some of the men of the Continental Army at a high ridge, looking at the dying city. Streaks crossed above like a bear's claw shredding through a victim's clothing. Another British ship fired violence, and then some screaming momentarily stopped where its message landed in New York City.

British sails appeared everywhere, like ants inside a decaying corpse. They told Mo there were about four hundred ships carrying a number of soldiers, greater than the population of the city itself. Mo heard whispered rumblings from leaders that the entire Continental Army had perhaps fifteen thousand soldiers. And only about half were truly ready for war, considering training, equipment, and the number of deserters who'd left because of lack of pay and returned back to their crops for their coming harvest.

Before them was the greatest assembly of naval ships the world had ever known. Just an iron-fist handful of those ships had more total guns to destroy than the number of guns the Continental Army had on land to defend the region. The colonies did not have a navy.

Days before, they'd read the Declaration of Independence aloud in various locations for the first time, and celebrations had ensued. They declared they were now their own nation. Mifflin said no one, in the growing list of lands conquered by the king, was fighting back against the king like they were.

But for now, the only fighting from the soldiers were their curses fired from their moving lips directed toward the greatest fighting force in the world, and their curses landed harmlessly at their own feet.

The new nation, a new baby born different from any other in history, was now pulled in different directions. Rebels. Loyalists. The king. Liberty. Fear. Fight. Run. Surrender. And now the most powerful beast released on earth began a strategy they all feared.

As fire and brimstone rained down from British ships, all knew that if the British took New York City, they would divide the colonies and then the newly born country would be pulled apart, dismembered, and fall. A new nation drawn and quartered as a living example for any other would-be rebels. Long Island was the key to defending New York, which was the key to defending the colonies—and that was where General George Washington was to make a stand.

The rebels' early success against the world's most powerful empire and army in the battles of Lexington and Concord had shocked the world. The battle at

Bunker Hill almost seemed to be another victory for the rebels because the rebels had inflicted upon the British such a heavy and bloody toll. It was now made known to the king that this was not going to be an easy war against an inferior army lacking enough soldiers, skills, and courage in fighting—as one sided as it was supposed to be.

Now the soldiers stood watching the wrath of the king sending messages from hell itself onto earth and upon their city. Mo clenched his jaw shut as he shook his head at the soldiers around him watching what was happening to their city.

I know what they are thinking. "Was that my wife's cry? Was that my child's cry? Are they okay?"

Mo was relieved he did not have to worry about any loved ones. Mo only had two friends in the Continental Army—Augustine and Henry. Elias had summoned Henry to fight with Mo for independence, so Mo had a bit of home with him.

Initially, Mo was not interested in fighting for the rebels, but Henry and Elias worked out a deal where Henry would go with and protect Mo. Somebody had to be there if anyone found out Mo was more African than desired. But as time passed in the Continental Army, Mo liked the idea of vengeance upon those who enslaved more than the ones he fought for, and he was convinced that any future liberty for all was more likely with the rebels than the king and his men.

His other friend, Augustine, was the son of a wealthy man in Pennsylvania without slaves. Mo refused to be friends with a man even associated with having slaves. Augustine was at first unsure of whether there was a God but started a radical shift toward believing in God, with the storm upon New York City. He did not hesitate to admit he was afraid to die.

As all three stared toward the explosions creating screams in the city, Augustine asked, "Mo, do you think some of that will be coming our way?"

Mo looked at Henry, next to him. "Is today a good day to die?"

Henry nodded.

"That is not funny," Augustine said. "I have not found my future woman. I know there is somebody out there that wants a handsome man like me." He smiled, with most of his teeth missing but illuminated what beauty a man could illuminate. He bowed his head. "I do not know how I will react with musket balls and cannon balls flying above and beside me like that. And did I tell you that I like having two arms and two legs?"

Mo shook his head and shrugged. "I will not see me and my people be free in my lifetime, so if I die today or tomorrow, so be it."

Henry nodded. "My mother's last words to me were 'Do what needs to be done.' Maybe you are right now doing what needs to be done. Subvert the king. Maybe this is not about you being alive to see your heart's desire. Maybe this is about fighting for others' children's children, enabling them to walk in the fruit of what *you* are supposed to fight for and accomplish. Maybe *you* won't make it, but this is about clearing a path to the promised land for the children coming after you."

"Is that what your Bible tells you?" Mo pointed his glare at Henry.

"As death approaches," Augustine said, "I have tried to read the entire Bible in the last six months. I did not know what many of the words were. I never read it before. Guys here have been teaching me. Have you ever read it?"

Mo looked away. "I never learned how to read. My master did not allow that."

"I have offered to teach you," Henry said. "But it is as if you do not want to read. Your friend Christopher sounds like he was a brilliant mind. You told me he was very smart."

"Well, no wonder you were not free," Augustine said. "At least that is what I am learning. There is a reason why your master did not want you reading God's Word. You start reading those words and start living His way, you will start to smell that tasty liberty, and the master's scraps fed to his humans on leash would never be good enough for you anymore. You would be a glutton for more. Gimmie more of that tasty liberty. I would die for some more of that. Fill this empty belly with an endless serving of liberty! That is what you would say. And you know what—you would then know how to go get that God freedom. Masters don't want you to know that. They don't want you reading that God book."

Mo reached into his pocket and pulled out some papers. "A few different times I made these copies of some original papers through all these years. My older friend Christopher was my master's house slave, and he died with these words in his pocket. I cannot read these papers. I did not want to read this. I rewrote the words as best as I could. Seven times over the years when I knew the words were fading. I learned and memorized what some of the letters to the words looked like, though I do not know what they are."

Augustine narrowed his eyes. "And you never tried to find out what they say?"

"I was scared . . . to find out. I know it is important."

Mo tilted his head to the ground and offered the papers to Augustine. Augustine took the papers as a messenger would take an important letter to deliver to a loved one.

Mo looked into Augustine's eyes. "Is it possible for a slave to be a learned man? That was Christopher. He was older than us, and he kept many secrets of how educated he was. I think the master's young son taught him well and helped him write. Christopher was smarter than the master, if you ask me . . . and I think I am now ready."

Augustine took the papers with his eyes still on Mo. Mo moved a few feet toward the city, scanning the horizon, and stood between the dying city and Augustine holding a letter from death behind him. Hell fell on earth in the city in front of him, and a fear of a wrathful God rose with what lurked behind. But Mo was ready.

Augustine, in the lights of the night, read aloud as Mo watched a city dying.

Dearest Moses,

I speak to you from the dead. I guess I did not live to tell you that our God is on the move. Though slavers bought and sold me while I still possessed dreams that I could never own, God is still alive, and He is a slave to no one.

How did I still possess hope even as they murdered me? One day I tasted freedom while in my chains. I stood before the only true King, examining me more than any potential slaver ever has or ever could.

He said to me, "I want you." My Jesus called me forward. He paid the price for my freedom from the original and first slave master. I am His and He is mine. My sins are no more. My chains are gone.

For the first time, someone I wanted to claim me, claimed me. He bought me. Though they murdered me before I got home, my Father God took me from the plantation and brought me home. I died and I live with God. They took me away from my family, but I live with my Father and His children, my family in my Father's house. My Father loves me. He claimed me as His own son, and I am glad.

Mo, there are many rooms here at our Father's house. You mother is home, now healed from the piercings through her body and glowing in her Father's presence. They stole your mother's distant relatives on ships from Luanda. You had a distant relative, the small one, with many broken bones, broken heart, and broken dreams, and yet they could not break her. She gave birth and birthed a Seed of hope upon these shores. Where the slavers wanted total control, they ended up spreading the Seed of that which they cannot control. I now see your mother with no chains. And I see her loved as she should have been loved.

You will die one day. Who will claim ownership over you when your sense of control dies with you? Who is it that you will die serving? In which kingdom will you reside when you die?

You are a threat, and Satan is hunting you. He is hounding you to do his will as he searches and attacks by land, air, and sea. It is as if his birds of prey rain down upon us from the sky, pecking at all our wounds until they fester with an infection that desires to consume our body and mind. They seek you at night, and if they do not find you, the weeds growing within will try to choke off the resistance taking root within you. I pray that the Lord God protects you and reveals to you who you are in Him. Redeemed ex-slave bought with a great price!

I learned these things when the son of the slave master, hidden in the slave master's home, read Bible stories for me. These words I give to you are for you at this appointed time. There is a reason why I spoke these words and the master's son wrote them for me to then give to you.

Imagine that! From the past to your present, through me, and through your slave master's offspring, He wrote these words to free you in the future!

The Author visits in my sleep. Each time it is the same. I am as if standing in a different world than our own. There is no sun in the sky. It is night every day. All day. Sometimes I see a rider who drops things unto the ground when he can elude the screeching birds of the night. They chase him, but the rider continues.

There is no life in the rocky and dead weed-infested hard ground. There is no great light to allow the ground to spring forth life worth living. There are many who try to take away what the rider drops. There is a small number of rebels who attempt to protect what the rider drops.

Then I see you. You are standing and wondering which of the two groups you belong to. The ones who want to destroy what the rider drops or the small number who give away their lives protecting and spreading what the night rider drops. I am then given eyes to see inside of your chest and in your head. The revolution I see coming in this world . . . I see inside of you.

With the dark surrounding you, the screeching above, lights flashing across the sky, I saw you standing and looking at a great light and weapon before you. Then the dream stops.

I have these verses to share with you.

The people spoke against God and Moses, and said, "Why have you brought us up out of Egypt to die in the wilderness? For there is no food and no water, and we loathe this miserable food."

The Lord sent fiery serpents among the people and they bit the people, so that many people of Israel died. So the people came to Moses and said, "We have sinned, because we have spoken against the Lord and you; intercede with the Lord, that He may remove the serpents from us." And Moses interceded for the people.

Then the Lord said to Moses, "Make a fiery serpent, and set it on a standard; and it shall come about, that everyone who is bitten, when he looks at it, he will live."
—Numbers 21:5–8

The Lord your God will raise up for you a prophet like me from among you, from your countrymen, you shall listen to him.
—Deuteronomy 18:15

I have hope because I know our Story. The Israelites complained as they traveled toward the promised land, and God sent snakes to open their closed eyes to see they forgot their God and how He saved them from slavery. They could be healed if they looked up at a bronze snake attached to a pole that symbolized their sins. God was telling them that there would be One who would be their sin and He would one day be lifted up high for their healing.

Despite their history of slavery, the slaves were going to a new promised land. One was going to rise up to save them.

What happened then is why we have hope now.

Just as the Israelites discovered there would be a Savior to come, so it is that today we have hope that our same Savior God is moving for us. I believe, like those on the Mayflower, He is creating a shadow of a new Israel in a new land. A new country to help the only Israel one day.

Mo, there is a bright light ahead for you. It can guide you if you choose well. Know it. Recognize it. I do not know if the freedom cry will be answered in our lifetime. But we fight for our future children. With our lives, we lay down the foundation for our God to build upon. Go and act as a free man. Know that I have prayed for you.

Your friend,
Christopher

Augustine moved closer to Mo, and they both stepped toward the edge of the cliff. Death in the sky violently expelled itself like burning rain, like angry predators in the sky hunting and diving toward their helpless prey. Screeching cannon fire aimed for those in the city. More screaming from those down below . . . then silence.

People were dead and dying.

The Continental Army could do nothing.

Augustine turned to Mo with his head bent toward the letter. "Your destiny is in that letter if you choose it. I am sorry about your mother. Did you know she had died?"

Mo closed his eyes and swallowed. "I think Christopher spoke from heaven about two different mothers. One was related to me and the other one was not. I was told that my real mother died after birthing me. But the other mother he referred to, she took me as her own. I did not go back for her after I escaped. I knew she was gone. I never had a chance to fight. To kill those who'd killed her."

Henry put his arm around Mo. "I am sorry for your losses."

Mo did not clench his fists when Henry touched him. He did not even flinch. He closed his eyes, as he had to take a pause at what was happening before him. His hands and feet began to prepare. His heart fissured in a new place for the families and the dying in the city.

They are not all slavers.

But he wanted to run to the ships and destroy the other slavers.

Mo's eyes alternated between the city and the ships. The city and the ships. He could not move. He wanted to kill somebody. But his commander demanded that they wait.

Mo turned toward Augustine and shook his fist. "We can't just stand here. When can we fight?"

Augustine shrugged. "I hope our leaders know what they are doing."

Mo waved both fists in the air. "When can we fight?"

They stood watching the power and patterns from the past becoming the future course of the world.

CHAPTER 37

MARY

Near Plymouth, Massachusetts Bay Colony
1750

Mary surveyed and walked around the home where Agnes stayed to reinforce what Agnes was already doing to protect herself from the father of her child coming back to kill her. Would he come without even trying to hide and just blatantly force his way into the house, or would he be patient and wait for an opportune time? There was no way of knowing, and Agnes often refused to talk about him and what had happened in the past. There was just too much pain in those memories.

Agnes worked with a handful of the other slaves and collected some of their food the last few days to feed Mary, who hid in various locations out of the view of their slave master. It had been months in the planning stages and days in the execution of the two-part plan.

And now it was the right morning to start part one. Mary stayed hidden and hoped that Agnes's master would come out to start his travel to the secret meeting with the leader of the Indians. She stayed hidden, and after several minutes, she began to worry.

Did he find out what we are going to do? When is he coming out?

Mary waited. He was not coming out. Where was he? If he did not come out soon, he would be late for the meeting. It would probably then mean he was not going to the meeting and that he did not want peace or he did not believe the message he received. Did the leader of the Indians also not want peace?

Where is he?

The front door opened.

Finally.

Then two of the man's friends stepped out with their weapons.

Did they even read the note? No guns.

After the two friends inspected their guns and ammunition, then the man stepped out. He was not armed.

He did read the note.

They gathered their horses for what Mary hoped was the meeting. She prayed that somewhere in her village back home that the chief was also leaving unarmed, likely with other men for protection, toward the meeting location at another Praying Indian's home.

The men mounted their horses several feet from the house. Agnes stepped outside from the house with a gun while the men's backs were turned. She lifted it up in the general direction of the men.

What is she doing?

Then Agnes's eyes turned and locked with Mary's.

What is she doing? Mary stood, waving her hands. She stared without blinking at Agnes and shook her head and mouthed, *What are you doing?*

Agnes mouthed back, *Is he not better dead?*

Mary pointed with both hands toward her and then herself and mouthed, *What about our plan for peace and your freedom?*

Agnes lowered the musket, paused, turned toward Mary, and moved her eyes from Mary to the men now trotting away. She lifted the gun in line with the departing men, with her finger on the trigger. She turned her head and locked eyes with Mary one more time, then lowered the gun as she gently sobbed. The men were now out of accurate range.

Mary resumed breathing and turned her head to the men, now farther away.

Something reflected the rising sun. Something sticking out of the man's sock and shoe.

He has a pistol!

The men strode away united, while Mary stood pulled in two directions.

Lord God, I have to trust You. Give Martha the wisdom to know what to do at the meeting. The man is armed. Forgive me for not being with Martha to protect and help her. But I sense Your presence with me now and that You want me here.

Agnes stood, trembling and crying. She wiped her eyes and stared at her weapon.

What is she doing?

Did Agnes need help? Mary crouched back down behind some bushes, trying to decide what to do next.

Chapter 38

THE YOUNG MAN WITH BIG BEAUTI-FUL BLUE EYES

State House, Philadelphia
Pennsylvania Colony
1776

The young man shook his head. Several in the room could not help but stare at the ocean-blue eyes of the young man as he stood off to the side of the room. *We are running out of time.*

The Continental Congress argued, debated, and yelled for some time, with a final outcome still in doubt. Would there be a new birth of a new kind of government, or would the king prevail, as he always did? After much discussion, they took what they hoped was the final vote.

Nine colonies voted for independence from England. Pennsylvania and South Carolina voted no. New York abstained. Delaware was split between its two delegates. The Continental Congress vowed that if they were to formally declare independence, it would have to be unanimous, allowing for abstentions.

Frustration boiled over, as they had spent days with no real progress made. Debates and arguments rang through the room as the members of the Congress stated their cases.

Was it better to hang for attempting treason, or to hang for blatant treason with one's own name on paper? Was it better to not do anything?

They would jump to one side or fall to the other side. There could be no fence sitting. But how could a sense of unity come from thirteen different entities? Even without formally declaring independence, the meeting was just one more reason for the king to kill those assembled and committing treason. What was the difference if they somehow united and formally declared independence?

Benjamin Franklin rose. "We must indeed all hang together, or most assuredly we shall all hang separately."

Knowing that the Delaware vote could come into play and a tiebreaker could be needed, a man approached with his head tilted, as if two ships sailed in the ocean-blue eyes of the young man before him.

"I heard you are an express rider who rides as swift as an angelic messenger from God. Is that true?" Benjamin said.

"I can fly."

"This is not going well. I think we will need Caesar Rodney from the Delaware contingency to break the unexpected tie between the two from Delaware. He would be the deciding vote for

Delaware and could be an important vote for a possible new nation. Go to Dover and get Caesar Rodney back to Congress before the next and possibly final vote will be taken."

The young man disappeared before any further chance of conversation. All knew that the ride would be difficult for the express rider as well as for Caesar Rodney trying to return to place his vote, let alone to cast a vote before it was too late. Patience was at its lowest point of unity, and frustration was soon to be unanimous.

The young man flew indeed. It seemed as if the pathway was parted like the Red Sea until hours later, he knocked on the door.

Caesar Rodney opened it and had a difficult time standing tall and with his eyes fully opened. He staggered closer to the entryway and opened his eyes wider. Caesar wiped his eyes but avoided disturbing a tethering green scarf on the side of his face. "I do not think I know you. By chance did you come to wish me a much-needed good sleep with whatever hours are left? Or did you come to wish me a wonderful rest for a body that still feels like it is bouncing in rhythm to a horse's whims from my just-completed long ride from Philadelphia back to here?"

"I have been instructed to tell you that the last chance of debating will start about nine this morning and the final vote will be taken afterward. What shall I tell them?"

Caesar smiled. "Eighty miles. A storm coming. My face hurts. Tell them that Caesar Rodney intends to save the day . . . or you can tell them I will be there as soon as I can."

CHAPTER 39

GEORGE WHITEFIELD

Exeter, New Hampshire Colony
1770

For the last several years, George Whitefield's body and his time were both winding down, like an old pocket watch running out of time. For now, he rested once again in a volunteer host's home. Rest for a few hours before his next day of preaching. Most days he spent more time riding on horseback to preach in a different location than he spent resting in bed.

Most people marveled, as they said his voice could carry over a mile at his outdoor revivals. He had spoken over eighteen thousand sermons to as many as ten million people. He was fully aware of the estimation that almost each person in all the colonies had either personally heard him speak or knew someone who did. Many listeners and newspapers named him America's first celebrity.

He rose from the dining room chair and steadied himself with the table in the cool morning. Though his voice influenced almost each household, leaders, and churches, he wondered if God heard his cry into the empty sky. His heart ached and was heavy, with his adopted orphan children back in his orphanage and his wife, Elizabeth, who did not travel with him.

All children, and of course his orphanage children, needed their real Father. Though George and Elizabeth's only child had died shortly after birth, George's orphanage children knew they had a Father, and this was what brought a smile to his face at the end of each day.

He pulled the object out of his pocket. Clarisa, a young teenage woman, during a pause in the throes of giving birth, had handed George the object, like a mother handing over her only offspring to a trusted relative. Death had begun to cover her eyes, and she knew she would not survive delivering her child. What a strange and short life she'd had. Years before, she had mentioned to George someone had told her she was born a twin in 1750 and she and her brother had been separated shortly after birth. She'd never met her mother or her brother. Clarisa gave birth when she was fifteen, and she died holding George's hand that held the object.

George squeezed the warming object, and his memory unlocked further.

Someone had shared with her that the object had traveled with a young female slave on a slave ship from Africa, and somehow years later Clarisa's mother had ended up with the object. The young woman had always been George's favorite. She'd worked hard. She had poor vision, and the other kids named her "squinty," but she saw through people like no one else he had ever met. Before she'd given birth to a beautiful girl, she'd locked on to his eyes and probably saw things that George refused to see in himself. And yet she'd still given him her most prized possession. It then became his own most prized possession for about the last five years.

He turned it over several times in his hands. *What is this?* It was not made of any material he was familiar with. The raised markings were not discernible. It reminded him of a foreign language of some sort. Who spoke or knew the language? The object sometimes emitted heat and seemed to transport him back to reliving different moments and the reoccurring dream that had visited him for the past several years.

Memory of the dream descended into him. In the dream he was riding the finest horse in the darkest dark but could not shake what was following him. It was getting more and more difficult to breathe as his breaths became shorter and less frequent. There were voices underneath him, initially moaning, unintelligible uttering, and now spoken words cut through him.

Two words entered into his ears and through his most inner spirit and moved him, like a deep thunder rumbling hard ground. It was just two words, but they spoke volumes. He knew that voice. Like a long lost friend from years ago. The voices continued to rise up from the ground.

He could no longer ignore them.

What did it mean?

George shook his head after returning from the dream. He knew it had something to do with the object. He turned it in his hand again, studied it, and imagined its history, then put it away. Hidden for years, but it would one day play a role.

With it now in his pocket, he realized just how weak he had become. He staggered to a chair closer to the front door and rested. Someone knocked. He remembered another time when he'd heard a knock in the early dawn hours while everyone else was still asleep. He paused. He prayed to his God. He slid his feet to the door and opened it.

A young man stood before him, eager to fulfill his job. "Mr. Whitefield, are you ready for me to take you?"

Lord God, can I make it one more time?

"I will be out shortly."

George stood and swayed for a few moments, searching for his balance. It had to have roamed off somewhere. There it was. *Come back here, you little ungrateful prodigal son.* He adjusted his balance.

But now it was his difficulty breathing that concerned him. Would he be able to speak to thousands one more time if he was having a difficult time taking in a single full breath?

As strength entered into him to walk, he turned toward the backyard of the Smith home, where he'd stayed the night. *I need to see the garden. Lord, remind me of how we started in the garden.*

He stepped outside holding onto the sides of the doorway and remembered the young boy from yesterday. It was many yesterdays ago when George had attempted to help his garden in the shadow of his parents' inn. And now Mr. Smith's young son sat in the middle of the garden, and George's heart sank. What could be going on in the mind of a young boy whose father had died just three months ago?

George's heart ached as he tried to move quickly while the boy sat motionless in the middle of the garden. He made his way toward the boy, as he was unable to focus on the Smiths' beautiful garden.

He walked and stood several feet in front of the boy. "My son, are you well?"

The boy did not answer but only turned his head toward him.

Is the boy mute today?

George moved closer, and when he reached the boy, he gazed at the garden and then turned his eyes to the boy. "I have heard of this garden. It is the finest I have ever seen. When I was your age, I wanted a fine garden like this one. I failed and was not a good gardener. I just was not good enough to ever bring new life. I bought the finest seeds I could find, and some grew into plants, but most just withered away in the shadows. I did not know what I was doing, but I tried my best."

The boy just stared at him without blinking or any other movement.

George continued looking around the garden. "I do wish I was able to have a garden."

The boy fixed his eyes straight through George's. "The seeds are sown. Will they survive in the shadow to come?"

George's eyes opened more fully. He smiled and prayed. With all his power, he looked through his cross eyes and tried to harmonize the beautiful sunshine with the shadow that he cast on part of the garden.

The voice.

What was he going to do with those two words in his dream?

CHAPTER 40

MO

**Gowanus Heights, New York Colony
1776**

It was time. The redcoats assembled at a distance right before Mo's eyes. Curses were flung in the direction of the British general Howe ahead of them. Mo shifted his weight onto his legs in a more stable manner, and his heart missed beats as the redcoats marched toward the Continental Army. Mo straightened his spine and turned his head toward Augustine on his right and Henry on his left. Augustine's left eye twitched uncontrollably, and Henry did not blink. The Continental Army was dressed in torn rags, and most had hunting gear as weaponry. Mo could not swallow, as there was nothing to swallow.

The seams and the colors of the redcoats moved in perfect precision and alignment. In perfect union of thought and purpose, with no apparent flaws. Mo and the men waited for instruction.

Finally, we fight. They will not own me or my brothers and sisters. I fight for the children today and future tomorrows who cannot fight.

No more waiting. No more watching the British destroying and tearing apart families. No more watching the skies open up and helplessly witnessing cannon fire from the skies raining down to earth. For the moment, no more slaves watching their masters beat family members. It was now time to inflict some damage. They would overwhelm the enemy, more than at Bunker Hill, and send them back home with missing lives and limbs heralding a threatening group of brothers-in-arms across the Atlantic.

Volleys of fire exchanged man-made threats of death sentences to the living. Musket balls whizzed above and beside Mo as cannon balls, like birds of prey, hunted targets from the sky. Several men nearby on each side of him collapsed with momentary cries. Executing precise and focused killing limited his peripheral vision, but his sense of hearing heightened, as he swore he could hear sickening thuds of corpses hitting the ground with their last breaths leaving them.

Like fellow slaves before their master, the ground trembled in fear with each cannon fire. Mo lost his balance stepping on limbs as he moved to protect himself while he fired and reloaded and fired again. There seemed to be a much higher proportion of his men falling than the redcoats. They just kept coming and coming in waves of unbroken lines.

Then as Mo and the men were moving back, a group fired on their flank.

How did they get there?

While Mo and the Continental Army fought the redcoats in front of them, seemingly another nation of redcoats spawned from the red-coated monster and attacked at their left flank. Where did they come from? With British ships likely waiting behind them and an ocean of water on their right, redcoats in front, and now with redcoats on their left, they could only run away to Brooklyn Heights, hoping there were no British ships behind them.

Mo did not want to run. He yelled "Stand and fight" as men around him ran away. No one listened. Mo turned his head toward the monster and his men running for their lives. He believed he could outrun the monster and the spawned offspring if he had to. Everyone ran with piercing sounds flying past them, some of those sounds ending in a thud. The hard ground exploded next to Mo and behind him.

I have to live to execute my plan to save future children.

The sounds of bayonets behind him ending pleading lives and Mo stepping on men who moments before were fighting, would forever singe in his memory with whatever time he had left. The redcoats now fired upon them in what seemed from almost all directions. His men moved like a wounded animal hunted by many hunters from multiple directions. They only had one remaining choice and that was to run in the opposite direction toward a trap with its jaws waiting open.

Where were Henry and Augustine? Where was the hand of God if God was moving for liberty? If hell could move, it was pushing them closer and closer to the water behind them. They knew there would be British ships waiting for them in the river. Whose hand would prevail?

Many of the men attempted to run through the marsh of Gowanus Bay. Most got stuck and either drowned or were shot from behind. Mo was disgusted with the cowards running. He was disgusted with himself, but his plan was bigger than his pride. It was time to run. There was no sign of Henry or Augustine. Maybe they ran up ahead and were still alive?

What happened to General Washington? Did he run away as well? Where was General Washington?

Then the hand of God seemed to intervene. At the front lines and from the surprise flank attack, British general Howe decided to halt the assault. Why did he stop the relentless and overwhelming attack? Did he want his men fully rested before the bayonets ended it all? Did he remember the slaughter of the redcoats at the battle at Bunker Hill? With far less than the original nine thousand rebel soldiers, perhaps about half of the entire Continental Army, pinned between perhaps twenty thousand British soldiers and the East River, with British ships soon to fill the river, where could they go? The war would end as it was just getting started. No army could lose half their men in one day and still defeat the most powerful king and nation in the world.

The night descended, reminding them that the hours of the day were disappearing like their lives.

During the nighttime pause, Mo and the others rested, wondering how long they had left. The men knew General Howe probably ordered his men to dig trenches as the redcoats ate, rested, and prepared for the final assault to end the war and be home by Christmas. If Mo was General Howe, he would rest and prepare his men, assuring that Bunker Hill would not be repeated.

In a strange dream months before, Mo remembered a voice from someone in the future saying that man would either be controlled by the Bible or the bayonet. Mo did not want either. He did not know the Bible or the Author of the Bible, but he knew of the slave masters who used the Bible to justify slavery. And Mo wanted to be the one to use the bayonet. But he also knew there were some Christians who used the Bible to argue against slavery. Mo did not want to be ruled by the threat of a bayonet to coerce him either.

What would it feel like to have a bayonet end his life? Mo held his stomach and tried to sleep and prepare for what was coming. But his rest was restless, with only hours left to live. Augustine and Henry must have fallen with the first part of the attack. His mother had been killed years ago. His adopted mother also gone. Elias was probably dead, as who won against the relentless cancer predator when it wants to end the hunt for its prey? Mo would never see home again.

What do I live for? Who do I live for?

But he knew he was not alone. He could feel it filling him up. What could he do with what was filling him when they would soon shoot him or run a bayonet through him?

Would he have time to execute his plan?

Then a fellow soldier approached him. The man looked familiar.

Why am I thinking of Betsy's laugh right now?

The man examined his weapon. "I recognized you a few weeks ago. I was with the men who chased you when you escaped. I was there when they killed Betsy. I will soon die, so what do I have to lose? I came to complete what my father aimed to finish."

He raised the weapon toward Mo.

Chapter 41

MARTHA

Near Plymouth, Massachusetts Bay Colony
1750

Martha and Mary seemed to always be together, but on this day, Martha was on her own. Martha had sent Mary to check on Agnes, and Martha prayed for the meeting that was about to take place. Months of conversations with a man from another land would soon settle the debt she had with him. Soon Martha would be free.

She was thankful for all the fasting and prayers of others that went into preparation for the meeting, as a strong spiritual sense permeated the area. The home they were using had a sweet spirit that occupied all rooms, as those who lived in the home stepped away for a few hours to pray. The entire region was about to change forever.

Martha saw the chief come to the entrance of the remote home, with about six warriors. They all had proclaimed to recognize a great spirit about Martha, and she knew they had no desire to cross her and the man from another land who was with her.

The man next to Martha, both contrasting and blending with her brown Indian complexion, then told the men who accompanied the chief that they could not enter into the house without him searching for weapons. The chief refused to enter unless the home was first cleared of any traps that could incriminate or endanger him. The man with Martha searched one warrior and allowed him to check the home. After several minutes, the warrior came out, nodding that all was clear. The man searched the chief and then escorted him into the home.

Another group of men kept the leader of the local colonists and his men separated until they had finished with the Indian chief. Martha recognized the leader of the colonists as Agnes's slave owner. The same procedures occurred with them, and when one of the colonists finished searching the home, he too was satisfied. The man with Martha finished searching the leader of the colonists and escorted him into the home where the chief awaited. No one but Martha and the man from another land were allowed with the chief of the Indians and the leader of the colonists.

Martha stood nearest the leader of the colonists. *So this is the man who rules over Agnes. Does he know what me, Mary, and Agnes are going to do? You will never see what is going to hit you, slave master.* Martha and the man stood as the chief and the leader of the colonists sat at a dining room table directly opposite each other. They had met before, through Mary's other efforts. They smiled at each other, almost like two old friends who'd had a disagreement in the past and were now placed together in a room.

"Mr. Colonist, how are you and your family? I hear your youngest boy is now about sixteen? And he has an Indian as a friend?"

"Ah yes. You have good people. We are all doing fine. My son's friend is a fine young man. Indian. Did I ever tell you that I am part Indian and European?"

The Indian chief laughed. "Multiple times. Did I ever tell you I am part British?"

With a big smile and wide eyes, the leader of the colonists shook his head. "No, I did not know that."

"Well, that's because that is a lie."

They both laughed again.

"There are many lies said about me and my people. I believe me and my people have also believed lies about you and your people. Maybe we have some things in common?" The chief gave a big smile.

The leader of the local colonists tilted his head. "How is your lovely wife? I hear she is tired of all the fighting."

"We are all tired of the fighting. But you and I both want the same two things. Peace. And this land as home."

"Perhaps that is where we are both wrong. What if this isn't home for either of us? What if we are both fighting for what isn't ours and we are only stewards of a land that belongs to God? We will only be home when we are with Him at the end of this life."

The chief nodded. "You may be right. We are both humble men when we open our eyes. I look forward to the day when we can act like brothers and sisters and not allow enemies of the Great Spirit to distract us by what others define family as." He smiled again. "I want to thank you for writing your letter to me. It took great strength to want to surrender for a truce of peace."

The leader stopped himself mid-smile and opened his eyes wider. "But I thought we were here because of the letter you wrote telling me *you* wanted to surrender."

Silence. No movement. Martha and the man with her looked at each other and then the two leaders.

Between me and Mary, we know these men well. This is where we think there can be peace. O God, move in the miracle we have prepared for. Please let there be peace when we have worked so hard to get the leaders here together.

The leader and the chief stared at each other. They then turned their heads toward Martha and the man with her.

The chief and the leader both laughed. The chief grinned. "The Great Spirit. I believe He visited me yesterday, and I believe He has something to do with this meeting."

The leader sat with lifted eyebrows. "Something happened to me yesterday as well."

"Those crazy Praying Indians may have started a miracle. I am only doing what God told me to do.

I mean you no harm." The chief reached down and pulled out a pistol and placed it on the table.

The leader raised his hands up in surrender and said "I mean you no harm" as he pulled out his pistol and laid it on the table. He then shook his head and fastened his eyes on the man next to Martha. "I am concerned that you let both of us enter into this house with a hidden gun. Perhaps your plan for us to kill each other failed because you underestimated God, heartfelt prayers, and us."

The leader then said, "We trust you, Martha. But we do not trust your friend with you. What he meant as evil, God meant for good. You lied to each of us and wrote that the other wanted to surrender just to get us here to kill each other. And the funny thing is, we are each surrendering to each other just like the letters said."

"You let us smuggle our guns here thinking that we would kill each other," the chief added. "The Great Spirit spoke to both of us separately, and if God is our Father—"

"—then you are my brother." The leader pointed his finger toward the chief and laughed. "My gun is not even loaded."

The chief laughed also. "Now I know why the Great Spirit told me to bring my unloaded gun as well."

Martha put her hands on her face to cover her beaming smile. *Things are going as Mary and I planned. We will soon all be free.*

The man next to her scratched his head and shifted his weight back and forth.

The leader turned his head to each person, with pauses at each individual. "Perhaps we are at different parts of the journey to know the one God. Perhaps we are at two different points in our walk with God?" He then showed downcast eyes that almost seemed to water. "I have not even been consistent with following the commands of the God I claim to serve above all. I have sinned. I have slaves, and I want to release them soon. I have committed crimes against God and those I took as slaves."

The chief nodded. "I have my sins as well."

The man with Martha then pulled out a gun hidden in a hole in the floor and pointed it at the two leaders. "Pick up your gun and point it at your own head."

"Wait!" Martha put her hand on the man's forearm holding the gun. "You lied to me. You are changing our plan. You allowed each of them to bring their guns, but you told me you wanted peace. This was your idea."

The leader shook his head. "I will not pick up the empty weapon—"

"—and make it look like I killed my brother," the chief finished.

The leader—the slave owner over Agnes—added, "Our subordinates had already been meeting before the fake letters. We want the spilled blood to end. You can kill us believing that you are killing whom you call murderer. But neither one of us is the murderer you are looking for. The Satan within you searches for whom he calls murderer, the one whom

God will use to save and to help free many in all the future generations. The one you call murderer will rise up, hidden before your eyes with or without us. You can't stop this. Even when you kill me, you have already lost."

The man narrowed his eyes. "The Dark Light told me one of you is the murderer intending to kill the power from the Dark Light. I oppose the One who uses you to attack the power we have taken." The man pushed Martha away, crashing her into a wall. He lifted the gun and killed both leaders.

"No!" Martha screamed, and pushed off her legs to steady herself as she wobbled against the wall.

The man placed each leader's own gun into his limp hand.

He ran out the back door, as the colonists and Indian warriors would soon be inside. Martha ran after the man. In the canyon behind the house, she collapsed when she reached him.

Surrounded by several elm trees, she lifted her head and pulled herself up. She separated some large black chokeberry shrubs, which shielded a waiting horse.

The man spoke while trying to catch his breath. He jumped onto his horse and tilted his head down toward Martha. "Martha, you did well. I knew only you working with Mary could get both leaders under one roof. This will continue the fighting until I find who I am looking for. The Dark Light just told me that neither of them are the murderer. But we could not have them working together. There can be no unity.

Maybe with all their coming fighting, they will end up helping us by killing the murderer we are looking for. In the meantime I need to find the murderer."

Martha's legs gave way and collapsed. "I believed you and thought you would force them to stay until they signed the peace accord. I thought this would buy more time for Mary to free Agnes."

The man smiled. "Thank you again. Now I know who the murderer is. The king will be happy." He smiled a crooked smile. "We did the first part of the plan—the leaders are now out of the way and the rest are left to their own seething vengeance . . . to devour each other. They will soon find you and decide what to do with the traitor."

Martha could not move. Her mouth was stuck open.

The man shook his head. "Though I found out neither of the leaders was the murderer, thanks to you I now know who the murderer is that the Dark Light speaks of." He leaned forward as his lower pant leg lifted up, exposing his darkened lower left leg. "I have to find the murderer, or the Dark Light will take over me."

The man turned his head toward the house behind him. "The Dark Light told me where I need to go to find him. The murderer must be stopped. I want to live."

Martha wept. "You lied to me. You told me I just had to bring the men together for the meeting so they could work on an agreement and you would leave me alone. My debt fully paid. You were not supposed to kill them."

The man chortled. "You served the wrong god. I cannot take care of *your* debt." He rode away.

Footsteps moved far behind Martha. Gunshots echoed in the house behind her.

CHAPTER 42

GEORGE WHITEFIELD

Exeter, New Hampshire Colony
1770

George Whitefield tried to catch his breath. His words were not clear, and his thoughts were elsewhere. He stood before thousands of men, women, slaves, and children who had come from faraway places. The organizers told him there were many from the Boston area and from other colonies and even other countries, to perhaps hear from the celebrity preacher one last time. In midsentence, he paused again to catch his breath and refocus.

George raised his arms, now seemingly weighted down by what hovered over him, and proclaimed so all could hear, "Will Your grace be sufficient for me one more time?" There was a quiet in the crowd as they once again hung on to each word as if God Almighty was inside George Whitefield, ready to begin a one-on-one personal discussion with each person at the same time.

Even with the buzz of the crowd, a slithering noise moved from behind him, toward him.

My Lord, can You give me strength one more time?

The sound of a sword unsheathed stopped the slithering noise's approach. Would the strength come one more time? He waited. He worried about the thousands who'd come in the midst of busy days and were now only hearing silence. He placed his right hand over the tops of his brows on this beautiful day, as if saluting all in front of him one last time before his departure. Individual faces blurred in the light and the shadows of the day.

Then the voice in his dream. Like from a father he always wanted and wanted to be. Those two words.

Free me.

He turned his head around him, anticipating that others had heard what was in his head. He thought of the slaves at his orphanage. His own slaves. And the slaves before him in the crowd.

It was the only way I could afford to run the orphanage to save the children.

He averted his eyes and bowed his head, like a child before his father trying to justify stealing from his father. The still pause increased the unease. Like blood from a well-used candle dripping to the ground, he felt his color draining from his face and almost dripping past the bottom of his feet and fertilizing the ground.

George, with unmerited favor and a new fire, stood straighter against the presence waiting and hovering around him like birds of prey circling the sky. "The same God who grants me unmerited favor to continue, is the same God who grants you His unmerited favor. Confess all your sins, the ones that God whispers, and when necessary shouts, and believe the Lord Jesus is your Savior, and commit to Him your life."

He continued to drop what was needed into the softening heart grounds before him in preparation for what was coming their way. *It is 1770. Does anyone here know what is coming to try to tear their family apart?*

After finishing his last public message to thousands in the grateful city of Exeter, he lost strength again. His horse in the distance waited and would need to wait longer, as he was not sure he could walk that long distance. He was not sure he could even ride his horse to the ferry that would take him to some needed rest at a friend's home in Newburyport, Massachusetts. If he could only make it to his horse.

Others realized his exhaustion and came alongside him to prop him up and walk him.

"Thank you, gentlemen. I preach independence from Satan and dependence on God . . . and a few helping hands."

With help, he made it to his horse. He stopped when he saw a young man, perhaps about twenty years of age, standing in the shadow of a large tree. George loved preaching for the slaves. He admonished those who did not allow them to read and hear about the Lord their God. Their Father. They loved George Whitefield.

George summoned the dark-colored young man to come to him, and the man would have sprung out of worn socks to come, had he been wearing some. The men gave extra support for George when his knees buckled as the young man approached.

George studied his face. Though he had never seen him before, he already knew the voice in him even before he spoke. George examined him as the light of God seemed to gradually move from his head to his toes. The young man bent his head, shuffled his feet back and forth, and closed his eyes.

"Young man, please open your eyes."

When his eyelids lifted, it was almost as if within the young man's eyes, the eyes of their common Father stared back at George. There were eyes within the eyes! George jerked his head backward as power emanated from the young man like a strong warm wind, and George lost his balance. Men beside him caught him and helped him regain his footing. *This man truly bears the image of our Father! God dwells within him!*

The young man, with a Spirit within that spoke for many, said, "Free me."

CHAPTER 43

CAESAR

Dover, Delaware Colony
1776

The dark night turned into a stormy night when Caesar Rodney left with his finest and rudest horse. Philadelphia was hours away. The young man who'd come to his door told him that the final vote to decide the fate of a new nation was balanced on the edge of a sharp blade of the finest sword. Strangely enough, even after falling and hitting the left side of his face earlier, the pain was not as bad as he expected, so he rode hard from home back to Philadelphia.

The storm riddled the ground with deepening puddles and sticky mud. His horse alternated between slipping and sticking to the ground. Would the fate of liberty against tyranny die with his horse falling and breaking a leg? Would the chains of the enslaved be tightened further and the short-leash chain around all of their necks shorten further with Caesar and his horse broken on the ground?

Then what could he do? Any hope of drafting a unanimous declaration of independence from the king would end like a slave master burning a book of liberty before the slave could read it. Where would the seed grow if it was not even placed on the hard ground soiled with the excrement of tyranny? Even arriving on time was no guarantee that a declaration could be drafted.

Lightning flashed from one end of the sky to the other. Thunder approached and seemed to chase him from behind, closing in. He rode as fast as the rain, mud, and his horse could go. She, though sometimes annoying, was the best horse available to him. He loved that horse. His face ached and burned more in the dark ride. Would he have to slow down?

After a few hours, the burning seemed to crawl from the left side of his face to his forehead and top of his head. As he continued, it extended down his arms and legs to the bottom of his feet. The pain was from a combination of the vibration and pounding of the ride and the stormy air both resisting and brushing up against his face. Or was the multigenerational, tyrannical king cancer, first ruling a small portion of his body, now spreading faster to other parts of his body? What was next—invisible flying creatures pecking at his dying flesh?

Caesar came across a stream swollen and flowing over the road he needed to cross. The road was impassable for a rider on his horse. There was only one choice. He slid off his horse and stood beside her. She pulled on the reins to go in the opposite direction. Caesar stroked her mane, and with her head she then pushed him toward the water. He guided her across the stream, now almost a small river. With less pounding, his face gained a short respite.

He then wrapped his arms around her neck, whispered words of encouragement, and found that the rocky road up ahead was too muddy and slippery to ride. He could not risk breaking her legs with a hard ride up that road. He walked her several yards and then mounted and continued until the next barrier.

Do we want to have independence? Are we ready to pay the cost with thousands of lives bleeding out and flooding onto what was an already thriving garden floor? We already have prosperity, and there is little to no material things to gain. Do we want liberty so much so as to see the blood of our young and old spilling like currents?

There was no other government in history, or in existence, that lived what the Continental Congress envisioned. Jolted when his horse misstepped, Caesar yelped. He immediately forgot his pain and focused on the horse that would help decide if a new nation with a new calling would be birthed. The mare staggered, but after about twenty feet she recovered. But for how long? There were still hours left on the journey. He adjusted himself to stay upright.

Would it not be better to not have our own blood spilled and remain in our riches? Perhaps things would be better when the king dies? Or would an even worse king take the reins of the same tyrannical beast of monarchy? Could I then be able to freely seek a cure for my cancer? No more pain. No more hiding behind a scarf and scaring others.

The sun was minutes away from breaking through, with the early beginnings of a new day. Up ahead a low-hanging branch partially blocked some of his visibility while riding full speed. At the last moment, he moved his head but still grazed his head on the branch. He overreacted and lost his balance as he leaned far to his left, almost falling over, before he was able to reclaim control and center himself and his horse. If he had reacted a second later, it would have been a direct blow to the side of his head and he would have fallen. It could have killed him.

What does it matter now? We have already committed treason without formally declaring independence. It is already too late for us.

In the early dawn skies, a screech in the sky flew above and passed him by. Then it seemed to turn back toward his direction . . . as if hunting something.

CHAPTER 44

KING GEORGE

Buckingham House, England
1776

The war against the rebellious colony children was proving more difficult than he ever believed it would be. Yesterday, servants in his court of power reported to him that his rich, spoiled children had declared independence. With a wave of his hand, he turned the servants away. What father wanted to hear again about his prodigal son leaving his faithful father and, from afar, wasting what was feely given to him, and was now blaming the father for his own poor choices?

The king lay staring at the ceiling above him in the partial dawn light. It happened again. He was wide awake, as something stirred in a nearby room somewhere down the hall. Sensing he was not alone, he stepped out of the bedroom, trying not to disturb the queen, and began his search. All was in order until he went to the main entrance and found the main door open partway. Who could have possibly left the door open without a watchful eye until the early morning hours?

He aimed muttered expletives toward his sub-servient staff still in bed. All knew the king had enemies, and someone left the front door open and unguarded? Who could be so irresponsible?

Something strange crawled up his spine.

Someone entered again.

He turned his head without moving his body. The hairs on the back of his neck and arms raised up, as if trying to flee from him and the room. He curved his body and head. He did not see the back of the head of the being sitting somewhere. At least not yet.

He would not be able to return to sleep, so the king sat and stared at the still-open door in from of him. He focused with what seemed to be one continuous, unblinking stare.

The markings on him grew. Would they eventually wrap around his neck to cut off any attempt at breathing? Sometimes he thought it was moving up to surround his head. Perhaps it was inside his body as well. Crawling inside of him and internal ground greater than what he could see on the outside. Would it wrap around his mind? Was it making him think the way the Dark Light wanted him to think? Was it setting up command inside from his toes to his head to do its own will? Or was it going to so greatly infect his mind that he would go mad?

The hairs on the back of his neck stood up again. What would happen to him, to Charlotte, to his legacy, to his people, if he went mad? Who could help him?

While sitting, he stared at the open door. Hours passed before he knew it. Some of the early morning staff began their work. Some stopped and refused to cross the path between himself and the open door. Some whispered to other staff members that the king was just sitting and staring at the door. Soon all avoided the area altogether.

Every once in a while, footsteps moved behind and beside him and carried on with their morning duties. No one dared to stop near him. As the morning continued on, when would the queen come around to check on him?

Soft steps approached from behind. They moved quickly, then paused, then moved, then paused again at a distance. The echoes of feet moving were even slower than those of the others.

She approached from his side. She bent closer to him for a better look and placed her hand on his shoulder. "My love, are you all right?"

He did not answer.

Please, Dark Light. Help me. Kill the ungrateful prodigal son who betrayed me.

Something stirred inside him. As if the other eyes within him opened. His eyes moved from side to side, as if searching for something hidden from most observers. Then it spoke in George's inner voice. *I see the murderer! The noose is tightening. The hand has lifted partway, and I see him! I will end the threat as I have ended all other threats. He will soon die by gun or bayonet. Or perhaps I will capture him and he will hang. The noose around him is tightening.*

George smiled with a sigh. Soon the murderer would be killed and the king would be free. The markings would disappear. He could then think more clearly.

Charlotte swallowed—preparing herself for what was next? "My love . . . I am getting worried . . ."

A knife cutting something echoed in his head. Whatever resisted the Dark Light slumped to the ground inside his head. George did not blink. His eyes did not move.

We found him.

CHAPTER 45

MO

**Brooklyn Heights, New York Colony
1776**

Mo's heart raced. The man before him looked older than he remembered, but the eyes gave him away. Edward was another of Mo's slave owner's sons. He raised his musket closer to Mo.

"I hated my brother for teaching Christopher how to read and write. His poison must have poisoned you too. I envied you. My father sometimes liked you, and you could have been a great slave. But I hated you more for escaping. Even after my father died, he is still with me. You were the only slave that ever escaped and lived. I recognized you weeks ago but knew you had not seen me. Your desire to kill wrecked your vision."

"I really don't care if you kill me. What do I live for if I am not free? I'm already going to hell. You will go to hell for killing me and all the other things you did to my people, and it will then be my turn to hunt you down for eternity, where you and I will have no place else to go. I will get to torture you over and over and over again."

Edward stood with eyes wide and unblinking. He shook his head, as if to wake up. "It is tragic what happened to both of your moms, Betsy, and your Henry and Augustine. I had planned earlier how I was going to avenge my dead father . . . my wretched father . . . but something stopped me. Maybe it was God Himself who told me to leave you alone. You have some sort of purpose and role to play out, and God will strike me down if I get in the way. I don't want to go to hell."

"If God will not strike you down, then I will." Mo pushed the gun aside and hit the man square in the face. Mo held his own bloodied fist and stood with a smile. The veins on the back of his hands pounded a war beat that summoned him to do more.

The man whimpered. "I wanted to kill him, but You told me to leave him alone. I do not like this war within me." He turned to his side and pulled his knees toward himself. "The slaves . . . I didn't know . . . I didn't know what I was doing . . . I didn't know any better."

Mo paused. *Something is telling me to stop.* Mo grunted and yelled under his breath. He stepped away. "I will not be owned and told what to do."

Mo walked to the other side of camp. His hands throbbed, so he rubbed them together. He sighed and then breathed deep breaths. He scanned the area and his fellow soldiers. When could they fight? They were united in their time left together and in death.

If he was leading the men, what would he do? What would General Washington do? Could he pull soldiers from New York City for reinforcements and leave New York City more vulnerable to attack? Were the attacks on his trapped soldiers just a distraction from a much larger attack elsewhere? Would he leave his trapped soldiers to fight on their own in a battle that they could not win?

Then, like there was the hand of God nearby, the weather worsened and a strong northeast wind howled, making it impossible for British ships to move behind the trapped rebels.

Mo stood. At a distance, the British ships, like birds of prey circling, waited for the wind to die down, as it looked like the Continental Army was waiting for General Washington's reinforcements from New York to arrive.

Someone turned to Mo and said, "I wonder if this is like when Moses looked at the walls of the Red Sea staying up as a passageway."

"But *we* are going to stay and fight the slave masters. We will bring justice. *I* will bring justice." Mo raised his gun. When could he kill to save lives again? The Continental Army could never win against what was coming, but at least he could inflict his plan and have vengeance on a few redcoats before they killed him.

Mo smiled as more reinforcements arrived while the British ships were held at bay. But where was General George Washington?

In the dead of the night, officers instructed all the men to not even cough. No speaking or making of any noises. Wagon wheels and oars were covered with cloths to quiet any sound that might alert the red-coats resting and preparing to end the Continental Army before the revolution truly started. This was to be a surprise attack on the sleeping redcoats.

As the hours continued, Mo noticed hundreds of fellow soldiers moving from the front lines toward the water behind them. Men, cannons, equipment all moved away from where the battle was to be.

Then like a sword impaling his best-made plans, it struck Mo. *This is not for battle. This is a retreat!*

Mo marched to General Mifflin and said loudly, "This is—" And then someone covered his mouth.

"Shut up and get back to your duty." Mifflin's eyes narrowed and cut through Mo.

Mo tried to keep from screaming, and the thoughts in his head were too loud to contain. "We must fight!"

The general ignored him and walked to another area to rule over others. Mo shook his head in disbelief. The soldiers were preparing a massive retreat that had never been done on such a scale before. How could they ever succeed? Evacuate nine thousand men before sunrise without being discovered?

Mifflin moved closer to Mo. "I have volunteered us to replace each man at the front, and we will protect each man up until the last man leaves. You best pray that your desire to fight today does not come true."

This is suicide! I am being sent to die for the small chance of just some of the men attempting to escape? How long will the British ships be kept at bay by the wind? The redcoats on land before us will soon notice that we are fleeing and then unleash their death earlier than planned, with even less resistance.

There was almost a quarter-mile-long line of men trying to leave. Washington had apparently ordered every available local boat to participate in the massive evacuation. Mifflin had explained this was to save the army, to then fight again to win the war. They would try and move under the cover of the night before sunrise, for all their intents would be fully exposed in the morning light. Mifflin looked like a man who knew he would not see his wife and children again.

In the long lines leading to the water and the escape boats, men started to fight amongst each other to be next to leave. They were losing time, and soon it would be sunrise. Even in the dark, the men could see the redness in George Washington's face when he found the men fighting each other. He cursed and grabbed a large rock and raised it above his head and threatened to sink the next boat if his men did not cooperate. All chaos stopped in fear of the best-case scenario of the general throwing the rock and eliminating one boat, which could end up costing some of them their own lives. Worst-case scenario was the angry and huge general crushing someone's head. To nobody's surprise, chaos turned into order.

But the men could still not move their boats to safety across the river because of the same wind that kept the British ships away.

Then the wind shifted, allowing their boats to leave. The retreat escalated in a race against the sunrise coming in a few hours. As more men departed, General Mifflin and his soldiers replaced the retreating army with others to the front lines in preparation for the start of the attack upon them from land. They would not be able to stop an attack, but they could give more time to evacuate others—all, of course, paid for by the lives of Mifflin and his men. And Mo.

Mo shook his head as the men retreated and the arrogant red-coated slavers in front of him rested and waited to attack and end the war in a slaughter.

How many redcoats can I kill before they kill me?

As the sun began to rise, a significant portion of the Continental Army was still on the Long Island side of the river. Hope fled like the single grains of sand at the top half of the hourglass emptying to be buried in the depths below. There was no way they could rescue every man before the sun rose.

But something arose from the lower depths nearby. A mysterious summer fog appeared and settled over the Long Island side of the river, covering the retreating soldiers. Visibility was about ten feet. Like a thick hand obscuring their escape, it also muffled sounds that the men inadvertently made in the still air that could alert the resting redcoats that they were retreating. But much of the army was still at risk on the wrong side of the river. Midmorning approached with the sun out above the summer fog.

General Mifflin then ordered the last of the men

to board the few remaining boats. In the chaos of the escape, Mo heard Mifflin curse under his breath because General George Washington was determined to be the last man to leave. For what purpose would the commander of the cause risk being captured or killed, therefore risking the entire cause of liberty from the king and all future tyrants?

He also did not notice that Mo, like a soldier protecting his country's most valuable asset, was nearby, eyeing the general.

Mo wanted to both leave and stay at the same time. But now was the time. Would many one day look to what was going to happen and proclaim Mo as a hero for the freedom of the world?

CHAPTER 46

MARY

**Near Plymouth, Massachusetts Bay Colony
1750**

Mary consoled Agnes after Agnes decided not to shoot the one who claimed to be her master and the other men as they'd left for the meeting with the chief of the local Indians. Agnes refused to talk to Mary about why she was so upset, and Mary remembered she had seen varying emotions like that before.

Mary always wanted to live those feelings while pregnant.

It was the late afternoon. With minutes disappearing for another day, Mary stood at watch again, to protect. Agnes had created space in a wooden shed for Mary to sleep at night, out of view of the master and his wife. The slaves fed her in secret. She could still hide during parts of the day and night and keep watch for the attacker coming back for Agnes.

Time was running out. The master would return from the meeting. What was happening with Martha supervising the coming agreement between the master representing the colonists and the chief of the Indians? Mary was awaiting for word on when they could start the second part of the strategy with Agnes while the master was away. Agnes was going to escape while some of her fellow slaves created a health crisis amongst themselves and thus compel the master's wife to seek medical help.

Mary needed to initiate the second part with the master gone. She should have already heard from her informants, but fortunately the master was not back yet. Were the two leaders able to finalize a new commitment to peace?

Something is not right.

Mary stood at the entrance of the shed, when one of her scouts ran to her. They both bent down out of view, and the scout paused to get his breath back. He gathered his energy and whispered that their plan was now finally ready to start. Mary sent the scout to run ahead to prepare for what would come next. She looked toward the front door of the house.

The master is still gone. We are now ready. We don't have much time before he comes back. Did Agnes succeed in distracting the master's wife from seeing us?

The master's wife staggered out of the house. Mary did not recall Agnes ever telling her that the master's wife had an alcohol or health issue before. But there she was staggering in a circle in front of the house.

The workers stayed at a distance from her and walked away while continuing their duties. It did not look like it was the first time workers had steered clear of her. Everything else before Mary seemed in perfect order. Even with the master's wife in disarray, the slaves continued working without distraction, which was remarkable, considering the master was also not present.

The master's wife tried to push a note into the hands of one of her slaves. The slave shook her head and raised her hands upward, as if in disbelief or not wanting to have anything to do with the note.

The slave said to the master's wife, "Please don't be angry with me. I don't know. Is this true? I do not know what to tell you."

The master's wife pulled the note back and showed it to another slave as she yelled, "Read it! Read this!"

The slave trembled and cried. With a shaking voice, the slave mumbled through her hands covering her mouth, "You know I cannot read."

The master's wife slapped her across her face. "Look what your people did. I have cared for you, protected you, and this is how you thank us?" She pulled the note away.

The young slave shook more and ran into the house crying while covering her face. The master's wife ran after her.

Did someone tell her of our plan?

Agnes appeared from the back of the house with the gun again and stomped toward the entrance. Agnes then stopped, turned her head toward where Mary stood, and this time ignored her and continued walking fast toward the house.

Mary ran toward the house with no fear of being seen or of letting her guard down for the approaching murderer. Before she reached the house entrance, a shot blasted through the calm and a gust of hot air brushed up against her face through the doorway. Mary bent over and stopped a few feet in front of the house as a sharp pain pierced her stomach.

With both hands holding her stomach, she did not want to stand up. She did not want to look at her hands.

O God, stay true to Your plan. Stay true to our plan.

What would happen to the grand plan for peace and freedom?

Mary stayed bent over. Her stomach and her hands throbbed as she thought she had to keep her insides from coming out. *I cannot move. I cannot go inside. I do not want to see what happened.*

Mary kept her hands on her stomach as she took a step to run away from more death. She was tired of all the fighting. The colonists with the Indians and the Indians with the colonists. The colonists with the king and the king with the colonists. Slave masters and slaves. Slaves and slave masters. Somewhere, in another place, life was protected and cherished. There had to be that place somewhere.

Mary bent again with a gasp. *Is this what labor pains feel like?* Perhaps it was best that Mary should never have and carry a baby into this world. She stepped forward.

A second shot stopped her in her tracks.

CHAPTER 47

THE CONTINENTAL CONGRESS

State House, Philadelphia
Pennsylvania Colony
1776

The Continental Congress had debated, argued, and yelled long enough. They had spent days and that morning together and divided, and no one knew for sure if unity or division would reign with the final vote coming. But enough was enough. Delaware's two present delegates were split in their votes, and they had waited long enough for Caesar Rodney, the tiebreaker vote for Delaware, to arrive. It was time to move. It was time to take a final vote.

A commotion in the back of the room disrupted the proceedings when a gentleman staggered in, with some assisting him. The man's spurs did not help in his effort. He struggled to catch his breath, as if he was chased by a dragon that had dominated the sky and that only he could see. All eyes turned to him, as it was difficult to discern who was standing before them under layers of mud and dripping water pooling under the standing man.

Fear cut through the room. Each neck seemed to be uncomfortably attached to ropes that someone was now pulling. All tried to catch a final breath.

Was this a scout or a random local about to tell them the redcoats were on the way? They would now never be able to vote for liberty. Were redcoats waiting to stain the hallowed halls with Congress's own treasonous blood?

They were probably now closing the noose after surrounding them and choking off any possible escape. All would soon be drawn and quartered as an example for the locals of what not to do. The king's long hand across the Atlantic gripped around each neck in the room and soon next to grip around each family member of the treasonous Continental Congress.

Treason.

The man shaking before them seemed to summon his last breath for his and their last words.

CHAPTER 48

MARY

Near Plymouth, Massachusetts Bay Colony
1750

Mary stood frozen in her steps several feet from the entrance to the house, trying to recover from the shock. Dusk moved forward. One gunshot. Then two. Then a scream.

Mary hid behind a tree next to the house. She could not bring herself to go inside. She bent her head toward her hands, and they were not bloodied. *Then what was that sharp pain? Was that Agnes's pain? Agnes! Are you still alive? Please come out so that I know you are all right.*

If Mary ran inside, the slaves who sided with the slave master, and were waiting for an excuse, might even blame her for whatever had happened inside. They knew the slave master did not like Mary. Mary turned her head toward the main road, where the slave master and his men could be coming any moment.

Agnes, come out.

Silence. No more noise came from the house. Perhaps the rest of the workers did not hear the gunshots? Or perhaps they already knew about the gunshots, as it was all part of a plan that Mary did not know about?

Was the attacker waiting for Agnes inside? Did he shoot her?

Mary alternated between leaning toward the house and running away. Agnes staggered out the front door. Mary did not even look in all directions as she ran to Agnes. Mary reached her just in time to prevent her from falling. As Mary propped Agnes up, Mary noticed that the liquid on Agnes's arms was warm. Agnes had blood all over her.

Mary walked her out of view and toward the bushes. "Agnes, what happened?"

"Somebody gave a note to his wife. She knows the truth."

A worker ran to Mary, and Mary whispered into the worker's ear. "Tell him we need to move now! Run and go tell him!"

The worker ran off. Mary half carried Agnes to a path that led away from the house. Mary then asked, "What truth? What happened? Why are you bleeding?"

Several workers ran into the house. Agnes spoke in between short breaths. "There is no one who attacked me and escaped, and no one is returning to kill me. The man who calls himself my master is the father of my child. Someone found out, and now his wife knows."

"What?" Mary covered her own face with her hands.

"He was going to tell his wife about what happened, and things were moving too fast for me. I was not thinking, and I am so ashamed. But this cannot stop our plans for peace and our escape. My mind is not acting good, but I knew I was ashamed of our sin together. The child I carry is because of our sin. This child deserves to live free of my mistakes. He should live free. I am not even sure this child will live. Other than me, who wants this baby? Nobody but you and me want this baby."

Mary could not take her eyes off Agnes. *I think she was forced into a relationship with the master. Or worse. Is Agnes telling me the truth now?*

Agnes gathered herself and wiped her face as they continued walking. "But does anyone live free of others' mistakes? Inside the house she told me we both could not remain alive with a European-Indian-African baby that looked like me and her husband in her home."

Agnes paused her walking with her hand on her chest. "She pointed her gun at herself, and I tried to take it away. During the pushing and pulling, it went off. While she was wounded, she tried to shoot me."

"God will judge as He sees fit. But why did you lie to me?"

Agnes averted her eyes away from Mary's gaze. "We needed to set the plan for peace into motion, and I could not let what happened with me get in the way of possible peace between our peoples."

Mary shook her head and closed and then opened her eyes.

Agnes's eyes brimmed with water. "I pray that our God is sovereign and full of grace and mercy and that He forgives all of us and would still choose to use anyone, any way, anywhere, any time He wants. Do you believe He can still use sinful people to do good?"

Mary turned her head away from Agnes as they walked faster. "I lied to you about the meeting of the leaders. Martha and I forged their notes to each other. Me and Martha wrote fake notes to the two men, just hoping they could get together for once and work out a deal."

Agnes let out a muffled laugh. She paused and shrugged and just let the tears roll. "Can God use lies to turn into good?"

Mary tried to quicken the pace, and Agnes coughed and winced. She spoke in a broken rhythm. "I did not know if you would stop everything because of what you thought of me or the man who calls himself master. Would I have to do things on my own, or would you help? I did not know what you would do to him or what you would think of me."

Agnes laughed again. "It seemed to be a perfect plan for a powerful leader with European and Indian blood in him to play a part in bringing peace between those of European and Indian blood. Then maybe you and I could work to free slaves."

Mary lifted a part of Agnes's torn dress. "Agnes, have you have been shot? Or is that her blood?"

"Quick, have I been shot in the stomach?"

Mary moved her face closer in the available moonlight. "There is blood all over you, but I do not see any blood on your stomach yet."

As Mary looked at Agnes's chest, Agnes sighed. "Then why does my stomach hurt more?"

Liquid dripped below Agnes. Was it water or blood? Agnes's eyes grew wide, and her face lightened in color. Mary turned away from the blood on Agnes's chest. A familiar weight pressed on her heart. Like after her husband had left her. Mary's vision blurred. "There is so much blood that I do not know if you were shot, and it would take too much time to figure that out for sure. But if you were shot in the chest, I do not think you would be walking with me right now."

Mary grabbed Agnes by her shoulders and locked eyes with her. "We just need less than an hour to get to the ocean, where they are waiting for us. I can almost hear the Atlantic from here. Finally, Agnes, our plan to get out of here when there is a peace accord in place with the leaders is going to work. The master's wife will not get in the way. We can free your fellow slaves soon. The plan is coming together."

"You should have stayed over there with Martha to make sure the plan was going as it needed to. And instead, because of me lying to you, you watched over me here. Are you even sure Martha is okay? Why aren't the men back yet?"

"Perhaps I needed to be here to witness you getting yourself and your boy to freedom. I trust Martha.

She will do what I would have done. There will be a time to confront the one who used to be your master." Mary smiled and gave a short laugh. "Right now our fight is to retreat and get you out of here to then fight another day. It has to be in His timing. He will make a way when man says there is no way. In the meantime, we continue on."

Mary grabbed Agnes's arm and pulled. "We need to run like when we were young."

They ran, though Mary sometimes slowed down for Agnes. *Agnes could not have been shot if she is running as well as she is.* Several minutes later, the ocean before them met the sand. As they raced closer, the rhythmic war beat of the waves perpetually attacked and then retreated from the shore. When their feet hit the water, Agnes's knees buckled and hit the water and partway into wet sand.

Agnes put her hands on her stomach and screamed.

Voices and barking dogs in the far distance answered.

CHAPTER 49

KING GEORGE

Buckingham House, England
1776

The dream was as real as the world that the king lived in. King George was in the expanding dusk, organizing a large group to search and destroy those who'd breached the wall and escaped. As they were ready to leave through the hole in the wall to chase the murderers, something was wrong. With the help of the flashes of light crossing above them, an unveiled trail of footprints went from the barren soil inside of the walls leading to outside. Feet running behind him and away from him within the walls echoed in his ears. He turned his head and body, and with another flash, footsteps and a trail led from the wall and through the area he stood on and toward several feet behind him.

The flashes increased in frequency and duration. In a sudden moment, a group of people stood before the king as the king's back faced the wall. They did not move, and they stared at him. They waited to see what the king would do. They wore clothing from a previous era. Clothing belonging to people over 150 years before. Though most were united in either placing their hands on a single book, or reaching toward it, there seemed to be two different main groups of people before the king,

Some were light, and others were dark in skin color. One group wore tattered clothing, and the other group wore shredded clothing or none at all. One group turned their backs toward him and showed raised stripes on their skin. There were dozens from the two different groups mixed together into one group. They were dripping wet. They looked like they had traveled on sea and landed.

Some had escaped, and some were taken away from their homes.

George gasped.

They did not escape . . . they broke in.

The king awakened from his dream with a gasp, reaching for air.

Queen Charlotte was right before his face. Her wide eyes narrowed and reminded him of when they'd said goodbye to their dying dog years ago. Air came out of her mouth, as if someone had punched her in the stomach.

He was still sitting before the front entrance to his castle. He must have been there for hours. What happened?

"My love, did you hear me? Are you all right?" Charlotte held his cheeks with her warm hands and again narrowed her concerned eyes.

He did not answer.

She held his face tighter. "My love . . . I am getting worried . . ."

He did not blink. He remained unmoved.

"Can you speak to me? I know the king will prevail, and I just want to hear it."

"The . . . murderer . . . is . . . coming."

The queen furrowed her brow, then covered her mouth with one hand. The king touched his forehead and thought he touched someone else's skin. Was it *his* forehead? He touched around his neck, as if something was crawling on him. Something tightened.

The king mumbled, like he was attempting to speak with a tightening hand on his mouth. The dream was no longer limited to sleep at night. He was wide awake in the morning, and the dream descended upon him. Trapped inside his body, he pounded on the walls of the waking dream, trying to persuade someone to pull him out. He tried to make someone wake him up out of the dream.

The dream descended. He was again in a place where a black blanket seemed to cover the land. There were only flashes in the distant skies. Then he was before the wall again, with a now larger hole in it. The murderer had already entered into the king's kingdom. Many soldiers appeared, ready to obey any of the king's commands.

He turned to them. "Go find them. Find what breached our walls and is now attempting to infiltrate all we have worked for. Find them and bring them to me to be hanged. Find what is shining within that murderer, and I want him drawn and quartered with all his people watching. I want them to hear the screams, the pleading, the whimpering of that dying light."

Then a voice, not his own, inhabited his thoughts.

A mighty hand has protected the murderer multiple times, but I now have him in my sight. I am moving through living and sailing vessels. I will further colonize one of my living vessels, just as I did in the beginning with Cain. He is mine and will soon execute my will.

The daytime dream stopped. The king smiled, and all other noises ceased in his head. His strength returned. The one with the other eyes within him, confident of what was to follow, sat down and allowed George to rise.

He smiled wider, and a gleeful sound of hope escaped his lips. He stared into his beautiful love's eyes. "The murderer is not here. He is in the colonies! We found him. We will soon celebrate the killing of the murderer I have been seeking. He will now die."

CHAPTER 50

MO

**Brooklyn Heights, New York Colony
1776**

The Continental Army continued the retreat during the pause in the fighting. One by one the ragged soldiers boarded the many boats—gathered in miraculous haste—to escape the coming inevitable slaughter. With the redcoats on pause and resting and preparing before them, it seemed like an invisible hand held back the British ships attempting to end the war before Christmas with a fatal rear attack. The mysterious summer fog hovered and protected the Continental Army from the view of the redcoats on land before them. The predators still could not see the prey escaping. Could the majority of the entire Continental Army flee to fight another day?

The men had moved toward the boats as Mo hid behind a large bush, studying General Washington standing alone, waiting to be the last man to leave.

Something slithered behind Mo and moved to right below him, crouching out of view. Mo's right hand held the knife, wanting to explode into a rage of justice.

There before him . . . a slave holder.

A slave master.

This war was about one group of slave masters fighting another slave master of another group of slavers.

Mo eased into enacting a role to execute the final part of the plan. What more powerful long-lasting antislavery statement to the world could he give than killing at least one of the most powerful of the world's slave masters standing before him now? If so, could he take off in a suicide run toward the redcoats to kill as many as possible before they ended his miserable life? Was there a more powerful way to give the voiceless a strong voice of liberty?

Mo wiped his eyes, as he would never have any chance of having children. Children who could be free. It ruined his life that he could not be a father. The pounding in his fists in rhythm with his thumping chest inflicted pain.

He remembered what had happened to his mom. He remembered what had happened to little Betsy. All the rest of the slaves he'd seen and heard about even before he was born. He remembered his master's yellow and smelly smile.

The rest of the men waited in the remaining boats for the last man to join them. The general stood still and alone at a distance, with his back facing Mo and the last of the remaining boats, with only his head moving to scan the horizon. Why did he not leave before the soldiers, like any sane commander would have done? Why would the leader of the rebellion against the king choose to be the last man to escape? One stray shot from a random redcoat could end any chance of freedom from the king for the fledgling nation.

What is he doing?

The general nodded, as if in conversation. Was he praying? Listening? The last boat waited in silence for the commander. The men leaned forward, resisting the urge to yell at him but clearly thought otherwise, so as to not alert the redcoats. And probably out of a reverence and awe of the man. He towered over their doubts.

They knew all the stories about how an unseen hand protected the general when there were too many times he should have died. They'd heard the stories of Indian leaders marveling at the Great Spirit protecting the man during the war between the French and British on North American soil just a few years before. They'd heard the stories of fellow soldiers describing how George Washington fearlessly rode into battle with elements of death hitting him and bouncing off him and death flying around him in the air while his horses were shot beneath him.

On this day, the fight against the king was not to be. No one else was brave enough to fight, so Mo prepared for his own personal assault. Somebody had to do things right. Future generations depended on it.

The slithering then moved from underneath him to upon him. It moved like an invisible mark, spreading on him from his legs upward.

Something is in my chest and in my head.

It filled spaces of emptiness within Mo. His chest pounded with a new increased swelling, and his head responded with echoes of throbbing. Yet he had an emptiness.

General George Washington had two faces and two different lives.

He fought for liberty.

He had slaves.

How could anyone have slaves? All slave masters must be killed for all men to be free.

A weight pushed upon Mo to move. Mo's feet descended into deeper mud near the large bush.

Firing his weapon would be the easiest way for Mo to execute his plan. But the sound of a gun firing would echo through the fog and still air and alert not only the Continental Army but the British, therefore endangering the rest of the men. Some were not slavers. If he ran toward the general with his knife, that might be riskier, as the general could then have time to fire his weapon. And if wrestling with the knife were to occur, the general was a much larger and stronger man.

If Mo waited for the general to walk closer on his way back to his men in the last boat, a surprise attack with a knife and a suicide run toward the enemy would settle the matter.

How many redcoats can I kill in silence after killing the general?

Midmorning approached, and Mo had seconds left to execute his plan before the general started his exit. He could not wait. His target was straight ahead with his back facing Mo. As he stood up from behind the bush and moved closer to the general, he noticed his own shadow. The same familiar shadow on a brand-new day. He stopped midstep and noticed the general's shadow in front of his. Then the clouds shifted, or the sun shifted, or perhaps the ground moved, but as they both stood still, the two shadows merged into each other. He thought of his dream. The shadows, now a single shadow, was proof of . . .

A great light.

Mo stood frozen in his tracks, with the general still not aware Mo was behind him. The dark cloud upon him moved toward the hand holding the knife. It then stopped when the dream began to play in his head.

In his dream he saw the shadows darker than the night moving. One shadow moved and swooped down and went into Mo. It went into him! Vengeance increased tenfold. He needed to fight. He needed to kill something. With what stood before him, he covered his eyes, and his eyes still burned.

I need to kill the light.

But he could not move his legs. For a brief moment there was another flash in the sky. The black blanket was lifted.

One light among the many others floated nearest Mo and made itself known. It stood still right before him. It was inside a figure silhouetted before him. As he stared into it while partly covering his eyes with his right hand, images moved in his head.

He did not know the locations or have knowledge of past, present, or future battles, but somehow he knew that images of the battles of Lexington and Concord, Bunker Hill, Trenton, Princeton, Saratoga, and Yorktown moved before his mind's eyes. Battles from future wars unveiled before him. A future War between the States of a new country split his vision in two. Families divided in two fought each other, and he saw free and enslaved people.

Many years into the future, he saw the new country join with other countries in a war against a tyrant attempting to kill all God's chosen people in another part of the world. He saw a nation return home and unite in a new way in their ancient homeland.

The dream showed that the dark shadows moved into alert and shifted in the sky with screeching and searched for what was below. Slaves with and without visible chains appeared.

Decades accelerated further, and his country gradually and progressively moved to give away their freedoms to the followers of a future dead man responsible for the deaths of over a hundred million people in one century. They then also gave their freedoms away to another leader, greater than the former tyrant, who desired to kill God's chosen people all over again on an even greater worldwide scale.

Different types of slaves had infiltrated all institutions. His future country rejected the One who'd created them, and they exchanged the Creator who'd died for their liberty for a slave master who deceived others to fight for their own slavery.

A new dream image moved into his field of vision, and a man in prison many years in the future was writing and sending his letters to join the letters of others instructing how to be free. Many hiding in underground churches secretly distributed the love letters. The man in prison, exhausted and broken, lifted the chains on his arms toward the ceiling and locked eyes with Mo's eyes, as if Mo was standing in the future in the prison with the man. A light was in the man. A fire burned within that man. His eyes! A great love allowed no room for fear in those eyes!

Something moved deep within Mo, and like a seed planted years before under a large tree, it moved, wanting to expand beyond the confines of time and location.

The man in prison moved his eyes to Mo's right side.

Someone was standing right next to Mo as Mo looked into the future in his dream.

He saw Jasper.

Then in the dream, a night-shadow rider carrying a dying light dropped something near the general and Mo and galloped away. The general picked it up.

Mo saw slaves lined up for inspection. All were poked and prodded like animals inspected before a slaughter.

Someone, or something, probed inside *his* heart.

The dream stopped.

He bent forward clutching his chest and tried to hold his knife tighter.

The general, still facing away from Mo, grabbed his own chest and bent forward and tried to hold his sword tighter. Sounds within Mo reminded him of dark markings screeching upon him and in him, screaming and screeching because Light impaled a dry and hard land under their feet.

He was not alone with General Washington.

Mo stood paralyzed and stuck in a bent-forward position.

The general could not straighten back up and cleared his throat.

CHAPTER 51

MARY

**Near Plymouth, Massachusetts Bay Colony
1750**

Agnes dropped to her knees, holding her stomach, with one knee on the wet sand and the other in the water. Mary looked behind to see how much time they had left before the fire lights, angry dogs, and voices caught up with them. She kept her hands on Agnes's mouth as Agnes screamed again through Mary's hands. Mary tried to convince herself that the pounding waves of the ocean would drown out the muffled screams.

In the far distance, the sounds of demons moved closer. In the dim moonlight, Agnes acted like she did not hear what was approaching, or did not care, while squirming in pain on her back. In between her waves of moaning and screaming, she said, "The father of this baby wanted us to be together and be right in the eyes of God. He said we would be together when his wife and her rich father cut off any inheritance. In my sin, I thought it was the only way I could bring forth the child who could free others."

Mary turned her head and was lost in thoughts. *I think Agnes was forced to have this child and is not telling me the truth. Should I pursue justice against that man?* Mary wanted to wipe her own eyes but then put her hands over Agnes's mouth in preparation for the next wave of pain.

Agnes shook her head away from Mary's hands and arched her back for a deeper breath. "And who would believe me when his wife is now dead after trying to kill me?"

Agnes pushed and then writhed in pain, waiting for the next wave. Agnes's eyes sparkled in the night. "I am now doing what God wanted . . . I knew you were never a thief . . ." Agnes paused to gather herself. "You will soon steal life from death for our Father. Next time ask for permission . . ." Agnes smiled a broken smile.

Mary laughed to reassure Agnes and herself. "That is nonsense. All three of us will soon be free."

Agnes smiled again and pulled something out of a secret pocket knitted into her dress. She paused again and took in a deep breath. She kept her gaze on Mary as her chest heaved up and down. "At least two of us have a chance to be free. They told me as a youth that this was smuggled on a slave ship by a relative of mine who carried it for her mother in-law and the young girl's young husband . . ."

Agnes pushed again.

"I can feel something," Mary said, anticipating what was entering into the fray.

Agnes continued. ". . . I still do not know what it is . . ."

Mary's face warmed, and Mary placed her hand on Agnes's chest. Agnes hit Mary's other open hand with the object, before the next wave of pain was to come. Mary closed her hand like a beggar taking money to pay off her final debt and moved her hand from Agnes's chest to cover her scream.

After the wave retreated, Mary tried to pull Agnes back up onto her feet. "Can you walk just a little farther? We are supposed to meet a little farther near the trees, under the big tree." Mary pointed several hundred yards in the distance.

Agnes was not moving as much as she had several minutes before. She appeared like she had run a long race and after years of running, finally needed to stop to rest. "Can a perfect God use sinful me to accomplish what He desires?" Her eyes searched Mary's eyes for an answer.

Mary turned behind her to see if someone she knew stood behind her.

Agnes smiled like an old friend who had come to say goodbye. "I only have Jesus to pay my debt. I am not going any farther . . . I escaped my master's plantation and will awake free in my Father's house."

Mary looked behind her, and for the first time the handheld fires appeared bigger. Had Martha successfully brought the leaders together to usher in new peace?

A man's voice shot through the invaded air from

the closing distance. "We know who you are, Mary. You failed. You and Martha succeeded in getting the leaders together, and then I killed the leader of the Indians and the colonists. Their peoples are at war again. I know who you are."

Mary tipped her head down and wept. *What happened with Martha? Did Martha betray me? Is he lying? The leaders were supposed to unite in a new peace.*

The man yelled again as the sounds of barking dogs seemed misdirected as they moved farther away. "I killed the leaders and peace, but I know you are the real murderer I am looking for. You know I will kill you and will sell the child into slavery as my rightful property."

Agnes whimpered. Mary put a hand on Agnes's shoulder. "There is no time to mourn. Get up. We just need to run to the tree among the trees, where I pray our help is waiting. We may then still have enough time to get away." Mary looked toward the voices and noticed a rising patch of fog above her and Agnes. *How long has that fog been over us? Maybe they haven't heard us as much through the blanket of fog? The fog seems to be confusing them. They cannot see us because of it.*

Agnes grunted and with one hand held her stomach and with the other tried to push off the wet sand to stand. Small moving objects, like birds of prey attacking from the sky, whizzed somewhere by them, and wet sand seemed to rise up in quick surrender several feet away.

Agnes screamed a new scream, and Mary again covered Agnes's mouth with one hand and with the other readied herself for the baby about to enter the ancient hunt it was already in even before birth. Another scream broke through the night. Agnes pushed. The distant barking grew louder. Mary prayed for the fog to remain as Agnes pushed for a few minutes. The voices still tried to figure out where Mary and Agnes were. Agnes pushed again. A new noise, like someone once safe and secure, screamed as it entered a war.

The baby appeared with a cry, seemingly attempting to answer other cries. *The cries in my head. This has something to do with the cries in my dreams.*

Agnes took in a breath. "The rescue is still alive and kicking." She then screamed again.

Mary took the baby girl into her arms. "Another one is coming out!" Mary looked behind her as the voices drifted the wrong way, as if a hand behind the patch of fog prevented them from coming directly behind Mary and Agnes.

"This one is coming out easier," Mary said. Within seconds another entered into the fray. "This one is a boy."

Mary placed both babies into Agnes's arms. One baby held Agnes's finger tightly.

"That is a strong grip. Your babies are strong . . ."

"They are yours . . . *your* babies . . . African . . . Indian . . . European . . . all mixed up the way God wants it . . . and more . . . They have it all in them and are now in your hands, Mary. Do not forget why you are here."

Mary shook her head. The trees seemed to be a hundred miles away. She held the babies and grabbed the object Agnes had given her. She shook her head and refused to see the truth in Agnes's eyes. She studied the object. She could not figure it out. It did not look like anything she had seen before. It was not metal but also not wood. It had markings on it.

"It came from across the Atlantic on a ship, and the ship landed not far from where we are," Agnes said, with a partial smile through her broken breathing.

Mary thought she heard mumbling from Agnes as new blood appeared near her chest. Agnes rallied and gasped. "Thy kingdom come . . . thy will be done . . . on earth as it is in heaven . . . My Jesus above it all . . . Jasper . . ."

Agnes closed her eyes. The babies cried as Mary wept.

I will see you one day. These babies are new and unlike others before. But will we survive? I only have You and these babies left. Save us.

Mary turned her head toward the voices and dogs approaching and then to the tree far in the distance.

Mary held her babies and ran toward the big tree.

CHAPTER 52

THE ASSEMBLED

State House, Philadelphia
Pennsylvania Colony
1776

The man shaking before the Continental Congress seemed to summon his last breath and any remaining energy. All looked from side to side as puzzled and questioning looks dominated the room. A common sense invaded the space. Every expression asked the same questions: Who is this covered in mud? Is this a loyalist who told the redcoats where to hunt treason while it was still in the womb?

With his legs wobbling and his body laboring, trying to gather his breath to push out new words, the man raised a fist into the air. "I vote for independence."

There was no more remaining doubt that Caesar Rodney, with a midnight ride and over eighty miles of storm behind him, had entered. With his final vote, the delegates from Delaware voted two to one for independence.

All had agreed beforehand that the final vote would have to be unanimous, allowing for abstentions, or they would not move forward in declaring independence. Caesar removed a layer of mud off his face and pulled out a damp scarf to cover his face. They counted the last votes one more time, and all voted for independence, with New York abstaining. No colony voted for continuing with the king.

After the counting of the final votes, silence covered the room. For a few moments, it was as if clouds had blocked part of the sun. No one moved or made a sound. Eyes brimmed with tears. Someone coughed. Some walked to the windows and looked outside. How many more times would they see the trees? The sunrise? The sunset? Would they ever kiss loved ones again back home?

"Gentlemen, the price on my head has just been doubled!" someone in the back said.

"He reigns in heaven," Samuel Adams proclaimed, "from the rising to the setting sun, may His kingdom come."

***

Brooklyn Heights, New York Colony
1776

A bright presence surrounded the general. It surrounded Mo. It seemed to command over both of them.

Mo winced, as if a finger with authority pressed on an inside part of his chest. He bent forward again with a moan at the same time the general bent forward again while his back was still facing Mo. They both moaned, trying not to scream out in pain, and then both stopped at the same time. They each straightened back up and stood taller, as if now lighter.

Mo's knife and the commander's sword lay on the ground.

The perfect greater Light broke through the two smaller flawed lights. It was beautiful.

Without turning toward Mo, the general said, "Hello, Moses." The general laughed. "It seems that the Supreme Commander General has our attention. If I abhor and do not tolerate those who rebel against good and righteous command, I can only imagine how the Commander of His army feels about me and what He is capable of."

He wiped his forehead and took a deep breath. "Who am I to have the same dream in sleep you have had? A night-shadow rider carrying a light and dropping things unto the ground. The night-shadow rider dropped living things in a dying world. Night fliers flew down and ate them. Some of what he dropped died on the hard ground. Thorns overwhelmed some of the other things dropped. Powerful men and women destroyed some. Many people ignored them. In the dream, I picked up one of the items."

He turned and stared straight through Moses. Something was in his eyes. The general bowed his head. "As a general assembling an army, my army is only as good as my flawed men. I pick the best of the flawed men available to me."

The general shook his head. "God is not limited, as I am. The all-powerful One searches His land for the humble who desire Him above all. Will not future generations give thanks to their God, as He will use any flawed man or woman, any way, any time, anywhere He desires?"

Moses knew he should flinch when the general pulled something out of his pocket. But Moses could not flinch. *I cannot move. Surely the stories are true, as the hand of God protects this man. Even when his horses were shot under him and he was shot in the French and Indian War, he lived. His enemies said the Spirit protected him. Is he now going to kill me?*

The general moved closer. He stopped with Moses's shadow separated from the general's shadow just in front of his own feet. He continued. "Great shadows are evidence of a greater Light. Grace is given to us. God's unmerited favor I do not deserve. It offends. I cannot control it, but how I cling to it." Then the general bent down with his hands in the joined shadow and scooped out some hard dirt. He placed what he'd taken out of his pocket into the hard ground and covered it.

General Washington then lifted his head and stood. "With all of my sins, I do not deserve to live. But He has chosen us. Moses, this is not in our timing. Today it is time to retreat to then fight and free another day. For God desires for me to live at this time, and you are to live and have one come through you one day. He will be a powerful voice for the voiceless. The fight and the freedom we seek is coming one day, would you not say?"

The internal probing stopped. Moses acknowledged and accepted the Author and His Story. He could almost see the markings on him and in him retreat and screech into the sky in search of the next person.

An internal yet almost audible voice moved within Moses.

I chose you and I paid for you.

Moses exhaled. All unnecessary weight lifted off him. No more slithering outside or inside of him. He nodded and tilted his head to see the general nod at the same time. The commander turned his head toward the British soon to attack and then toward his retreating men. "The fate of unborn millions will now depend, under God, on the courage and conduct of this army. Your offspring will grow in the prepared soil."

Their eyes locked. Moses opened his eyes farther. The general was not the Light. But the perfect Light stood within the flawed general.

It now burns within me. Did God bring me here to see Him use a slave holder to plant a seed that will help destroy slavery?

They stood across from each other as their shadows had crossed into each other like two splintered beams intersecting and impaling the hard ground. They picked up their weapons and walked to the last remaining boat waiting for them. About nine thousand men evacuated, and the last boat left as the remnants of the unusual summer fog lifted.

***

State House, Philadelphia
Pennsylvania Colony
1776

The Continental Congress was still silent, like after a lifelong bullied child having punched his bully in the mouth and now waiting for what was next. A mix of reverence and reality spread throughout the room. It reminded Caesar of someone dying and yet birthing life at the same time. Clouds moved as the daytime sun now seemed to darken. Caesar drifted to a window. This time he refused to sidestep and approached the window directly centered. A new reflection stared back at him. Something new in his eyes. He ran his fingers over the scarf on the left side of his face.

What have I done?

In the reflection, there was no doctor. There was no cure. There was no Dorothy. He stood alone. With a roomful of men sharing a moment while each stood alone with invisible ropes at their necks and also seeing a day with a chance of no ropes around any necks.

Caesar did not blink as he stared right back into the eyes in the reflection. He took in a deep breath and removed his scarf.

***

Exeter, New Hampshire Colony
1770

George Whitefield stood with the young man who had walked toward him from the great tree. He remembered Scripture in which Jesus, after His death and resurrection, asked Saul, who was soon to be Paul, "Why do you persecute me?"

Through blurred vision and after wiping his cheeks, George pulled out the item he had held for several years and studied it. *What is this?*

It was not exactly wood. It was not a metal he had ever seen. It was handmade but from what, or for what, he still did not know.

George sighed and offered it to the young man. "A young woman gave this to me a few years ago as she was on her bed birthing a beautiful baby girl. We care for the little girl to this day. It turned out to be the young woman's deathbed." His lips trembled, and his voice cracked when he added, "She was one of *my* slaves."

George shook his head and bowed. "She said that she'd had this item since her birth. She lost contact with her mother, who she believed died giving birth to her and her twin brother, but she never lost this. She gave it to me, and it became my most prized possession above my few possessions. I believe our Father desires that I give this to you."

The young man studied it, and tears escaped his eyes down his cheeks. He turned the object in his hands over. His lips trembled as he used his shirt to hold it. "God showed me this in a dream, and it came from under a tree in another land and in another time. It is hot in my hand. I cannot read, so what do the markings on this mean?"

"I can read. But I do not know. But I do know I met your parents years ago, and you will be known as the 'African Wonder.' What is your name?"

"My name is Harry Hoosier." The young man turned the object in his hand over and over with his eyes closed. His eyes rolled side to side under his closed eyelids. He at first shook his head and then nodded with a smile. He gestured with his hand toward all the people from the crowd still standing near them. "Know in your final hours that the seeds you helped plant will grow. The thorns and most of creation resists. But the seed will grow in many here. You have helped prepare the soil for the blood that will soon spill and for the great loss of blood in the next several years. Kings and masters resist, but the seeds will grow from generation to generation as it always has."

As if night turned into day, the two men shook hands as George, cross-eyed, studied their two hands together.

Free us, Lord God.

***

Near Plymouth, Massachusetts Bay Colony 1750

A voice in the dark several feet in front of her yelled out. "Mary, we have the horses ready."

Mary ran toward the big tree in the available light. Whistling cut through the night and the air around her. Sand popped up when the whistling found a target. She pulled the bundle housing the twins closer to her chest.

How have they not hit me yet? A quick flash of a woman praying at a tree reflected the surrounding light and then disappeared. Through blurry vision. Two men ahead. Standing and then bending at the tree. Full of light but hidden into the night. How did her legs run so fast? She'd never run like this before. There was still several more feet ahead before she reached the men.

Can I make it? I have to for the children. More whistling cut through the night next to her and above her. She collapsed at the feet of the men, heaving for elusive air, and could not speak.

One of the men reached out and took the babies. He shielded them as he said, "You stole them from death."

The other man tilted his head toward the approaching voices and said, "They are after these babies, whether they realize it or not. They are almost here!"

Mary's head throbbed with each exploding heartbeat as she attempted to understand what was happening.

The man with the babies ran toward some horses at a speed she had never seen before. He almost flew toward the horse. He was already several feet away from her as Mary cried out for her babies.

The other man assisted her onto her feet. "We must run!"

Another shot whistled toward them and hit something more solid than sand with a thud. Mary fell. Another thud made Mary forget her pain. The man next to Mary fell.

What happened?

Mary's back and chest throbbed. On the dry sand, her hand holding her chest was getting warmer and more wet. She heard growling dogs approaching faster than the voices of the men. One of the men with the dogs yelled to the others with him, "Shoot him! Do not let him go!"

Mary's vision dimmed, like just before falling asleep. Another shot buzzed by Mary and toward the man with her babies. The man holding the bundle flinched, and something deflected off his shoulder as he neared the horse. He was not going to drop the illegal contraband. He jumped onto the horse in one hop. Mary's eyes closed farther. *Who moves like that?*

He jumped onto one of the horses, when something dropped from the babies. Shots whizzed past him and clanked, as if deflected after hitting something invisible. He turned his head toward the man leading about ten men with guns and dogs. The man, while holding the babies, jumped down in a single motion and picked up the object Agnes had given Mary. Then, like ropes were attached to his body, he swooped back up and landed on the horse, still holding the crying babies. The man handled the object like it had just been pulled out of a fire. He gathered a cloth around his hand and put the wrapped object securely into a back pocket.

Mary, from a distance, watched the rider with a dimming light in his arms. She mustered her strength one last time as one of the men hunting her stood above her with a gun to her head. Someone put words onto her tongue that were too hot to keep in her mouth.

She smiled. "You cannot stop my children . . . You can't stop this."

The man with the gun to her head paused, as if wanting her to see what was going to happen to the last failure of her plan. In the distance, the dogs surrounded the man on the horse with the babies just before he tried to take off. They barked and growled and bit one of the horse's legs. The horse gave a death stare and kicked the dog, and it whimpered several feet into the air. The other dogs stopped, almost in reverence. The man and the babies, and the snarling horse, the last remaining night-shadow rider, rode into the night with the brightening light.

Inspiration and Sources

"Battle of Long Island"—Wikipedia

The Light and the Glory—Peter Marshall and David Manuel

Seven Miracles that Saved America—Chris Stewart and Ted Stewart

Killing England—Bill O'Reilly and Martin Dugard

1776—David McCullough

"Praying Indians of Natick and Ponkapoaq"—natick-prayingindians.org

"George III"—Wikipedia

"Benjamin Kent"—Wikipedia

"Praying Town"—Wikipedia

"Praying Indian"—Wikipedia

"George Whitfield"—Wikipedia

"Deer Island: A History of Human Tragedy Remembered"—Julianne Jennings, ictnews.org

"By the King, A Proclamation, For Suppressing Rebellion and Sedition" (1775)—encyclopediavirginia.org

"Franklin's Contributions to the American Revolution as a Diplomat in France"—ushistory.org

"First Great Awakening"—Wikipedia

"Major General Thomas Mifflin 1st Quartermaster School Commandant October 1776-November 1777"—quartermaster.army.mil

Caesar Rodney statue—aoc.gov

"How an Enslaved African Man in Boston Helped Save Generations from Smallpox"—Erin Blakemore, history.com

"The French and Indian War (1754–1763): Causes and Outbreak"—William R. Griffith IV, battlefields.org

ABOUT THE AUTHOR

As a storyteller and a physical therapist, Charles Anthony Solorio works with people who are physically and sometimes emotionally broken. He believes that stories can confront the raw side of our brokenness and bring about healing by seeing our own lives through the lenses of both faith and a faithfulness woven into our history. Charles lives in Southern California with his wife and adult children. You can meet Charlie at charlesanthonysolorio.com